# MAIN LINE MAVERICK

# MAIN LINE MAVERICK

▼

*Sally Gibbs*

Authors Choice Press
San Jose New York Lincoln Shanghai

Main Line Maverick

Authors Choice Press
an imprint of iUniverse.com, Inc.

For information address:
iUniverse.com, Inc.
5220 S 16th, Ste. 200
Lincoln, NE 68512
www.iuniverse.com

Cover designed by Lori Gilbert

Edited by Lori Gilbert

ISBN: 0-595-19715-9

Printed in the United States of America

*~ With heartfelt gratitude to my dear friend,*
*Lori Gilbert*

# CHAPTER I

▼

# WHAT TO DO ABOUT BRENDA

"Sex is nasty, Brenda," Mother said. "Men get you where they want you, then toss you aside like a rotten apple."

Brenda had just finished her eye exercises, which Mother made her do every day to correct her walleye. Brenda didn't think it was doing any good. The eye still went out on its own whenever it wanted.

"I don't know why you think sex is nasty," Brenda said.

Her friend Ruth Anne said she'd gone all the way and it wasn't that bad. And she wasn't being tossed aside. In fact, she had two more boys after her now.

"Ruth Anne told me-"

"Don't talk to me about that girl," Mother snapped. "She's much older than you...besides, I think she's fast."

Being "fast" on the Main Line back then was about the worst you could be, it seemed.

"But you and Dad do it, don't you? You must have done it a couple of times to get Ted and me."

Mother flushed. "Brenda, how dare you say that? It's not the same. Your father and I are married."

"So, it's okay to do it if you are married. But shit, Ma, I don't see–"

Mother pounced. "Brenda! I told you not to use that nasty word. If you say it again, I'll have your father wash your mouth out with soap!"

Brenda knew this to be an idle threat. It had been offered before but never materialized. And, why make such a big deal out of a word? Besides, "shit" was one of her favorite words, inherited from the twins. They had a new word, which began with an "F." Brenda didn't like the sound of it. It sounded like something nasty being sucked down the drain.

Mother was scowling. "You're not to use that word and that's final! I'm going to the greenhouse and don't wrinkle your brow. It makes you look old."

Brenda was twelve.

She watched as Mother took off across the lawn to where her carnations awaited her, warm and cozy, under the glass. Mother was a flower person. She liked them better than people. She thought that most people were boring and full of themselves. Flowers simply bloomed and were beautiful.

And was Mother off the beam about sex? Was it really that rotten? Though Ruth Anne's description of what they did to you kind of turned her off. Maybe Mother was right. And she certainly didn't want to get tossed aside like a rotten apple.

That night, Brenda was at her nighttime listening post outside Mother and Dad's door as they lay in bed. There she learned a lot of interesting things about herself.

"Jason," Mother said. "What are we going to do about Brenda?"

"What do you mean?"

"She's so lumpy."

'Lumpy is right,' thought Brenda. A round bottom, fat hips, plus suffering from a disease called "lack of a waist line." Why couldn't she have looked like Mother? Blonde, slender and elegant. People stared at her when she and Brenda walked down Chestnut Street to the Philadelphia Orchestra on

Friday afternoons. They stared at Brenda too, who looked slumpish and peculiar, tagging along behind. Her long hair tucked inside her coat collar in an attempt to make it look bobbed and make her appear older.

"But she does have lovely legs," Mother said.

"Yes, poetic," Dad said. "Just like mine."

Dad was beautiful too, with his black moustache and aquiline features of an Italian aristocrat. He always claimed they had a Venetian ancestor.

"But she's so romantic and silly-headed," Mother said. "I hope that she isn't going to get into trouble with men."

"What!" Dad sounded jolted.

"Yes. She keeps her eyes fastened on that good-looking first cellist at the orchestra. I think she's in love with him."

"A childish crush," Dad said. "All adolescents get them. Could we go to sleep now? I've got to go to work tomorrow."

"I tried to tell her about sex today," Mother went on. "But I don't think it sank in. She worries me."

Mother was a worrier. She worried about Jancy, their black cook, over-cooking the chicken and making it shrink. She also worried about Jancy's parrot, Coco, who'd taken to imitating Jancy's little farts, which she claimed eased her insides. Coco augmented these sounds into real boomers, which floated out of the third story window. "What would the neighbors think?" moaned Mother. Then she worried about Dad playing tennis at the Main Line Tennis Club. He might get hit in the eye with a tennis ball or he might come home late for supper.

They seldom discussed Ted, Brenda's brother, who was good looking, sweet natured and no worry to Mother. She kept him busy studying art at the Academy of Fine Arts.

Brenda loved Ted, though he teased her a lot. And she did enjoy the funny things he did, like spending hours teaching Coco to say, "Go to hell." That human-like sound, echoing from the third story window, caused passersby on the road below to crane up and one man was heard to yell back, "Go to hell yourself, you son-of-a-bitch!"

But Brenda seemed to be an inexhaustible topic of conversation.

"I shall just have to keep Brenda busy," Mother continued. "I've made up my mind that she's not going to come out. It's a waste of time with her talents. Besides, her stuffy cousins will probably try to knife her in the back like their mother did me."

"Margot was just jealous of your beauty," Dad said.

"She was more beautiful than I."

Brenda didn't care much for Aunt Margot. She had a way of looking down her nose at you and talking through clenched teeth the way a lot of Main Line women did. It seemed as though they were afraid the words would get away from them and get them into trouble, or that they had constipation of the mouth or something.

"Margot always tried to steal my men friends. Of course I didn't care, but—"

"Of course you didn't," Dad said. "You were waiting for me."

Brenda could tell that Dad was smiling and stroking his silky black moustache. Dad loved Mother a lot. It was her beautiful blonde hair and that dimple when she smiled. He was even jealous of F.D.R. because Mother thought he was attractive.

"Mama says she'll pay for Brenda's coming out but not one penny for dancing lessons."

"We don't need your Mother's money," Dad said. "And I do think coming out is a way of meeting people."

"What people?" Mother scoffed. "A bunch of snobs."

Dad was a people person and enjoyed the company of his golf and tennis playing cronies and fellow architects. Mother didn't like people except for her immediate family. What she loved was the arts, her piano, the greenhouse and their home. The house Dad had designed, with its pretty white columns like a Southern mansion. He called it Upsan Downs because it was built on the side of a hill. Brenda loved Upsan Downs. She figured that no matter what life had in store for her (and she was sure that she could mess it up somehow), there would always be Upsan Downs to come home to. Rich Grandma had had the house built on her property and had given it to Mother and Dad as a wedding present. Dad said it was a mixed blessing. Grandma wanted to keep Mother near her so she could run her life.

"Mama's such a snob," Mother went on. "She thinks Margot's wonderful because she's descended from that Civil War general."

"History says he was no great shakes," Dad put in.

"And the way Mama pampers Jake, giving him money all the time, which he squanders on his horses and women."

Brenda didn't think much of Uncle Jake either, though he was funny. He was small, red-faced, always dressed in riding clothes and looked like he'd just parked the horse outside. He liked to pinch Brenda on the neck. Mother said her brother was over-sexed and wouldn't let Brenda go to the movies with him.

"My mind's made up," Mother said. "Brenda doesn't belong with those social people anymore than I did. I want her to have a career."

Brenda's ears sharpened. This was the first she'd heard about her career.

"Doing what?" Dad asked.

"I think Brenda should be a dancer."

Dad chuckled. "For once, I agree with your Mother. I don't think Brenda's good dance material."

"I always wanted to be a dancer," Mother said dreamily. "But I had no talents."

"You play the piano beautifully," Dad remarked.

"I was always too timid to play for people."

"An inferiority complex induced by your Mother."

"I'm bound Brenda won't have one."

"Brenda has a talent for writing," Dad said. "That poem she wrote about the apple seller showed real talent. Of course, the opening line had to be changed."

The opening line was, "He stands on a cold corner polishing his red balls."

Brenda couldn't understand why Dad had burst out laughing and suggested she change the word "balls." She changed it to "globes."

"She could write, too," Mother said. "But I think—"

Dad interrupted. "Be realistic, Lillian. The stage is no place for a sensitive, impressionable child like Brenda. Now…could we go to sleep?"

"But I do think she could be a lovely dancer—"

Dad sounded irritated. "For goodness sake, Lillian, your dream of her being a dancer is far fetched. Brenda has many attributes, but face it. She's fat, wall-eyed and pigeon-toed. She'll never be a beauty."

Brenda slumped against the door.

"What was that?" Mother said.

In an instant, the door was wrenched open. Mother in her pink nightgown looked at her accusingly.

"Have you been listening?" she stormed. "How could you?"

"You said I was fat, pigeon-toed and ugly," Brenda blubbered.

"You're not ugly," Dad said.

Mother said severely, "Jason, she must be punished."

"I don't think—"

"Now!"

"Very well."

Brenda found herself being propelled toward her bedroom. The whack on her behind didn't hurt much. Softy Dad wasn't big in the punishment department. What hurt was she knew that from now on, the door would be guarded against her. She loved the sound of their drowsy voices discussing her. She loved to know their inner thoughts. Now, that would be denied.

But she took a chance and sneaked back to see if there was more to hear.

Their lights were out. She heard Mother's voice.

"Jason, Brenda's been a trial to me always. In fact, she almost did me in trying to get her born."

This was well known to all of them and Brenda always felt guilty about having almost killed Mother by taking so long to come out.

She heard Dad say, "But she's been worth it, hasn't she?"

There was a long silence, then Mother said softly, "Oh, yes. Brenda's wonderful. I love her."

Brenda's heart leaped. Mother wasn't much for making flowery speeches or showing affection. But it seemed that in spite of Brenda's being such a trial…Mother loved her!

At that moment, Brenda loved Mother so much that she'd even try, for her sake, to make it as a GREAT DANCER.

# CHAPTER 2

▼

# DANCE, DAMN YOU, DARLING!

Mother now put in motion her plan to promote Brenda's dancing career. She enrolled her in Miss La Rose's Dancing Academy on Chestnut Street in Philadelphia.

In the sweaty smelling studio, Mother sat along with mothers of the other pupils, measuring every bit of progress of Brenda's plump form as she laboriously tried to hoist her bulk to twirl on point, trying to be a toe dancer. All she got out of it was toe shoes with bloodied ends. In spite of the lamb's wool stuffing, her toes just couldn't take the stress.

Brenda didn't think she'd make it. Mother did.

Furthermore, Brenda knew she'd never make it as the social success that Grandma wanted her to be. She knew it definitively after Grandma offered to pay for Miss Wothington's Saturday Evening Dancing Class and Mother consented to let her go. Here, according to Grandma, Brenda would meet the right boys and girls who would be a boon to her in later life.

The venture was a total flop.

Brenda sat on the sidelines with the other hefty wallflowers receiving wary and insulting looks from the huddled boys in their tuxedos who would only dance with the skinny girls. Brenda could imagine the remarks that those goofball boys were making about the fatsos. She did not see how any of these people could possibly be a boon to her in later life.

Tiring of watching those poops struggling around the dance floor and after catching a glimpse of herself in the tall mirrors, in the awful ruffled dress Mother had made for her at John Wanamakers, with Dad's corsage beginning to droop on her shoulder, Brenda charged into the girl's room. She grabbed her evening bag in which she'd stored a copy of Lady Chatterley's Lover in case of just such an emergency.

She spent a pleasant half hour on the john reading, then dashed outside where Aldo, Grandma's Italian chauffer, was waiting to drive her home.

She refused to go to Miss Wothington's again.

"Those damned boys!" she raved. "Looking like stuffed asses in those dress suits!"

Dad smiled. "I guess our Brenda isn't cut out to be a social success."

"I should think not," Mother declared. "A waste of time with her talent for dancing."

"And her talent for writing," Dad chimed in.

He'd submitted several of Brenda's poems to a literary magazine and one poem had been accepted. He was all pleased.

"I predict she'll go far with her writing."

"Writing is all right," Mother said. "But dancing is her real talent. And I'm going to see that she pursues that."

That summer, with a nod to Dad's ambition for Brenda to become a writer and to placate Grandma for Brenda's social flop, Mother came up with a great idea. Brenda was sent along with maids and steamer trunks to the Grandparents' summer cottage in Cape May.

Brenda hated Cape May, New Jersey.

"What am I going to do down there?" she wailed.

"Why don't you write?" Mother said. "No one will bother you."

Grandma bothered her with lectures on deportment. Brenda guessed that Grandma loved her. Mother had said that when Brenda was born, Grandma was so thrilled about having a namesake that she had a gas attack. But Grandma was always picking on her. It was a bore, as was the topic of eating. When Grandma wasn't eating, she was talking about it.

Brenda was lonely, so she ate. Her curves burgeoned and looked awful in her Anette Kellerman one-piece bathing suit Mother had bought her. Grandma disapproved of this object as too revealing. Revealing was right. Every bulge of Brenda was on display as she made a dash for the Atlantic Ocean, hoping not to be noticed by the bronzed lifeguard with whom she was in love.

Her hope was realized. Why would he notice Brenda when those beautiful skinny teenagers clustered around his stand?

Brenda's legs continued to be slender and graceful, so she tried covering up her upper part with a beach robe when she strolled to see if the legs could arouse any interest. She received one wolf call from an aged Jewish gentleman and so, gave up and spent most of the time hiding under the boardwalk with a book. She considered suicide by drowning but figured, what the heck, with her blubber she would probably float.

On the beach one afternoon, she ran into a girl from Miss La Rose's Dance Academy who told her that a local summer stock company was looking for talent.

"Why don't you try out?"

"Sure!" replied Brenda.

Thrilled, Brenda squeezed herself into a girdle and her most thinning outfit and, avoiding Grandma, sneaked over to the Yellow Barn Playhouse. This was a glorified storage shack with a stage added on. Brenda, tall and looking older than her fourteen years, was hired. They must have been hard up for players.

Mother praised Brenda's initiative in getting herself a job, for which she would be paid five dollars a performance.

Grandma raised the roof. "I will not have my namesake an actress!"
Ted grinned and said that she was worth at least ten dollars.
Dad kept quiet.
Grandpa, being such a fan of movies and the theater, was delighted! He got Aldo to drive him over for the shows, probably hoping to see Buster Keaton. What he ran into instead was Brenda playing a hooker. Followed by her big role as an ingénue.

In the latter, she crapped out completely.

Her big scene was with leading man, Eric De Lima, a South American-German or something. He had burning dark eyes and a luxuriant black moustache covering his upper lip. He also had a cleft in his chin, which Brenda found fascinating. Rumor had it that he was in his fifties and dyed his hair, but he had a heart-stopping foreign accent. Brenda totally forgot about the lifeguard and fell in love with him.

In their big scene together, Brenda was supposed to kiss De Lima. During rehearsals this was a glancing encounter. Not so on opening night. How was Brenda to know what danger lay under that luxuriant foliage on his upper lip? How was she to know that beneath it lurked a lethal tongue?

At the opening, this old pro (probably for fun and games), taking advantage of Brenda's inexperience, grabbed her and stuck his tongue into her mouth with such force that she became dizzy and forgot her next line. And old De Lima didn't bother to help her get back on track. In fact, he seemed to enjoy her frantic groping for lines. Finally the prompter in the wings gave forth Brenda's words in a loud voice that produced much laughter from the audience.

After this happened a second time, the director, a young eager beaver, said that Brenda seemed to suffer from memory lapses. Besides, she was a bit too hefty for the part and would have to be replaced.

Mortified, Brenda departed into the ocean breezes, muttering, "The hell with acting."

She wasn't too sorry. It was boring to have to learn all those lines and having to hang around for hours while people read theirs. Also, her ardor for De Lima hit bottom when he'd been so shitty about that tongue business. Besides, she'd discovered that he had halitosis and probably false teeth.

Mother thought Brenda had quit and was pleased. She said that she didn't like Brenda being kissed by strange men. She might pick up something.

Brenda was glad to go home. But what to do now?

Dad wanted Brenda to go to college. Mother did not. Dad said Brenda should write and needed a proper education so she could. Mother said, "I won't have her turning into a frumpy intellectual. She's capable of more."

The argument heated up. For two days, Mother and Dad hardly spoke. Silence prevailed at the dinner table. Ted, as per usual lost in his dreams, didn't seem to notice. Jancy looked worried as she passed the overdone chicken. Dad offered to move to the Club. Brenda felt guilty.

Harmony was restored when Mother came up with the solution. Brenda was to develop all her talents, not just the writing. Brenda must be prepared for anything theatrical. To this end, she became a human yo-yo, bounding from one lesson to another: singing, drama, ballet and tap. She was driven in a bewildering number of directions but was focused mostly on the dance.

Brenda figured that since sex was nasty and boys didn't like her anyhow; and since she hadn't really made it as a poet and had totally flopped as a social success and actress…maybe Mother's ambition for her to become a great dancer might actually pay off.

Wasn't Mother always right?

# CHAPTER 3

▼

# VALSE TRISTE

Every year, Miss La Rose hired the Academy of Music stage for her spring concert. The pupil's mothers paid all expenses. These ladies would have paid anything to see their little darlings on that renowned stage, wobbling through Swan Lake and other ambitious endeavors.

Brenda, knowing that she continued to look like such a schlump in the dancing game, was surprised when one day Miss La Rose informed Mother that Brenda was to dance a solo, the Valse Triste, at the concert.

Mother was delighted.

Not so Brenda, who had visions of herself thumping around that enormous stage while the other mothers made snide comments. How come fat Brenda was getting a solo while their darlings, who were much better dancers, didn't get one?

That was easy to answer. No doubt, Miss La Rose felt she had to repay Mother for those big bucks she was squandering on the private lessons Brenda was getting and to insure that the lessons would continue.

"I hope I'm not going to have to do it on toe," Brenda complained.

Miss La Rose said Brenda was more suited to an interpretive dance, based on her height. This dance form, Brenda learned, entailed a lot of running around and making dramatic gestures.

On the great night, the house was packed with Irish, Italian and Jewish mothers with their families. Brenda was not particularly nervous. In spite of practicing her routine like mad, it was bound to be awful. But what the hell…she'd get through it somehow. Mother, standing in the wings, waved encouragingly as Brenda stalked on stage and took her place.

As the curtain rose, she lay on some kind of rickety old couch Miss La Rose had dreamed up. It was covered with a red drape and Brenda was in a white, flowing affair, which mercifully concealed her bulge. She was supposed to be dead. But as the strains of Valse Triste began, she hoisted up slowly, waving her arms like Isadora Duncan.

Isadora Duncan was no lightweight either. Mother had taken Brenda to see Isadora on one of her farewell tours when Brenda was seven. The sight must have left an indelible impression, for as Brenda rose, she was suddenly transformed.

Brenda became Isadora. She threw herself into the rhythm of the tinny piano, running wildly around the stage; beckoning to a phantom lover, rejecting him, whirling up a storm and in her excitement, forgetting the routine and making up steps of her own and finally ending in absolute exhaustion.

For Brenda had discovered at a rehearsal that the Academy stage had a horrendous tilt to the rear. At the end of the dance, there were a series of pirouettes circling the stage. To accomplish this, Brenda had to climb that hill several times. Gearing herself for the onslaught, she charged into the turns with such ferocity that, to her surprise, the audience let loose with a burst of applause.

That did it! Brenda suddenly became a changed person. She was beautiful, graceful and noticed. Her blood surged intoxicatingly. This was it. She would never be the same. Screw the wispy girls and the boys who had ignored her. She had something they would never know…applause from a full house.

The end of her dance required her to swoon back dead on the couch. She did, and "dead" was about it. But once more, greeted with applause, she was galvanized to her feet. Imitating Isadora, Brenda bowed with the poise of an old pro (someone remarked), throwing kisses to the balcony and then bounding off stage.

Mother rushed over and hugged her. "You were wonderful, dear."

Her face was flushed and Brenda saw that Mother had danced with her every step of the way.

After the show, the mothers were lavish in their praise and Miss La Rose put forth her seal of approval. Brenda had the makings of a fine interpretive dancer.

Dad had been in the audience and gave Brenda a hug. "Bravo! I thought you'd never make it around that last bend."

"Me, too." But Brenda saw that Dad was proud.

This was her day and Mother's. Brenda finally thought she knew where she was going. She wasn't going to have to come out and be messed up by the snooty cousins. She was going to be the great dancer Mother promised. A BIG STAR!

# CHAPTER 4

# THE GREAT IGOR PLOTKIN

More than ever in hot pursuit of Brenda's career and of a loftier outlet for it than Miss La Rose's, Mother found what she was looking for. She learned that the great Igor Plotkin was about to open a dance studio in Philadelphia.

At the breakfast table, she informed Brenda and Dad of this exciting news.

"Just think...he was once Pavlova's dance partner! I'm going to enroll Brenda in his classes."

"Oh, must you?" Dad buried his face in the newspaper. He added, "Plotkin must be ninety if he was her partner. I'm surprised he can still walk, much less dance."

"He was just a child when he danced with her," Mother defended.

"It must have been hard on her, changing his diapers between acts."

"Oh Jason, why must you always take such a negative view? I've heard he's only about fifty."

"Well, bless his arabesques and plies."

"Just wait. You'll see that I'm right."

Dad buried his head in the newspaper. He was of Ted's opinion that when Mother got onto something, you might as well give up.

It turned out that Maestro Plotkin was only in his fifties, maybe late ones. You would never have known it. He was boyish, dynamic, fiery and frightening. He wore immaculate white ducks, a striped shirt and a colorful bandana to hide his balding head. His set of aquiline features poised dramatically above his leaps and perfect entrechats. When his white tennis shoes rapped out rhythm on the dingy floor of the studio, it sounded like the report of a revolver.

The old studio was draped with musty and picturesque hangings from the Maestro's glory days in Russia, and shades of Diaghcleff haunted the shadows. Also haunting the shadows were those mothers who had deserted Miss La Rose for this more rarified atmosphere. Along with Mother, they sat on folding wooden chairs, resembling a kind of Greek chorus, commenting on the pupils' progress and, of course, gossiping.

This gossip intensified when the Maestro brought from New York a pale Russian beauty called Kratcha Valotna. This aroused much conjecture among the mothers. Was she the Maestro's girlfriend? Of course she was. That's why she got to dance the leading routines when their Susie, who was a much better dancer, should have, etcetera. And didn't someone glimpse Kratcha in the Maestro's dressing room, on his lap while he fondled her?

Kratcha fascinated Brenda. An aura of mystery seemed to surround her. Her long, hipless body seemed summoned out of some source of a Plotkin dream. Her graceful, slothful arms made music of their own to ornament the Nutcracker or Lake of Swans. She smoked a lot using a long white cigarette holder, spoke little and had a heavy Russian accent. Though she ate a lot of chocolate, Kratcha was thin in a voluptuous way. To Brenda, she had it all.

The Maestro's manager, Mr. Blumov, also enthralled Brenda. He'd been with the Maestro in Russia and was determined to give the Great One a success in America. His dark eyes flashing behind horn-rimmed spectacles, he informed the mothers that the pupils would do great things. There would be recitals and productions for the opera company. Everyone was thrilled and the pupils doubled their efforts for these marvelous prospects.

In the center of the studio, there was a pole, probably to prop up a weakening ceiling. The Maestro used the pole to demonstrate his prowess in the art of mime. At times, he'd grasp the pole and make love to it. Sometimes he'd make like a monkey, scratching his chest and uttering sounds like a lovesick orangutan. Another trick he pulled was to single out some unfortunate pupil to serenade in his raspy voice, with lyrics such as, "Brenda, Brenda…you are not very slenda," to music of a Strauss waltz.

His humor was lost on the bewildered pupils, who didn't know whether to laugh or to cry. He picked on Brenda quite often, but she thought that it was funny. The mirror told her she looked slumpish trying to make with the grace and glamour. She was surprised when Mr. Blumov told Mother that the Maestro said Brenda had talent. Mother triumphantly relayed this news to Dad, who buried his face in the newspaper.

The first performance with the opera company was to be 'Aida.' Brenda made a solemn vow that before the show, she would pare off some lard. However, every time Jancy passed the French fries or Baked Alaska, they cried out to Brenda for a second helping. So on opening night, she was as bulgy as ever. Unfortunately, she had to wear a skimpy costume. It was of red satin, exposed a bare mid-riff and was high on the thighs, revealing most of what Brenda had, which was plenty.

On the big night there was wild excitement among the mothers and hysterical bewilderment among the pupils as they (in backstage dimness) dodged scene changes, Egyptian warriors, cursing stage hands, tenors tuning up and a white horse that pooped while waiting to carry the fat basso on stage.

As the curtain rose, the Corps de Ballet was seated downstage, pretending to pluck phony little harps. Brenda was miserable. Why had old Plotkin placed her down front, where the opera glasses of Dad's club and golfing cronies and their wives could easily size up Brenda Marr's size? She tried to make herself scarcer by pulling in her stomach, an impossible feat.

As the orchestra paced out the galumphing ballet music, the dancers rose, plucking their harps and moving sinuously across the stage.

That Academy stage definitely had it in for Brenda. As she started to trip gracefully on her way, a nail, left by a careless stagehand, came into contact with the toe of her slipper. Trip was right! She went down, the harp crashing under her.

The audience must have thought that it was part of the act to pep up 'Aida' (which could stand a little pepping up). There was applause and a lot of laughter. Brenda remained prostrate, utterly humiliated. Then another emotion took stage. Defiance. 'So, I'm a fat, clumsy comedian. So what? They seem to want a comedian, so I'll give 'em one!'

She hauled up, confronted the howling mob, made a funny face, then turned and showed her behind, skipped by the startled faces of the ballet girls and bounded off stage.

More applause and laughter.

Blumov, in the wings, let loose a flood of angry Russian. Brenda was certain that it was obscene. Mother grabbed her hand, rushed her into the dressing room and into her clothes, and down to the parking lot where Aldo was waiting.

"I tripped over the damned nail," Brenda protested tearfully.

"It's all right," Mother soothed. "It could happen to anyone."

What couldn't happen to everyone was what happened to Brenda at the breakfast table. Instead of gloom from Mother in her pink negligee, she received a radiant smile.

"Oh, Brenda. You're all written up."

"Yes," Dad said. "Looks like my daughter's a sudden celebrity. Here...read it."

There it was in black and white in the Daily Post.

"In last night's performance of 'Aida,' Brenda Marr stole the show with her mime of a ballet dancer's dilemma. This touch of comedy was either provided by the genius of Maestro Plotkin to enliven the turgid ballet, or was the creation of Miss Marr. She seemed to enjoy her trip and carried it off with aplomb. It created a lively diversion."

"You see," Mother said, "You carried it off. You're a real performer."

Brenda expected to be fired from the ballet, but she guessed that Blumov had decided that he did not want to lose a good source of income provided by Mother. He'd also probably read the write up. In any event, nothing happened except that the mothers gave Brenda funny looks and the girls giggled. The Maestro had a ball with her in song at the next class. To the strains of a Chopin waltz, he sang, "Brenda, Brenda fell on her tummy. Brenda, Brenda looked very funny."

At the end of his song, Brenda turned around and showed her behind to the class. Everyone laughed. Even the redoubtable Blumov managed a snigger.

About this time, something miraculous occurred. Brenda's toes began to turn out and, due no doubt to Mother's persistence with the eye exercises, Brenda's walleye began to bounce off the wall and take its rightful place. But more miraculous, she began to show signs of thinning around the middle, possibly due to the massaging it got when her dance partner grabbed her love handles to hoist her into the air. She was even able to get up on point with ease, and her reflection in the mirror in leotards began to look more willowy.

Her face thinned and high cheekbones began to appear. The effect was nice and, encouraged, Brenda began to lose interest in eating. She took to eating almost nothing. Imitating Kratcha's diet of spinach, hard-boiled eggs and chocolate gave Brenda indigestion so…she cut out the spinach and substituted French fries. This gave Mother indigestion.

Brenda began to pattern herself on Kratcha, sleeking down her dark hair and imitating Kratcha's walk, which was kind of a graceful Garbo slouch. She wore boots, Russian blouses and took up smoking with a long cigarette holder. She looked so much like Kratcha that the Maestro began serenading her in class. "Brenda, Brenda, she's looking very slenda. She's pale like Valotna and has lost her little potna."

So, Brenda had her image now and it was proving to be a success. She began getting leading roles in the ballets and was written up in the papers as "That talented daughter of Lillian and Jason Marr." When people stared at her now, it was because she was looking good. And she did enjoy it when men gave her an appreciative glance. It gave a big boost to her moral. She decided that what she needed was more men in her life.

# CHAPTER 5

▼

# MEN AND BRENDA

### The Lawyer With the Sleepy Blue Eyes

So far, Brenda's encounters with the opposite sex had been with boys of the feminine gender at Plotkin's. Now something new was added: Jordan Kirsh, a Philadelphia lawyer.

This happened at an Opera Supper Dance following the performance of the 'Jongleur de Notre Dame,' in which Brenda played the role of the Madonna. Due no doubt to her Madonna hairdo, she had been chosen to play the part over other girls at Plotkin's.

The role required her to stand motionless, high above the Academy stage while the Juggler, a famous Met soprano, performed her juggling act. At the end of this, the Madonna came to life. As the Juggler prostrated herself before her, the Madonna opened her arms in blessing.

It was kind of nerve-wracking to hold still for fifteen minutes with Dad's cronies training their opera glasses on her to see if she'd twitch. But she managed to restrain a violent desire to rub an itchy nose. However, when she bestowed her blessing on the Juggler, emotion summoned a flood of tears. These dripped down onto the hand of the electrician holding the halo over the Juggler's head. This prop man was heard by Brenda to mutter, "Where the hell's the rain coming from?"

Brenda managed to restrain hysterical laughter until, mercifully, the curtain descended.

Now, sitting next to Jordan Kirsh amid supper party chatter, Brenda remained withdrawn, still in character and pretty beat from being so holy up on stage. She was also pondering that maybe she should drop the Valotna image and shoot for the Madonna image. The hairdo would fit it quite well.

This thought was fortified when Jordan, a popular bachelor around town and a lover of the arts and pretty women, turned to her and said, "You make a lovely Madonna."

Brenda came out of her trance and found herself looking into the sleepy blue eyes of an attractive "older man."

"Thanks."

"But why so sad?"

"I'm not."

"I'm glad. Anyhow, I'm addicted to Madonnas. How about lunch next week?"

Brenda felt a flutter. It was the first time a man had asked her to lunch. Yes, the Madonna image was definitely paying off.

"I guess it will be all right," she said. "I'll have to ask."

"Who?"

"My mother."

A light danced in those eyes.

"Would you like to bring her along?"

Brenda said with dignity, "My mother doesn't go every place with me."

This was pretty much a lie. She did get to go to the bathroom alone and that was about it.

"At the Bellevue? Say Tuesday at one?"

"I guess it'll be alright."

Mother and Dad went into a conference. Dad had heard of Jordan and that he had an important government job.

Mother said, "I doubt if this Mr. Kirsh knows Brenda's age. She looks so much older."

"What's the difference?" Brenda moaned. "It's only lunch."

"I think we should meet this Mr. Kirsh, Jason."

"Before or after lunch?" Brenda remarked sarcastically.

For her date, Brenda wore her Russian boots, a peasant blouse, and a tall fur hat and looked as though she were about to dash on stage for a quick balalaika. She sported her new cigarette holder and flourished it gracefully as Krotcha did. Jordan ordered her a sherry. She gulped it down and it immediately made her woozy, as she was unused to alcohol. She ordered an egg salad sandwich and hoping to impress him, told Jordan about her poetry.

"I must read it," he said. "I've always wanted to know a lady poet."

Those sleepy eyes could tease.

"And I understand you're a solo dancer with the Plotkin Ballet and were written up for your fine performance. So, you're multi-talented."

Somewhere Brenda had read the line, "Enough about me, let's talk about you."

She sprang it on him. He knew his line, too.

"But you're so much more interesting."

He raised her hand to his lips. She pulled away.

"What was that for?"

"Because you're a lovely, talented and charming child."

Her fur hat, which was too big, had slid down to her eyebrows. She pushed it back. "I'm not a child. I'm sixteen–almost."

His eyebrows raised a fraction.

"Did you think I was older?"

"Well–yes."

"How old?"

"Maybe twenty."

She flushed with pleasure.

He was smiling. "I think I've fallen in love with you–for life!"

Jordan passed muster with the family. Dad thought him a decent sort and invited him to play tennis at the club. He became a frequent dinner guest and when he asked Mother if he might escort Brenda to the theatre sometime, she surprised Brenda by saying it would be fine. She said he impressed her as being a gentleman of the old school. She would trust Brenda with him anywhere.

Jordan liked glamorous ladies of the theatre and spent much time in New York and L.A. in pursuit of them. But when in town, he squired Brenda. To her annoyance, he called her "Baby." She liked his importance and enjoyed dressing up and being taken to the theatre in his chauffer-driven limo.

But how could you fall in love with someone who didn't even try to kiss you and called you "Baby"? Besides, he was too old.

## The Maestro With the Halo On Top

Brenda's next male encounter took her out of the baby class when she finally met HIM. She was now seventeen and her dancing career had progressed quite well. She'd been asked to dance at the Academy Pension Fund Concert for the Philadelphia Orchestra.

Those Friday afternoons after school, sitting next to Mother, and emotionally primed by seductive and passionate orchestral strains, Brenda dreamed. The dreams mostly had to do with the male objects before her eyes.

And mostly to do with HIM.

Now, as she waited for her cue to go on, there he was in the wings, across the stage from her. There was the beautiful form and the bright halo of golden hair, which since childhood she had worshipped as he hurled thunderbolts of sound from his long, graceful fingers or drew soft, sensuous strains from the violins.

And HE was watching her.

The orchestra in the pit, conducted by a second in command, gave her intro. She swung out in her newly thinned-out form into her Oriental dance. Wearing her Ruth St. Dennis black and gold skirt, her arms swaying sinuously, she gave her all for HIM.

Once again tilting at her old enemy, the Academy Stage, Brenda made with the pirouettes. Climbing that hill, her skirt billowed out spectacularly and its flash as she circled brought on a burst of applause.

As she whirled off stage, the din of applause in her ears, the Maestro stopped her. In delicate, precise and accented English he said, "Bravo, my dear. You are indeed talented."

"Thanks," she panted, barely able to breath from the exertion plus the effect of his piercing eyes.

As the orchestra pounded into Traviata and a soprano let loose, the Maestro drew her into the backstage shadows.

"My dear, I'm working with a ballet company in New York. Would you be interested in joining?"

"Oh, yes!"

"Why not stop by here next Wednesday. I will be rehearsing and after, we could have a little lunch and discuss everything. Would you like that?"

"Oh, yes."

Wednesday at eleven, she sat just offstage while the god worked his magic. Violins soared and cried. Basses leaped and moaned. Sometimes he would stop them sternly.

"Not so heavy." Or, "Pour in the sound. I want more sound."

He wore a turtleneck sweater and dark trousers. His waist was slim; his shoulders, wide; his halo, a golden, fluid flame, which trembled and danced to the music. To her worshipful gaze, he was every inch a god.

The rehearsal over, humbly waiting with her dance bag in hand, as she would be going to class later, the Maestro joined her. He took her arm and guided her through the mysterious cavernous backstage, which she knew quite well. Past the stars' dressing rooms then up a dark stairway, which echoed to their footsteps. She had not known this venerable building housed a private inner sanctum under its roof, the Maestro's lair!

It was a bright room filled with Oriental rugs and modern paintings slashed with color, like wounds. From a refrigerator concealed behind a screen, the Maestro produced lettuce, tomatoes and raw carrots, which he placed on a long, low table in front of long, low divan. This was so low, in fact, that they were almost lying down.

Munching this rabbit food and sipping dry, white wine, his knee occasionally touched hers in a way that sent a quivering signal to certain parts of her anatomy.

'Where is he going to touch me next?' she wondered, as Mother's warning gong reverberated in her ears.

After their second wine, the Maestro queried gently, "Tell me, little one, have you love in your life?"

"What do you mean?" she stammered.

"You are young, but surely with your attributes, some man has–"

Casually he picked up her hand and turned it over.

"In your palm I see many loves to come to you in your life."

She summoned a smile to trembling lips.

"The boys I know are kind of boring."

"Ah, yes." A faint smile. "In other words they are, shall we say, too short."

"Some of them are tall."

The smile lingered. "I didn't mean that."

"Oh, you mean that their capacity is short. They're limited."

"Exactly. How well you understand. Your need is for something much beyond what they can offer."

He raised the inside of her hand to his lips and she felt the trace of his tongue upon it, sending a frantic shiver up her spine. 'Why he's licking my palm,' she thought, 'and why is it making me feel so queer?'

She withdrew her hand.

The smile still lingered in the curve of his full lips.

"You are a lovely child, and intelligent. I would love to be the one to–"

Thinking about 'the thing', she jumped to her feet, stammering wildly. "Maestro, I must leave. I have a rehearsal and—"

He also rose, unhurriedly, graceful god with the halo on top.

"Must you, my dear? Well, I will let you know about the ballet. I hope you will join. Meanwhile, if you ever feel you would like to visit me, please do. You perhaps know where I live, that little house near Camac Street. Just come around and ring the little bell and I will know it's you.

Cheeks flaming, she fled, stumbling down those mysterious stairs. Her god had fallen from grace. The halo had feet of clay. Besides, his hands were not that beautiful close up. The fingers were kind of stubby and his accent sounded phony.

To the family and Jordan, she told all amid hoots of merriment from Ted.

"Come ring the little bell, Brenda," became Ted's theme song around the house.

Mother was furious. "That man may be a genius, but he's horrid. He's seduced half the women in this town, more fools they. Don't you ever go near that place."

"But I want to be in his ballet. I want to live in New York."

"At your age, you're not going to live alone in New York."

"Maybe we could get a nanny," Ted suggested.

Mother's look silenced him.

"Jason, back me up on this," she demanded.

"New York is out," Dad said sternly.

# CHAPTER 6

▼

# MARTIN, MAN OF MYSTERY

Brenda's next experience in the romance department was with one Dad dubbed "Man of Mystery."

And Brenda was all for mystery.

Dad met Martin M. Schrull through a fellow architect. Martin was a playwright and looking for a quiet spot to indulge this hobby. It seemed he spoke several languages and had no visible means of support except for an occasional French or Spanish lesson he managed to scare up. Mother, always a sucker for the struggling artist, particularly one with charm, allowed him to live rent-free in the small house she owned next door if he would keep the grass cut.

Martin said he would and fell in love with Mother.

Mother said Martin wasn't so good looking, but he had sensitive hands. Mother was all for sensitive hands. She began to invite him to dinner because she was afraid he wasn't getting enough to eat.

Brenda wasn't impressed by his looks. He had a fair build, but his eyes were too far apart. This gave him a kind of wistful expression, which she later dubbed "shifty." His neck was too short and his mouth was kind of small and girlish. He also had this funny accent, kind of German or Jewish or something.

Martin did a lot of hand kissing of Mother and Brenda, which Brenda thought annoying and affected. She felt like saying, "Kiss my foot." Mother ate it up. Ted remarked, with his usual quiet insight, that he thought Martin's foreign airs put on, as though he were acting a part. And what kind of name is Schrull? Once at dinner when Ted asked what Martin's middle initial M. stood for, Martin replied, "Mortimer."

"Mortimer!" Brenda hooped. "Like in Mortimer Snerd!"

"Mortimer is an English name, is it not?" Martin said with dignity.

Mother gave Brenda a severe look. "Certainly, and a very good name, too."

Ted told Brenda later, "I knew his name was phony. Probably made it up and comes from Minsk or Pinsk. Thought he could get away with being English by calling himself Mortimer."

Ted was incapable of dislike toward anyone, but he'd pegged Martin as an adventurer type and was afraid he'd louse up his little sister.

But Brenda was all for adventurer types. Also, Martin gave her her first chance to exercise her womanliness. This she did by teasing him about his spats. "What's those funny things on your feet?" And about his loused up English such as, "An eye for an eye and a toot for a toot."

But Martin knew his women and men, having hauled himself out of some back alley in Middle Eastern Europe by his ability to charm. He saw through Brenda's ploy and that it spelled, "Notice me. Come get me." He saw this little Main Line maiden was ripe for the plucking. And, he intended to pluck.

He began his campaign by wooing Mother with compliments and candy. He cozied up to Dad, running his errands and supplying him with magazines and the chewing gum Dad enjoyed since he'd given up smoking. He couldn't do enough for them.

He might have liked to woo Brenda's grandparents. But when Mother took him to the other house in his natty gray suit, Grandma kept peering through her lorgnettes. "Who did you say he is, Lillian?"

Mother tried to explain he was living in the house next door. But Grandma got it into her head he was a car salesman and said she was perfectly happy with her nineteen, twenty-five Buick. Grandpa thought he was an actor and asked if he knew Buster Keaton. Mother didn't take Martin up the hill again.

Mother decided that since it was the slack season at Plotkins, and to please Dad, Brenda should stay home this summer and write. That was great with Martin. He had acquired an ancient Chevrolet and began taking Brenda on drives in the country, during which he told her how beautiful and talented she was. Brenda knew this from Mother, but hearing it from a man made it sound real authentic. He also told her of his sad childhood of an aristocratic but impoverished French family and how he was orphaned at fourteen. His one desire had been to come to America, land of his dreams. But he had struggled here, even gone hungry. He wasn't an American citizen yet but hoped to be one soon.

Brenda ate this up. It was better than a novel and she was playing the sympathetic heroine.

To insure they were constantly together, Martin came up with the idea of giving Brenda French lessons in the evening. Mother thought this great. Dad was less impressed. Martin never seemed to know when to go home and would linger in the hallway endlessly.

"Martin," Dad would say, leaning over the banister, "I know parting is supposed to be sweet sorrow, but I'd like to lock up and go to bed."

"Yes, Sir," Martin declared. "Just leaving. I was trying to teach your daughter how to say 'bon jour.'"

"I think bon soir would be more appropriate."

But Dad wasn't always around to monitor the goodnights and the week a business deal took him to Chicago, Martin made his move.

Now, after the lessons, he bestowed a lingering good night kiss at the door. Brenda didn't mind. Those sensitive, girlish lips seemed to fuse so sweetly with hers. In fact, they tasted sweet. Had he just sucked a cough drop? The operation seemed esthetic, soothing, like listening to Debussy. Surely nothing to which Mother could object.

Then Martin asked Mother if he could take Brenda to dinner and dancing.

"You mustn't spend all that money on Brenda," Mother told him.

"It is the least I can do to repay you for your generosity," he said, kissing Mother's hand. "And I think Brenda will enjoy it."

"Just don't bring her home too late."

Ted wondered where he'd gotten all the money. "Maybe he robbed a bank," he commented.

"Don't be silly," Mother said. "He told Brenda he has an aunt in the South of France who sends him a check once in a while."

"A likely story. Probably some woman but not an aunt."

"What's the difference," Brenda said. "I'm getting a free meal out of it."

Brenda was excited, her first dinner date, and in a French restaurant. Pale and Krotcha-like in Russian boots and an off the shoulder peasant blouse, she sailed in, noting how Martin slipped the Maitre D' a tip for a good table and then ordered the dinner and wine in French. She was impressed. Later at the nightclub, they danced the Tango, at which Martin was adept, while people stared admiringly. This was great. This was really living! Brenda hated the night to end.

It didn't. Martin had more plans in store.

Mother had left a light on in the hall and Brenda, sleepy with wine, allowed Martin to lead her into the library for a last cigarette. Beside her on the sofa, he held her hand and talked about her beautiful shoulders.

"Do you mind?" he said, leaning over and bestowing on her shoulder a light kiss.

"Not really." Brenda felt like yawning.

"Lovely Madonna. Lovely Main Line Madonna."

He took her in his arms and there were mouth kisses, delicate as usual, nothing Mother could object to. The kisses grew deeper. Martin's tongue parted her lips. This woke her up. She thought, 'Oh-oh, another tongue sticker like old De Lima.' But, unlike that other, this was a soothing caress, which she found was causing a delicious kind of weakness to invade her body.

She thought of Mother's words. "Never let a man put his tongue in your mouth. Wet kisses lead to other wetness."

She was curious about that.

Then that sensitive hand Mother admired stole inside her blouse.

After the first shock, this new operation began to feel pretty good. Her breasts liked the feel of this and Brenda began to agree with them. While this was going on, Martin's other hand crept under her skirt and up her thigh. She thought of protesting, but her mouth was full of Martin's tongue.

She remembered Bunny's words. "He kind of fooled around with his finger."

She thought of pushing the hand away. Mother certainly wouldn't like this. But she was curious. How far could this go? Then the hand went all the way up and the finger took over.

Oops! What gives? Mother certainly wouldn't go for this!

The finger soothed and caressed and, like Bunny said, it wasn't too bad. You could get used to it. What now?

What now was Martin, unzipped and whispering, "Hold me, Darling," and placing 'the thing' in her hand.

Soft and hard, like Bunny said. It felt strange, like some live, pulsing creature.

"Move it, Darling," he whispered.

She didn't want to, but there seemed no way out. Moving it broke his soothing finger's spell. Also, Martin began making weird little squealing sounds, kind of ridiculous. The more she moved it, the more he squealed. Finally he let out a big squeal and 'the thing' exploded.

With all this, Brenda's romantic illusions exploded too. So this was what love was like. Rudolph Valentino must have done this too. It was a mess. The hot wetness, all over her hand.

He whipped out his handkerchief. "Sorry, Darling."

He tried to mop up. She gave him a shove.

"Darling, where are you going?"

She was up and running to her room and slamming the door.

The stuff was all over her dress. In the bathroom she scrubbed, but it wouldn't come off. It would leave a stain. How would Mother like that? But Mother must never know. And she was right. Sex was rotten. Now she'd probably look haggard and old, and Martin would drop her like a rotten apple.

She wouldn't give him a chance. She'd drop him. He was rotten. She hated him.

Where was Martin?

He left a phone message with Jancy. "Tell the family I have to go to New York on business."

That was a week ago.

Dad had returned and they were at dinner.

Dad said, "It seems odd of Martin to take off like this."

"I hope nothing's happened to him," Mother said. "I sent Jancy to check his place, but nothing's missing.

Mother was missing Martin's charm and compliments.

She continued. "That night Martin took you to dinner, did you quarrel, Brenda?"

"No."

"He took Brenda to dinner?" Dad questioned. "How could he afford that?"

"You sure none of your silver's missing?" Ted offered.

"He could of at least phoned," Mother said.

For the last few days, Brenda'd been in a stew. After making her feel so rotten, then just taking off. Where'd he get the money? Did he have some woman in New York, like Ted thought?

"Maybe it's just as well he's gone," Dad said. "Bob Weller told me that though Martin seemed nice enough, he knew nothing about him. He seemed upset Martin was here so often."

Mother said, "People are so quick to think wrong things. Martin is perfectly nice. I'm sure we'll hear from him."

"I'm sure we will," Ted put in dryly.

They were finishing dessert when in walked Martin in a new suit.

"Well," Dad said. "Man of Mystery, where have you been?"

Mother looked happy as Martin bent to kiss her hand.

"We were worried about you."

"I did try to phone," he said. "But your line was busy."

'Liar,' thought Brenda, 'our line is never that busy.'

"Have some dessert," Mother said.

He pulled up a chair next to Brenda.

"I have some good news. A producer friend likes my play. He's going to put up some money to keep me going while I finish it."

"That's wonderful!" Mother exclaimed, her eyes fastening on Dad. "You see!"

"That is rather unusual," Dad said.

"I know. I'm very lucky."

Ted got up and said he was going to the movies, but nobody noticed. While Martin launched into a description of his storming of Broadway, his knee kept contacting Brenda's under the table and giving her those odd feelings.

Sure, what he'd done was rotten and sex was nasty, but she hadn't noticed herself looking that haggard. She guessed she didn't really hate Martin that much and things had been pretty dull without him. She looked at his mouth and remembered how it felt kissing her. She looked at his hands and remembered how they'd made her feel. Even if his neck was too short, he looked really sharp in that new blue suit.

She decided that even though sex wasn't that great, it had its moments. And, after all, all the girls did it. You could probably get used to it. Brenda decided to give it a whirl.

It happened often, in the car at night, on country roads. Down by the pond when they were supposedly having a French lesson.

Sometimes Brenda had pangs of guilt, but she rationalized they were not doing the "real thing." Martin wasn't too happy. He wanted the real thing. Sometimes he tried for it.

Brenda held out. "You might get me pregnant."

"Of course not. I'll take precautions."

Sure, if he got her pregnant, she'd have to marry him. Great for him, he'd have a home and could eat regularly.

They began to quarrel. Sometimes she lashed out.

"You claim to love my family. They wouldn't want you to do this."

He had an answer for everything. "Darling, if they knew how deep our love, they'd understand."

She could have stopped it. She didn't want to. She was bored trying to write. She wanted excitement. He was supplying it.

The hot summer dragged on and Brenda grew pale with so much loving. She lost her appetite and with the guilt feelings, grew nervous and tense.

Then, the inevitable happened. Dad caught them kissing in the library. Brenda thanked God that was all they were doing!

Dad cleared his throat and they jumped apart.

He said sternly, "Brenda, go to your room. I want to talk to Martin."

She made for the stairs but returned to listen at the door.

Dad said, "Martin, Mrs. Marr and I feel that you should go away for awhile. You're seeing too much of Brenda. She's too young to get involved with anyone and certainly not with you. You've been living hand to mouth, giving those lessons, taking your meals with us–which I certainly don't begrudge, times being hard with the depression."

Martin's voice, very low, "I'll never be able to thank you enough for what you've done for me."

Dad said, "The fact that there are a lot of unknown quantities about you. For instance, this mysterious aunt you receive money from, and the producer friend…could they be one and the same person?"

Martin sounded flustered. "To be truthful, this friend in New York is kind enough to help until I get on my feet."

"A lady friend?"

"Yes," he added quickly. "Of course I intend to pay her back every cent."

Dad asked coldly, "Is this lady in love with you?"

He said quickly, "Believe me, it's purely a business arrangement. She believes in my play and—"

The words came in a rush. "Mr. Marr, I'm in love with your daughter."

Dad said angrily, "It's presumptuous of you to fasten your sights on an innocent girl like Brenda. You have nothing to offer."

Silence, then Martin said slowly, "I was afraid you'd say that. Believe me, I would never hurt Brenda or you and Mrs. Marr. I'm devoted to you all. Coming here is the most wonderful thing that ever happened to me. You see, I was orphaned young. I never had a real home—" his voice trailed off.

He was really pouring it on. 'There ought to be violin music to go with this,' Brenda thought. But was Pop swallowing it? Not Dad.

"It's too bad, Martin, but that's the way it is. My advice for you is to leave here and look for a job. The sooner, the better. And you're not to spend any more time with Brenda. Understood?"

Brenda couldn't resist a peek at them. Martin's neck seemed to be growing shorter as it tried to retreat into his collar.

Brenda took off for her room, surprised to find she felt only relief at this turn of events. She guessed she hadn't really been that in love with Martin. She felt that life had better things in store for her. Interesting things away from here, in New York, wherever. Things weren't very interesting around here right now.

In fact, they suddenly became downright lousy when Mother announced the "great news."

# CHAPTER 7

▼

# ONE BIG HAPPY FAMILY

They were at the dinner table when Mother uttered the words.

"Mama just told me Margot, Jake and their brood are coming to live with her for a while. She wants us to come to dinner."

"Lord," Dad said.

Ted continued to eat, but Brenda knew he was thinking, 'What have we done to deserve this?'

Grandma wanted them all to be one big happy family and made them come to those dinners. It was awful, everyone trying to pretend to like each other. Still, Brenda was curious to see what they'd all be like after the two years they'd been gone. She figured, now she was older and could handle anything they could dish out.

"I guess Margot will try to make my life a misery again," Mother said.

Mother never discussed Aunt Margot in front of Brenda and Ted. She must really be upset.

"She's always disliked me," Mother said.

"She's jealous of your beauty," Dad put in.

"I don't know why. She was considered the greatest beauty in Philadelphia."

Dad said, "She's too fragile for my taste. She can't compare with you."

"Her girls are considered beautiful too, according to Mama."

"I don't think they're beautiful," Brenda put in.

"They certainly don't have any of Brenda's talent," Mother said.

"They're dumb," Brenda said.

"Hush."

"Grandpa doesn't like Aunt Margot. He calls her 'the whited sepulcre,' whatever that is. To me, she always looks sick."

She did, too, Brenda thought. That dyed black hair and dead-white skin.

Mother said, "She tried to ruin my life the year we came out."

"Your mother said you had a wonderful time," Dad said.

"Margot tried to steal the men who were attentive to me. Not that I wanted any of them."

Dad smiled. "You were waiting for me."

"And that gossip she spread about me is still going on."

Dad had box seats for the Metropolitan Opera at the Academy of Music. Sometimes Mother made Brenda go. Brenda hated opera, those fatsos sitting on phony rocks and yelling in a foreign language about how they loved each other and trying to get close enough over those stomachs to kiss.

To Mother, this was all great. She would rest in the afternoon to look her best. Then in her gold dress and brocade cape with the ermine collar, she would sail into the box, trailed by Dad, tall, erect and black bearded. Beauties. No wonder people stared and tongues wagged.

On this night, they had really wagged. Those whispered words came back to Brenda.

"Isn't that Lillian Marr?" one woman said.

"Yes, she came out my year."

"What a queer woman. Margot Woodruff says she's a regular hermit. Just plays the piano by the hour."

Brenda glanced around. Gossipy old biddies. Who cared what they thought?

Dad hadn't noticed, but Mother heard. Brenda remembered her hiding behind her rose colored fan, her face flushed, her evening ruined. At this moment, Brenda began to understand a lot of things; that Mother was no match for malicious tongues like these and Aunt Margot's. So that was why Mother hid from people. Damn Aunt Margot anyhow!

"Forget it," Dad said. "It's not important."

Mother wasn't eating her soup.

She said, "Mama says they plan to stay East permanently so the girls can go to the right schools, have a proper training and marry the right men."

"God help the men," Dad said.

"Margot only dragged Jake to Wyoming to get him away from some woman."

"A losing game," Dad said. "Jake will always have some woman, or women."

According to Mother, Uncle Jake was a rake. The only rake Brenda knew was the garden kind. This other must be something pretty bad. Though Jake didn't look like much, he must have something going for him. Scandals followed him: young girls pregnant, their families raising hell. This drove the parents bananas, as they had to shell out hush money to the injured.

Jake was always into some get rich scheme, like the cattle ranch in Wyoming that never made it. Grandma could refuse him nothing and the result was that in spite of their good income, they were often broke. Then Grandma would call on Mother to run things and to help them save money. Brenda blamed Mother's stinginess on Jake. She valued money so much because of all Jake had connived to grab what should have been hers. Uncle Jake would stand on the terrace under Mother's window, yelling that she didn't own Grandpa's money and how dare she say he couldn't have any. Mother said she always got the short end of the stick.

There was never enough money for her piano lessons but always enough for Jake to buy a polo pony.

Uncle Jake liked Brenda and was always pestering her to go to a polo match with him. Mother didn't want her to associate with him. She said he had no morals and might put nasty ideas into her head. Mother was strong on morals.

Her soup was cold by now and she told Jancy to take it away.

"What's wrong with it?" Jancy sounded hurt.

"I don't want it."

"I don't know why you let Margot get to you," Dad said.

"Mama had me on the phone all morning, excited about them coming. She'll regret it. Margot'll start complaining about Jake's affairs and then I'll have to listen to that."

"You could hang up."

"Mama caters to Margot."

"She's always been impressed that Margot's descended from some Civil War General who, history has it, was no great shakes."

There was a statue of that General in Fairmont Park. Brenda enjoyed it when they drove by the statue and how Dad always tipped his hat in mock reverence.

Mother said, "As for Margot's girls, I never want them in my house again."

Jancy, passing the overdone chicken, thrust out her lower lip and muttered, "Them girls expecting me to wait on 'em hand and foot like they done before."

On one of their visits, Cousin Billy got the measles and Grandma dumped Margot's three girls on Mother so they wouldn't catch the germ. They ordered Aya and Jancy around and made everyone miserable, particularly Cynthia. Prettier and meaner than the others, she had a special place in Brenda's memory.

At thirteen, Cynthia was already a heart-wrecker and was entertaining a couple of the "right" boys in the parlor. Brenda, lured by curiosity, ventured downstairs in her jammies, the kind with the flap in the back.

She peeked around the corner to be greeted by a whoop of derision from Cynthia. "Ooh, look at fatso Brenda in her jammies! Keep your flap up, Brenda!"

The boys guffawed. Brenda fled and cried.

Mother said, "Margot always puts her children up to being mean to mine. Remember how Billy got those boys to throw stones at Ted when he was coming home from school? Brenda flew at Billy and ripped the buttons off his shirt."

Brenda said, "I wanted to give him a black eye. But he beat it."

Ted was smiling. "That's my sister."

"You should have more of Brenda's gumption," Mother reproached. "I worry about you."

"I don't see any point in fighting over nothing," Ted said. "And you don't have to worry about me. I'm taking boxing lessons at school."

"Ted can take care of himself, Lillian," Dad said.

"You mustn't do those things, Brenda," Mother said. "It makes dissension. Try to be nicer to Billy this time."

"I don't like him. He's rotten."

Like that time he said he'd show her his if she'd show him hers, and she punched him in the stomach.

Mother said, "No, I won't have Brenda coming out. Those girls'll knife her like Margot did me. As I've said, I want her to have a career."

"How about as a prize fighter?" Ted put in.

"Drop dead," Brenda said.

Mother was cutting up her chicken.

"Jancy, it's overcooked again."

Jancy pursed up her under lip, which was kind of big.

"It was only in an hour."

"It's not bad," Brenda said. She liked her eats, even dried chicken. "Anyhow, the food'll be good at Grandma's."

The food was always good at Grandma's: roast duck, applesauce, candied sweets and asparagus with Hollandaise.

Grandma was at the head of the table, her fat little fingers crowned with their diamonds' glitter, her curly white hair around her pink face. Brenda guessed it was her cute giggle and dimples that got grandpa to marry her and let her rule him. Dad said that Grandma had a Queen Victoria complex, whatever that was.

Grandpa, at the other end of the table, blew in his whiskers and stamped his foot every so often, making people jump. Brenda knew he did this because these people were making him nervous.

Aunt Margot on his right, looked sick as ever with that white stuff on her face. In Brenda's opinion, she put it on to impress upon her girls how helpless and delicate she was. The girls still looked like pale imitations of their mother, except Cynthia, who was really a knockout and mean as ever, Brenda was sure. Of course, they were nice and skinny. But who cared? She noted that her legs were better. They all had fat ankles like Aunt Margot's.

They still made her nervous, but she vowed she wouldn't show it. They had this way of looking you up and down critically, waiting for you to speak first. This time, Brenda did it to Cynthia, who was sitting next to her.

Finally, Cynthia said, "How are you, Brenda?"

Brenda noted she imitated her mother's way of speaking, that slow drawl through clenched teeth thought attractive by Main Line ladies. When Brenda heard it, she always felt like saying, "Speak up if you've got something to say."

To her, their speech sounded like a cross between brain damage and lockjaw.

"Faan. How are you?" Brenda replied, trying out an imitation of the clenched jaw.

"Putting on a little weight, aren't you?" Cynthia said.

The girls across the table gave those smiles.

"No. Are you?" Brenda said.

Old Billy at the other end of the table imitated her. "No, are you?" and laughed.

"Oh, shut up," Brenda said.

"Brenda," Mother reproached.

Brenda saw Dad and Ted exchange glances and saw they were going to keep a low profile. She decided she'd better only open her mouth to eat.

Being nice, Dad tried to make conversation with Aunt Margot about the beauties of Wyoming.

"A dreadful place!" Aunt Margot exclaimed. "I was glad to leave. The girls must get into a good school here." She turned to Brenda. "Where are you going to school?"

Aunt Margot had a wonderful way of timing a question when you had a full mouth.

Mother took over. "Brenda's going to Mrs. Jenner's Academy."

Apparently, this didn't overwhelm Aunt Margot.

"Why do you send her there? It's a boarding school, isn't it? A place for girls from out of town."

"It has a fine scholastic record," Dad said.

"Yes," Mother said. "And they specialize in the arts."

Grandma chimed in. "I told Lillian Brenda wouldn't meet the right girls there, but she insisted."

"Brenda's going to school to learn, not to meet people," Dad said. "And she's doing very well."

Aunt Margot seemed to lose interest.

"I'm thinking of sending my girls to Shady Lawn Academy."

"A good choice," Grandma said. "It'll get them into the right set."

Conversation dwindled while they ate. Billy was skinny, but Brenda saw he was putting it away. He looked like a pig with his nose in a trough. Then Aunt Margot said her girls needed new clothes and Grandma said she would take them to Wanamaker's and outfit them.

"And I will need something new for the Assembly Ball," Aunt Margot added.

"Yes, you must have something lovely," Grandma said. "I'm so glad you're going."

Brenda saw Mother's blonde eyebrows rise. If there was anything she couldn't stand, it was the Assembly Ball. This Philadelphia Ball was said to be America's oldest and most exclusive party, dating back to 1748 when members of the city's first families put their names on the original subscription list. Apparently, it was a way to pep up the long winter months. To belong was supposed to be an indication of first family status. Mother had gone in her debutante year, escorted by an uncle who was "in."

"The whole thing's a farce," Brenda'd heard her exclaim. "People all gussied up, bowing and curtsying through that receiving line, trying to act like royalty, dancing till their feet fell off and ending up eating lukewarm scrambled eggs at 3 a.m."

"So, you're going to that, are you Margot?" Mother said stiffly.

"Of course Jake won't go with me, but the Newsomes have invited me to go with them."

Brenda'd heard Mother say the only smart thing Jake ever did was to refuse to go to the Assembly.

"Lillian and I will take you to our dressmaker for your ball gown," Grandma said.

Brenda knew Mother was thinking, 'Indeed I will not.'

Grandma added, a bit wistfully, "The Assembly is a lovely thing to do. We could have belonged, but Papa never wanted to."

Grandpa blew and stamped. "Bunch of damn foolishness! Never could stand it!" He stroked his whiskers gently while Grandma gave him a dirty look.

Mother gave him a beautiful smile. "I quite agree with you, Papa."

Brenda loved Grandpa's whiskers. They were so bushy and nice. She'd never seen him without them. It seemed, one Fourth of July to celebrate, he shot off the old family cannon on the lawn. It backfired and burned him badly and he never shaved again.

Aunt Margot didn't say anything else. Brenda guessed she wanted to stay on the right side of her father-in-law. After all, he was the one with the money and, in spite of Grandma, had been known to tighten the purse strings. Her phony sweetness never cut any ice with him. He wasn't so nutty.

The conversation took a slump. But Uncle Jake, who could always be counted on to pep things up, made his appearance from the downstairs powder room where he had been eating his meal of shredded wheat biscuits and whole milk.

Uncle Jake never ate with them. He was supposed to have a Woodruff stomach and the gas attacks like Grandma and Mother. Even though he lived on his skimpy diet, he seemed to be strong as an ox and could spend hours on the hunting and polo fields and never tire.

Tonight, ornery as always, he paced around the table making remarks like, "What's that you're eating? It'll only make you fat." He had a point there.

When Annie, the pretty, young waitress appeared, he gave her one of his quips. "Hi, Annie. Still snatching those mackerels every Friday?" Annie was a Roman Catholic.

She giggled. "Oh, Mr. Jake, that's not nice."

Brenda thought he would have liked to pat her behind but restrained himself. This he seldom did. He didn't care who he insulted. He seemed to care only about satisfying his whims and sexual desires. But at least he was honest about himself. Brenda once heard him say, "All I want out of life is to be in a position to tell everyone to go to hell."

He danced over behind Mother. "Well, Sister, still playing the pi-a-no? That won't get you anywhere."

Mother ignored him.

"Oh, Jakie, do behave," Grandma said, looking at him fondly.

Jake really made Grandpa nervous. He stamped and blew. This only seemed to provoke Jake to new efforts and sent him to the hall to pick up Mother's hat, put it on and return doing a buck and wing. This, he must have picked up watching all those burlesque shows he went to.

He made some of them laugh but not his brood. They pretended he wasn't there. Brenda knew they couldn't stand him and felt he wronged their mother, which she frequently pointed out.

Finally, he quit the vaudeville act and said he was going to the movies.

"Like to go with me?" he said to Brenda, and pinched her neck.

He was a neck pincher.

"No, thanks."

Grandma said, "Jakie, I wish you wouldn't go to those movies. They're full of germs."

"Well, I'm off," he said.

As he passed Aunt Margot's chair he leaned over and kissed her on the neck. He was a real neck man.

Margot drew up stiffly. "Jake, you're impossible."

Behind her annoyance, even Brenda's young eyes caught something else. A certain sparkle? Brenda later knew that in spite of Jake's sleeping around and other faults this descendant of a U.S. General had, this social beauty queen with morals above reproach was fascinated by her husband. She was never able to subdue him, and to punish him, she turned his children against him. When she annoyed him, he just went to his horses and women. Unable to tame him, she was wildly jealous and in love. And he knew it.

"Don't eat too much," he said. "It slows down your sex life."

He danced off.

Grandma smiled indulgently. "He'll never grow up."

Brenda knew Mother was thinking, 'too bad for him.'

He really was a case of arrested development.

Now the conversation died completely. Everyone was exhausted from eating too much and trying to get along. Brenda thought, 'Thank God it'll soon be over.'

Usually after those dinners, stuffed to the gills, Grandma would make them all go into the high-ceilinged living room with its tall gilded mirrors and antiques. Then, at Grandma's urging, Mother would play Dad's accompaniment on the lace-draped upright piano and he would sing 'Oh, Promise Me' in his beautiful baritone, while the Grandparents nodded and Aunt Margot and the cousins looked bored out of their socks.

Tonight, this was not to be.

They were finishing their baked Alaskas when Aunt Margot turned to Brenda with her sweetest smile.

"I've been meaning to ask, Brenda dear, did you put your nose in the flour barrel?"

Brenda'd been experimenting with make-up, trying to look like Myrna Loy. She'd probably overdone it a little.

As Margot's claque snickered, Brenda felt a rush of annoyed blood.

Out of her popped the words. "You should talk. You look as though you put your whole face in the flour barrel!"

There was a stunned silence. Grandma's voice rang out.

"Brenda! Such behavior! You are to apologize to your Aunt Margot, then you may leave the room."

Poor Mother. Brenda saw her face, flushed and unhappy. Dad's face was bowed over his plate and Ted was chewing on something. If they were smiling, it was inside.

Somehow, Brenda managed it. The inborn ham took over.

She rose and bowed to Aunt Margot.

"My apologies, Aunt Margot. I'll be happy to leave the room. In fact, I'll be delighted."

Feeling a little shaky in the knees, she marched out. Then, lingered by the door to listen.

The remarks were plenty.

Grandma said, "Lillian, you'll have to do something about Brenda. She's completely out of hand. It's terrible the way you let her act. Putting make-up on at her age!"

"I never let my girls wear make-up," Aunt Margot said.

"Quite right," Grandma said. "It's this theatrical thing you indulge her in, Lillian."

"The child likes to play act," Mother said. "I don't see any harm in it."

"I certainly wouldn't let my girls play act, as you put it," Aunt Margot said.

"She sees too many movies," Grandma said.

Grandpa stamped and blew. This was his and Brenda's territory. They loved to go to the movies together. Next, Grandma would be forbidding it. Brenda knew he was thinking, 'Why don't these damn women shut up and let us alone.'

Grandma said, "Margot's quite right. The child should not be allowed to indulge such fantasies. No telling where it'll lead."

"Oh Mama!" Mother exclaimed. "Brenda has a vivid imagination, that's all."

Brenda knew she was thinking, as Dad was, 'And, that's more than Margot's children have.'

Margot's children were eating this all up, Brenda getting the business. 'Dumb clucks,' Brenda thought.

Mother followed Brenda into the living room. She looked woeful. "Brenda, why did you?"

"I'm sorry," Brenda said. But she wasn't.

Dad and Ted came in.

"Get your coats," Dad said. "I've said our goodnights."

"Yeah, let's get the heck out of here." Ted grinned. "I'll never forget Aunt Margot's face when Brenda said that. I thought that white enamel mask she wears would crack."

They laughed. Even Mother managed a smile.

It was a brisk cool evening, but spring was coming. As they walked down the hill, the lights of Upsan Downs beckoned warmly.

Ted put his arm around Brenda's shoulder. "Nice going, B."

"No, it wasn't," Mother said. "I'll never hear the end of this."

"It wasn't very diplomatic of Brenda," Dad said. "But Margot deserved it."

"She certainly did," Brenda piped up. "She started it."

"And you finished it." Ted grinned.

"What kind of bringing up will they think I give you, Brenda?" Mother questioned.

"Who cares?"

"You should care. This does it. My mind's made up. I won't have Brenda coming out and exposing her to them."

"What are you afraid of, Mother?" Brenda asked. "Aren't we as good as they are?"

"Better," Dad said. "I think you're making a lot over nothing, Lillian. I think we should drop the subject."

They were quiet a moment, the sound of their footsteps coming along with them down the gravel driveway.

Mother said, "Margot always tried to make me feel I don't belong. That I'm different."

"Thank God you are," Dad said.

"Sometimes I don't know where I fit in." Mother's voice sounded small.

Dad took her arm. "I'll tell you where we all fit in. And that is in a world where people create, write, paint, and make music. A creative world those people wouldn't understand."

As Dad's words sank in, Brenda had a new insight into Dad's world. Successful, strong and understanding, he would fit in anyplace.

"Our children are unusual and talented," Dad said. "Brenda's an outstanding student and Ted's showing a marked talent for painting."

"And, of course, Brenda's a wonderful dancer," Mother put in.

"Now I have a piece of good news," Dad said. "I understand Jake has badgered your parents into buying them a house. They'll be moving soon."

"Poor Papa," Mother said. "I'll bet it set him back a pretty penny."

"Thank God we won't have to see much of those people anymore," Ted said.

"I never want to see them again," Brenda put in.

"Now, Brenda," Mother said. "They're family."

"The hell with family."

"Jason," Mother said. "Will you make Brenda stop swearing?"

"Stop swearing, Brenda," Dad said.

"Okay."

Brenda skipped ahead and paused to hear Mother say, "Brenda's not only a wonderful dancer, but she has a lovely singing voice. I think the time has come to develop her singing, if she's to have a stage career. And she's certainly capable of it. I've just heard of a fine singing teacher in New York, a Mrs. Tacconi. I'm going to send Brenda to her."

"Okay, if you say so, Mom." There was a smile in Dad's voice.

"Yeah," Ted teased. "I've always wanted a show biz singing sister in my life. That, or a prize fighter."

"Aw, shut up," Brenda retorted. "And when am I to start on my new wonderful career, Mom?"

"I've already contacted Mrs. Tacconi," Mother said. "You're to go over next week."

"You mean you're allowing me to go to New York by myself?"

"Yes. But you must come right home."

# CHAPTER 8

▼

# BRENDA IN SHOW BIZ LAND

## The Audition

Brenda thought how great it was to walk up the canyons of Broadway, enjoying the glitter of costume shops, theatre marquis and milling crowds. She even enjoyed the tacky Roseland Building with its theatre types lugging dance bags, and those shoddy corridors echoing to the beat of bands, Flamenco heels and howling blues singers.

Mrs. Tacconi, her singing teacher, had dyed red hair, heavy eye makeup and was no longer young. From the soprano Brenda's former teacher said she was, Mrs. Tacconi seemed bent on turning her into a bass. Soon Brenda was howling out the blues with the best of them.

"You've got good strong lungs," Tacconi assured her. "It's a gift."

Brenda didn't really like the sound she was making, but it seemed the "now" thing to do.

On one of her excursions up Seventh Avenue, Brenda ran into Larry Bronson. Handsome and sleek looking as ever, he was enjoying a smoke at the stage door of the Winter Garden Theatre.

He hailed her. "Hi Brenda. Looking good. Kid sister all grown up now."

"Why sure."

Larry, a classmate of Ted's at Penn charter, had kicked the Main Line for a life in the theatre and was now stage-managing a new musical. Little Brenda, once enamored of him, had worshipped from afar Larry's casual manner and great looks.

"Where are you heading?" he asked.

As she told him, his dark eyes took in her slinky figure in the new form-fitting outfit Mother had provided for fall.

"Say, we're casting today for singing show girls. How about trying out? You've got the looks. Can you sing?"

"I can bellow."

"So much the better."

After bellowing for Mrs. Tacconi, Brenda rushed to the theatre where Larry, list in hand, was busily directing backstage traffic. A lot of showgirl types and assorted dancers were nervously waiting to be called.

Larry waved to her.

"Okay, kid, I'll call you in a minute."

It was dark and musty smelling in the wings, and rows of empty seats stretched back into a cavernous dark. A naked light bulb was suspended from above and an accompanist in shirt sleeves was seated at a battered piano, just like in the movies. And who were those two men? One fat, one skinny and sharp-faced, sitting in the first row, scanning the harried performers like Oriental potentates preparing to say, "Off with their heads."

"What's holding things up?" the fat one said, irritated.

Larry hurried a blonde girl to the piano. She was beautiful and had an outstanding chest. In a screechy voice, she began to render 'Cherri Berri Bean.' It was pretty awful.

A button-nosed dancer-type next to Brenda whispered, "She couldn't sing her way out of a paper bag, but she's sleeping with the fat old poop."

This information widened Brenda's eyes. So that was the way they did it here.

Finally, Larry called Brenda and hurried her toward the piano. She didn't expect anything to come of all this except a fun experience, so she wasn't too nervous. She waved off the accompanist, plumped herself down on the piano stool, opened her music and let go in a loud, confident Tacconi howl with 'Love Your Magic Spell is Everywhere.'

To her surprise at the finish, the thin Mahoff, after consulting with the fat one, said, "You sing good, dear. Come back Tuesday."

Brenda, suddenly weak in the knees, tottered into the wings. Larry squeezed her hand.

"Nice going, kid. You can tell them back in Philly you made the big time."

Brenda could hardly wait to rush home and tell them the news. It happened that Martin came to dinner that night. He hadn't yet found a job and Mother insisted he stay on and work on his play until he did. As Brenda enthusiastically described her experience, he sat with glum eyes fixed on her.

"Isn't it wonderful?" Mother said. "Just think, Brenda singing on Broadway."

After a silence, Martin said, "Mrs. Marr, are you convinced you want a theatrical career for Brenda? You realize the kind of people she'll be thrown with?"

"What's wrong with them?" Mother asked.

"Dear lady. I see you're blinded by the glamour of Broadway but innocent of its pitfalls, the men–"

Dad smiled. "I think Brenda can handle herself. Besides, I think she'll soon be bored with the life. It's probably best to let her get it out of her system."

"I think I'm the best judge of what I want," Brenda flared. "Whose life is it anyhow?"

Martin said abruptly, "Excuse me. I hate to eat and run, but I have work to do."

When Mother broke Brenda's news to Grandma, she blew her top.

"How can you do such a thing? Let her perform on Broadway! I forbid it!"

Grandpa was delighted. "Maybe she'll get to meet Buster."

That night, after Mother and Dad had gone to bed, Martin sneaked over from the cottage and knocked on the French doors. Brenda, in the library, let him in. A mistake.

He clasped her. "Darling, you can't leave me like this!"

She pushed him away. "It's no use. My career's important."

"What career? As a singing show girl? And your talent for writing, are you just going to throw that away? And, what about me? You should know I'm your man. You belong to me."

"I don't belong to anybody."

He said angrily, "The trouble with you is you're afraid of life. You've got no guts." He went on to enumerate all the things that were wrong with her. When he saw he wasn't winning, he went down on his knees. How dramatic could you get?

"Please don't do this to me!" The 'too far apart' eyes gazed up at her soulfully.

Her harsh voice surprised her. "Martin, it's no use. You'd better go."

He got up slowly, dusting the knees of his natty gray pants.

"The trouble with you is you're not a real woman. Who do you think you are, some kind of Madonna?"

"Shut up!"

She ran from the room. Whatever made her think she liked him?

On Tuesday morning, Mother, Dad, Ted, Aya and Jancy stood on the porch to wave her off. She felt a little sad, as though she were leaving her old life behind.

As Aldo drove her past the cottage, she saw Martin sitting on the porch. His shoulders were hunched as he bent over a notebook. He seemed to be scribbling furiously. He wore a white-visored cap, which made his neck look even shorter.

She stuck her head out the window.

"Bye, Martin!"

He hunched his shoulders more and shook his head. The cap looked funny on him. She felt kind of sorry for him.

# New York, New York, New York

# CHAPTER 9

## THE GORGEOUS GIRLS

There were six singing showgirls in the line-up. Solomon, in all his glory, was not better arrayed. They were swathed in cloths of gold and silver, satin, brocade and lace. They were covered with rhinestones, sequins, beads and tassels. Some numbers were slinky and slit to the upper thighs; some were bouffant and cut to the navel. Anything to titillate the palettes of jaded New Yorkers or to deliver shock treatment to out-of-towners from the Corn Belt. They wore picture hats, pillboxes and turbans. They were dubbed the "Gorgeous Girls." All they had to do was stalk about and occasionally sing. The singing came out in kind of a squeak, a bleat, a bray, a lip-sync murmur and a Tacconi deep-throated bass. That didn't matter because they were so gorgeous.

At least Brenda thought they were.

She was completely awed by them. They seemed exquisite creatures from another world with their talon-length, blood-red finger nails, the thick, black fringes of their eyelashes, their outstanding busts, their tiny waists and shining hair of many hues. Their eyebrows were plucked in a thin arc, which gave them an air of perpetual surprise she found fascinating.

They had improbable names. There was Gloria Sweet, six feet tall, regal, with a fantastic shape. She wore big hats and was conceited and rich. A Jewish princess whose uncle was one of the show's backers. There was Happy Waters, the buxom blonde Brenda had heard audition who was the property of the fat mahoff. There was Titania Russ, a beautiful, doll-like creation; so fragile, she looked as though she would break in a strong wind. She spoke in a barely audible whisper and was sleeping with the composer of the show's music. There was Jenny Darling from the Bronx, loud, good-natured. She called everyone "my little chick" and seemed to be sleeping with the skinny mahoff. Then there was Sally Winsome from Paducca, Kentucky, with a big time Southern accent. She was too, too elegant but when roused, could swear like a truck driver. She was constantly knitting at something that resembled a pink potato sack. She was sleeping with a saxophone player named Morty Auer.

And last, but not least, was Lucky Gamble, a flaming red head from Nevada. Slender, beautifully formed, she always wore an ankle bracelet and a mink coat, even in summer, with nothing under it but a bra and panties. Under her arm she carried a tiny Chihuahua called Twiggy. This minute creature wore a diamond collar. It was said to have been presented to Lucky by a famous producer. Since Lucky was an animal lover, she seemed to Brenda more approachable than the others. She was rumored to be sleeping with some powerful underworld figure, all very hush-hush.

Though Brenda wasn't sleeping with anyone, she congratulated herself that though she'd never done the "real thing," she almost had and felt she knew the ropes, too. They were all a few years older than she, had been in shows together before and had in-jokes she couldn't get. To Brenda, their lifestyles seemed utterly glamorous. Men were always showering them with diamonds, flowers and furs. She didn't ask herself this question: 'Would she have slept with any of their mahoffs, fat, skinny, cigar smoking and otherwise unattractive?' She had diamonds inherited from her Great

Grandmother, which she kept in the bank. She even had a practically new mink coat, handed over by Mother when she bought herself a new one.

Later, when she started sporting these heirlooms to get into the swim of things, the girls' eyes bulged.

They commented, "Gee, Brenda, where'd you get the mink?" or "Get a load of that diamond. Who is he, Brenda?"

"Who?"

"The guy."

"Oh, a friend of the family."

In the beginning, Brenda was pretty much alone except for Larry, who took her to dinner when he could break away from the dancer he was sleeping with. But Brenda was never lonely. There was too much going on. Living at the hotel across the street, she hung around the theatre a lot. An aura of ancient glamour seemed to cling to its ornate columns and draperies and, wandering the cavernous emptiness, she would imagine the greats whose voices had resounded through the vast space. As Larry said, this was big time. It smelled professional, from the lady star with her famous jewels and sables to the sharp-eyed, cigar-smoking doorman who guarded the inner sanctum like some hoary old dragon. She lived in a state of excitement, with the fittings at famous costume designers, rubbing shoulders with the stars and being photographed for the publicity. She didn't even mind the hours of waiting, content to watch the marvel of an intricate musical revue being spliced together, with the confusion of split second scene changes, the huge revolving stage, the dancers, singers and soloists being juggled around like puppets at the command of their leader, the Great Director.

When she went home weekends, she was always eager to get back. Home was pretty dull, now that Martin had accepted the inevitable and gotten a job at a resort hotel in Jersey, where he worked as a night desk clerk.

During this time, Brenda didn't see much of the gorgeous girls. They didn't bother with boring preliminaries. They'd seen it all. Living on

Central Park South at sugar daddy's expense, they would saunter in in the afternoon. Brenda guessed their nights were pretty strenuous. They stuck together, laughing and joking, sometimes at her, Brenda suspected. When she approached, they would clam up. She suspected, to them she was an odd ball and they kept a wary eye on her. Or rather, they had no eye communication. Their glances passed her and wandered on to other things. Brenda thought conceited Gloria expected her to be Main Line snooty and was out to get in the first snoot. Certainly they had all read the little piece in 'Variety' about her. "Philadelphia Main Line Socialite, poet, dancer, singer and daughter of well-known architect, Jason Marr, joins Broadway musical 'Let's Live'."

How Brenda wished to be one of them. Was this hunger to belong a hangover from early days when Mother had cut her off from her peers? No way would these girls let her into their club. She tried to be like them. How could she? She wasn't from the Bronx or Brooklyn. They spoke a different language. She absorbed their speech and mannerisms. She bought an ankle bracelet, piled on dark lipstick, tried to grow long fingernails and plucked her eyebrows into the surprised line. To try and imitate their fabulous curves, she invested in a waist cincher and pulled herself in until she could hardly breathe. But still, couldn't seem to be as one with them.

About a week before the opening, they were assigned a dressing room. It was here that Brenda was initiated into the secrets of the sisterhood.

The girls immediately set themselves up at their stands with professional-looking makeup kits containing every sort of rouge paint and eye shadow. Brenda had little in the way of makeup and not much know-how on the subject. But she wasn't about to ask their advice unless they offered. They didn't.

The room, on the third floor, meant that when they had a fast change, they had to begin disrobing on the way up and zipping up on the way down. The room was small and cramped with one window, which looked down on the bustle of Seventh Avenue. An overheated radiator cooked them in winter; in summer, they were cooked by blasts of hot air, dust and gas fumes from below. There was no air conditioning back then.

They were packed in on hard wooden chairs before makeup tables, long mirrors and bare light bulbs that glaringly illuminated their reflections. Gloria, Tatania and Sally sat along one wall. Brenda was wedged in between Jenny and Lucky Gamble. Lucky liked to place Twiggy beside her make-up kit, but he often ended up with his mousy feet in her cleansing cream or on the lettuce and tomato sandwich, which she shared with him. The crowding was even worse when their costumes arrived on long metal racks. It was a squeeze to get by them and out the door.

To save crowding in the wings, on the last days before the opening, they were required to remain in the dressing room until called, sometimes for an hour. This posed a problem for Brenda. She had thought that in such close quarters they might loosen up a little. It was not that they were unfriendly, they just acted as though she were not there and addressed all remarks to each other.

'Okay,' Brenda thought, 'I'll act as though I'm not here.' She smoked, read the paper and made no attempt to talk. But she observed and made some interesting discoveries about the Gorgeous Girls.

In the first place, they were not as gorgeous as they seemed. Their long lashes were glued on, as were their fingernails. Most of their glorious fronts were padded, as were their curvy bottoms. Their full mouths were works of lipstick artistry. Layers of paint, powder and rouge accomplished miracles for them. In fact, with these accoutrements removed, they were rather commonplace looking. But when they swayed and postured on stage, exquisite womanhood was achieved to dazzle the eyes of the rich, famous and infamous, inhabiting the front row, center.

Listening to them, she made a further discovery. They were rather limited. Their main topics were on how to improve parts of their anatomy.

Such as:

Sally: "I'm planning to have my ass lifted."

Jenny: "It is kind of droopy."

Sally: "You should talk. You don't even have one."

Laughter from the others.

Lucky: "I'm thinking of getting a nose job."

Gloria: "You don't have much nose now. What's to cut off?"

Lucky: "Not cut off. Add on."

Gloria: "Where do you plan to add it?"

Lucky: "On my behind, silly."

More laughter.

A whisper from Tatania: "Do you think my boobs could stand some silicon?"

Jenny: "Don't do it. They say it hardens into lumps."

Gloria: "Might be an improvement on those buttons she has now."

And more laughter.

Another important topic was their men friends. Lucky seemed discontented with the one she had now.

"I'm fed up," she moaned. "He's so damned old. All talky-talky, no doey-doey."

Sally Winsome: "You're lucky. I'm worn out. You know what they say about my Morty. Every hour, on the hour, Morty Auer."

So they jibed with their in-jokes, little cats on the back fence. And in spite of their camaraderie, Brenda felt they were not really that close and when the show closed, would part without a qualm.

Another thing she learned was their casual nudity. They often had male visitors, hoping, no doubt, to get a stripped down look at the gorgeous ones. Brenda was always buttoned up to the chin in her makeup robe, but the others, sometimes in bra and pants or even less, didn't bother to cover up. Sometimes Larry wandered in or the tenor who dressed across the hall. Also, when his manager-wife wasn't around keeping a watchful eye on him, they had a visit from one of their male stars, Fredly Bodly.

Fredly was famous for being funny and for his dancing. His legwork and tap were dazzling. Off stage, he was just as funny, breezy and friendly, sometimes too friendly. When his wife wasn't looking, he'd manage to give the girls a squeeze, a pinch or a tweak on any available area.

The girls dubbed him "Friendly Fredly Bodily."

"Probably not getting much at home and looking for a little," Lucky remarked.

"Yeah," Jenny said. "She's got a frozen puss. Probably frozen elsewhere, too."

Their response when he gave them a goose was, "Bug off, Fredly. Put your hands in your pockets."

Maybe Fredly was intrigued by Brenda's Main Line reserve, but she seemed to come in for more pats on the behind than the others.

The girls noticed.

"Watch out, Brenda," Jenny said. "I think he's after you. Wifey wouldn't like that."

It got so Brenda was always looking behind her to see if he was creeping up. Perhaps because she was impressed that he was famous and was flattered to be noticed by him, or maybe because she was embarrassed and didn't know what else to do, she responded to the pats with a faint smile.

It turned out those smiles were a mistake.

Another frequent visitor was a contortionist known as "Stevie the Smoker." This character, attired in a purple jump suit trimmed in sequins, performed the most marvelous double-jointed contortions to a Strauss waltz. He became a human pretzel while holding a cigarette inside his mouth and blowing smoke through his ears.

Stevie, too, formed an attachment to Brenda and persisted in giving her meaningful glances while pretending to rape a door or any other upright object. He really was repulsive, but Brenda couldn't help laughing. When his shiny, black eyes lit on her, she automatically clutched her robe closer.

This delighted Stevie. "What's the matter, Brenda? Got something you're afraid to show me?"

One day, fed to the teeth, she retorted, "No. You got something you're afraid to show me?"

This was the wrong retort.

Stevie beamed. "Really? You interested?" He began to unzip.

Brenda sprang up furiously. "Will you get the hell out of here and quit bugging me!"

Delighted, the girls hooted with laughter.

"Atta girl, Brenda!"

"You tell 'im, Brenda!"

"Ooh, Brenda used a bad word!"

She swung around. "Yes. And, I'd appreciate it if you people would quit bugging me too!"

"Ut-oh, Brenda's mad," Gloria gibed.

"You're damned right I am! And you would be, too, if you were on the receiving end of all this crap!"

She had the satisfaction of seeing their mouths drop open. So, the timid little Main Liner could fight back.

She took off for the john.

Sure she was mad. But she was learning. Fast. Boldness and frontal attack was all they understood. Morons. Who did they think they were? They'd probably never even read a book. Why was she laying herself out for them to walk on? So, they disliked her. Who cared? But she did care. What was it that always made her think others more beautiful, cleverer than she? Why did she strive so hard to please? Was there some residual in her, planted with poison darts from Aunt Margot and the cousins? But why hang on to that?

'Get rid of it,' she thought. 'Grow up.'

Her anger faded and with it went her awe of the gorgeous ones. So, they weren't that fabulous. And if they were limited, it probably wasn't their fault. Brought up on some back street, they had never known the beauty and ease of an Upsan Downs, never read great poets, thrilled to the music of a great orchestra or had parents like hers. Theirs was a small world of grease paint and competition for men. What they did have was guts and stamina to have gotten this far. Some might even make the grade, a good marriage if they were lucky. Others, when beauty faded, would go down the drain. Show biz was not all glamour. These people were tough, street smart. They knew she didn't belong here. She was invading their space and had better toughen up if she wanted to stay. Of course, she always had Upsan Downs to run home to. But did she want to run back now? It would be admitting failure. And wouldn't Martin love that?

As she heard Larry calling them to the stage, she thought, 'It's a challenge. Can I meet it?'

She was about to get a chance to find out.

## The Great Director

He was famous. Top-notch musical shows had borne his imprint for years. A genius, he was aging and irascible, graying and fine-featured as a woman, with pale, womanish, expressive hands. He delighted in cutting up the Gorgeous Girls (but not the Gorgeous Boys) in the chorus line. One misstep or missed cue and he stopped the whole works, as he lashed out in a high-pitched tirade that could have been heard on Times Square, and reduced the unlucky girl to abject sniveling. This was the purpose, of course. Watching this performance a few times, Brenda swore this demon would never make her cry. Actually, he had been rather nice to her. Learning she had some experience in summer stock, he gave her an understudy to the leading lady in a couple of sketches. Naturally this caused raised eyebrows and "Who does she think she is to rate that?" among the Gorgeous Ones. Encouraged by the director's show of friendship, Brenda presented him with an autographed copy of her poems. Foolish. Whatever made her think she rated above the others? She was sure he looked on them all as bovine nincompoops, fit for nothing unless it was to screw the producers and backers and keep them happy.

She had to learn the hard way.

They had a new and complicated number that the director, in one of his genius brainstorms, decided to try out at the last minute. Many of the routines had been set on what was called a "double revolving disk," a huge turntable that was new to them. The Gorgeous Ones, sheathed in silver with long beaded trains dragging behind, and balancing enormous, unsteady headdresses on top, were called on to descend from a high platform onto the revolving turntable and to peel off, one going right, one left.

Brenda's headdress, not securely fastened, began to slip. Endeavoring to straighten it, she turned right when it should have been left.

Shades of Plotkin's 'Aida'! She had goofed again!

"Stop! Stop!" the waspish voice sang out from the front row.

The turntable ground to a halt. Trembling with fury, the voice trilled on.

"You! Whatever your name is! Brenda! Brenda from Philly! Brenda the socialite poet! What the Christ do you think you're doing? Don't you know your right from your left? You're reputed to be intelligent, but I see no sign of it! What the hell are you doing? Speak up! That is, if you can speak."

Nothing would have made Brenda speak up. She managed a stern countenance while the lightning bolts continued to strike. Apparently, her willfulness in not weeping shook him up. Anyhow, he suddenly stopped yelling and in a dramatic and aggrieved voice said, "You are excused from this number. Go to your dressing room and try to figure out which is your right hand."

In the deadly silence in which the cast stood transfixed, Brenda gathered up her train and managed to exit with dignity.

In the wings, Larry pressed her hand.

"Don't let the old fart get to you. He just likes to let off steam."

His sympathetic tone let loose the floodgates and the girls, rushing upstairs to change, found Brenda huddled over the makeup table, weeping.

Jenny Darling patted her shoulder. "Come on, my little chick, don't mind him. We've all had it. Better hop into your next outfit. This is the fast one."

She began to unzip Brenda down the back. Brenda smiled at her gratefully. This was the first time she'd felt a bit of warmth from any of them. So, they could be a little human under the tough façade.

"I kinda liked the way you didn't let him break you up, honey," Lucky said.

"Yeah," Sally Winsome drawled. "He's rotten. Just a dirty old faggot."

Brenda had always thought a faggot was a piece of wood. She turned a mascara-stained face to Sally.

"Faggot. What's that?"

They laughed uproariously. Even snooty Gloria deigned to address her. "Come on, Brenda, get with it. Don't they have faggots on the Main Line?"

Lucky, renewing an eyelash, explained. "A faggot's a fairy, honey. Light in the heel, a homo, a fruit, you know."

Brenda laughed, too. Though they were laughing at her, she felt they were laughing with her. As she dried the streaky mascara and hastened into her gown for the 'Things' number, she began to feel better. So she had to get it in the neck to win the girls over a little. Okay, so if that's what it took. It could have been worse.

## The Star

Until the dress rehearsal, they hadn't gone through the 'Things' number with the benefit of custard pie. But the director must have felt that before the opening night, they'd better iron out the pie business.

They had been briefed that when the pie was hurled, they would be splattered, and their gowns would have to be rushed to the cleaners to be ready for the next performance, particularly a quickie on matinee days.

In 'Things,' the Gorgeous Ones, in long, flowing gowns, sat or stood around an elaborate tea table with silver teapot, cookies, the works. The star, in tail coat, cravat and gray striped trousers, treated them to a rendition of 'Things.' The girls were supposed to present a deadpan look during this. But, it was a struggle to keep from laughing as his quavery falsetto screeched to the topmost galleries.

At the end of his song, statuesque Gloria was supposed to rise and with dignity, hoist the pie and slam it into his face.

This male star, completely different from Friendly Fredly, was a complete enigma to Brenda. He never seemed to be aware of anyone and while backstage waiting to go on, would sit, head in hands, as if sunk in deepest melancholy. But, at his cue, would leap to the stage, personality raying from him like a floodlight. It seemed he was only alive in front of an audience.

At this rehearsal, things went as usual. The star's ugly, marvelously plastic face was arranged in its ladies-tea-party-exuding-charm expression. And, as usual, his voice quavered and screeched as they struggled to keep their faces blank. As the song roared to its audience-convulsing climax, Gloria rose majestically and hurled the pie. Brenda was in the line of fire. It missed the star and slammed into her.

She had not realized what a disaster a custard pie in the face would be. Shocked, blinded, dripping goo, she staggered and swayed as the entire cast, orchestra and stagehands roared. She even heard the director's laugh and his voice yelling from the auditorium: "Poor old Brenda from Philly! Get her off! Dry her off! Get her out of here!"

Worse than her trip in 'Aida' was this humiliation. Right on Broadway, a colossal boo-boo! Had Gloria done it on purpose, her revenge on Brenda's Main Line-ness?

'Oh hell,' Brenda thought. 'So I'm a comic freak. Well then, let's be a comic freak.'

Trying to brush the stuff out of her eyes, she faced front where the director sat with the mahoffs. She stuck out her tongue and, in an exaggeratedly gluttonous display bulged her eyes and with gusto, licked the goo from around her mouth, smacked her lips, then turned, showing them her backside in a nasty wiggle and walked off stage.

"Leave it in!" someone yelled. "Leave it in!" As there came a burst of applause and laughter.

In the wings, the girls clustered around her.

"Brenda from Philly got it again. Poor Brenda, come on, let's get you out of this custard."

They rushed her upstairs. In the dressing room, Gloria surprised her by apologizing.

"Gee, Brenda, I'm sorry. I guess I just got nervous."

She managed a smile. "You've got a lousy aim. I forgive you, but don't let it happen again."

Mopped up and getting ready for the next number, she pondered the woes of being a famous comedian. How would she like to endure the humiliation of having a custard pie slammed into her face six nights a week and twice on matinee days, just to amuse people? No wonder the star was melancholy.

# CHAPTER 10

## OPENING NIGHT
## AND
## BYE-BYE MARTIN

The family couldn't make it to the opening. Ted was arranging for an exhibition, Dad was in Chicago for a new building project and Mother wouldn't have been caught dead in New York. As far as Brenda knew, she'd never been there. However, a huge bunch of flowers arrived from them at the theatre and Grandpa sent a telegram: "Gook luck to my wonder child. Please remember me to Buster."

Probably due to the director's temper tantrums and because he knew exactly what he was doing, opening night went without a hitch. No missed cues, turn tables revolving as planned and Brenda had learned her right from her left. Friendly Fred brought down the house with his flexible legs and the other star got the pie in the kisser where it belonged.

As the curtain rose, the Gorgeous Girls were discovered in long, golden gowns, their heads in velvet tricorn hats. With Lucky bleating on one side of her, Sally lip-syncing on the other and mumbles and squeaks from the others, Brenda let herself go full blast trying to cover their deficiencies.

"Live, live!" she boomed. "You gotta wake up and live!"

She'd been in front of enough audiences not to be shaken by the full house of New York sophisticates, gamblers, socialites and hit men. She noticed a good-looking man in the front row whose eyes seemed glued on Lucky. She also noticed, and this did throw her for a moment, Martin in the second row, his eyes glued on her. She knew he was thinking 'I hope she falls on her face.' With this in mind, she was determined to give a perfect performance.

Though Brenda felt no jitters, this was not so of Lucky who was in a high state of excitement as she confided in the dressing room, "Did you see that guy in the front row? It's Brick Schwartz. He's loaded. I've decided I'm going to marry him."

It turned out that Lucky did marry Brick. Poor Lucky. He was a well-known gangster. Years later, Brenda read he was on the run from the law and Lucky had been found hiding out with him in some sleazy hotel in Philadelphia. Jordan Kirsh and Ted loved to tease Brenda about her gangster friends.

But on opening night, Lucky was feeling high. Brenda wasn't. She'd heard Lucky was giving a cast party after the show and everyone was invited, everyone except her.

However, as they were getting ready for the finale, she turned to Brenda. "Oh Brenda, I've been meaning to ask. Want to come to my place after the show?"

"Sure. You bet. Love to."

But how about Martin? She knew he'd be at the stage door. He was, with an orchid.

"Hi," she said. "I saw you out there."

"I must say, you pulled it off. You looked lovely, kiddy."

It annoyed her when he called her that. It sounded so corny.

"You staying in town?" she asked.

"I checked into your hotel."

Who needed this?

"I promised your Mother I'd come to the opening. She wanted me to see that you were all right."

This was a laugh, Mother sending Martin the seducer to protect her little girl.

His eyes went over her critically. She knew why.

The girls were accustomed to going out after the show without removing their makeup, too much trouble. Of course, Brenda went along with the gang. It was sort of fun being conspicuous. Her false eyelashes were black and stiff as spikes and her cheeks blushed heavily with rouge.

"I'm taking you to dinner," Martin said.

"Oh, Martin, I can't go."

"Of course you're going. I'll wait while you remove the goo. Go get ready."

"I am ready," she retorted. "I'm going to a party."

"You mean you're going looking like that?"

"Sure. We all do."

He looked disgusted.

"What is this party?"

"One of the girls is giving it."

"I can imagine what that'll be like." He sounded superior.

"What does that mean?"

"Those girls are all kept women. Is that the kind you want to associate with? My God! I'm sure your family would be pleased to know about it."

"It's my business with whom I associate," she snapped.

"You mean I came all the way from Jersey for this? Some welcome. I'm not going to let you go." He grabbed her arm.

"Let me go!" she said furiously.

Sally, Jenny and Lucky came by in their grease paint.

"Like to ride up with us, Brenda?" Lucky asked.

She pulled free of Martin.

"Sure. Thanks."

She saw Martin taking in Lucky's ankle bracelet, Twiggy in her arms, and the mink coat, half open, revealing her lacy bra.

Lucky took him in too. It seemed he passed muster.

"Like to bring your friend along?"

"Want to come, Martin?" Brenda challenged.

He looked furious. "No thank you." He stalked off.

"What's with him?" Jenny said. "He mad at you or something?"

"He's kinda cute," Sally said.

"He's a pain."

"Not to worry," Lucky said. "There'll be plenty of guys around."

Lucky's Central Park South apartment was spectacular. A large, nude oil painting of her hung over the mantelpiece. In the painting, her rosy flesh was extended full-length on a sofa, reposing on a scarlet drape. A seductive smile hovered on her lips. Lucky's piano was white, as were chairs, sofas and the wall-to-wall carpets. On the tables were exotic Oriental lamps and there many satin cushions strewn about. Huge carnivorous-looking plants hung in baskets. Twiggy, underfoot, was being fed hors d'heuvres, which he dropped to be ground into the carpet. Everything looked like something Aladdin might have dreamed up.

Brenda left her wrap in Lucky's bedroom. This was done up in white, too. The bed sported a black satin spread. Brenda peeked under it to see black satin sheets. On the ceiling above the bed hung a mirror. She wondered why.

Back in the living room, other members of the cast had arrived. Jenny, Gloria and Sally had now accumulated escorts. Brenda noted, thankfully, that Stevie the Smoker was not there. Lucky had changed into a diaphanous see-through hostess gown. She was clinging to the arm of Brick Schwartz. He wasn't bad looking, tall and well built. He wore his hair sleek as a tango dancer's and sported a Miami tan of an odd brick-like hue, hence the nickname, Brenda supposed. He was surrounded by a group of odd-looking men, sharp dressers in checks and plaids. Some wore hats. They looked like something out of a Twenties' gangster film. She had a feeling they were guarding Brick and thought she would steer clear of them.

Having heard raves from stage door enthusiasts, everyone was feeling friendly and happy. People were embracing and some, who'd never given her the time of day, grabbed and kissed Brenda.

"Gee, Brenny, I think we got a hit on our hands."

"Did you see Winchell in the front row laughing up a storm?"

"Looks like we'll be eating for the next few months."

It was good to be caught up in the wave of warmth, and Brenda, totally exhilarated at being included, proceeded to pin one on. Two martinis drove her to the piano and sent her banging away and bellowing out 'Dark Eyes,' the only piece she knew by heart.

If she wanted attention, she got it and wished she hadn't. A burly gangster-type with dark, curly, greasy-looking hair, a loud checked jacket and brown pointy shoes leaned over the piano.

"You sure can tickle those ivories, honey."

Oh-oh. Was this like a Humphrey Bogart flick, or what?

Pointy toes edged in beside her on the bench and stuck out a hairy paw.

"Louie's the name. I seen you beside Lucky in the 'Live and Love' number. You caught my eye. I said to myself, 'There's a chick with class.'"

His hand felt like a hairy, cold fish. He leaned close and she got the benefit of the garlic he'd had for dinner on his Caesar salad.

"Tell me about yourself, sweetheart."

He even lisped like Humphrey. And Brenda could have sworn that hard thing pressing against her was a gun in his side pocket. It couldn't have been anything else. It was in the wrong position. She tried to edge away, but no-go. His arm crept around her cinched-in waist.

"Nice," he said. "But what's that iron thing you're wearing around yourself?"

She mumbled something. Damn if she was going to discuss her underwear with him. "Say," he lisped. "I seen on the program you're understudying the star."

"Yes," she said, averting her head from the garlic. He lowered his voice. "She's the dame with all the rocks, ain't she?"

"What?"

"Jew-els. Rocks, you know."

Their female star was famous for her jew-els.

"I guess so."

"Anytime you like, I could get rid of her." He added, "For a few days."

Her head swiveled. "Why?"

"Give you a chance to go on. Do your stuff, honey. You know, get discovered."

Lord, was this creep saying he intended to bump off their leading lady so she could go on? Jeepers! She didn't want to go on anyhow. Just the thought of it threw her into a panic.

"Excuse me, I've got to go to the—"

She fled to the bar and downed another martini. A lot more people arrived and all the girls seemed to have found admirers and were being pawed over and propositioned, it looked like. It was turning out to be some party. An unnatural hum buzzed in her ears. Were the martinis trying to tell her something?

Then she saw Friendly Fredly Bodily come in without his wife. Uh-oh. He spotted her and moved in her direction. She tossed down the rest of the martini and went to the bar for another. There, she ran into Louie the Louse.

"Listen honey, like I said, if you want me to—"

She took off in what she hoped was the direction of the john, her escape hatch. Friendly Fredly barred the way.

"Where are you off to, little one?"

By now, she was really flying. So, what the heck? Fredly liked her. Maybe she was lucky. He was famous. Maybe he could advance her so-called Broadway career. Everyone was into this scene. Why not she?

When he patted her behind, she didn't even flinch.

"Oh, hello," she said, in what sounded to her like a casually seductive tone. "I didn't know you'd be here."

"I came because I knew you'd be here."

She blinked her false eyelashes. Heavy with mascara, they stuck on one side, which made her look as though she were winking at him. She reached up and unstuck them. At the same time, dizzied by that last martini, she swayed off balance and surged into his arms.

He grasped her. "Hey, this is nice. Could we go someplace and talk about it?"

His agile body propelled her into the bedroom, which was empty at the moment.

Friendly Fredly was a fast worker. He had to be. He didn't get away from his wife that often. He could move with lightning speed when his libido was aroused. Before Brenda knew what was happening, he'd closed the door, shoved aside coats, pulled her to the bed, pushed her back and was on top of her, biting her neck.

"Hey!" she shrilled. "Stop it!"

"Stop it," he muttered. "What d'you mean? You've been wanting it from me ever since you saw me."

"I have not." She gave him a shove.

"Oh, a tease, huh? Well, that makes it more interesting."

"Let me up!"

"You gotta be kidding."

The thought flashed through her mind. 'Dear Mother, if you could see me now.'

Then she felt the thing. It was pressing against her and it was big. He was an expert at this. While he held her down with one arm, his other hand was pulling up her skirt, pulling down her pants, unzipping himself, pulling down his pants and trying to get at her. But he had a confirmed virgin to cope with.

Brenda's legs were locked shut, and on her back, staring up, she saw the reflection of the star's wildly bouncing bottom. So that was what the mirror was for. Seen from this angle, sex was a joke. Why would such a sight excite anything but mirth?

Hysteria overcame her and a loud and awful sound burst forth, something between a laugh and a primal scream.

The bray startled Friendly and arrested him in mid-motion. She grabbed the opportunity to give a tremendous heave that propelled him backwards and crashing into a chair. This gave her time to pull up her pants and pull down her skirt. With rare presence of mind, she grabbed purse and wrap. She flung open the door into the surprised faces of a couple that were probably seeking a convenient bed. They must have gotten an eyeful of Fredly with his pants down and exposed to the hilt.

The smoke filled room was jammed, as loud drunken voices engulfed her. Sobered, she shoved through the mob, out to the elevator, down and into a cab.

At least she'd kept her head. She thought, 'No big deal.'

But in her hotel room, she flung herself on the bed and wept. How could she have gotten so drunk and in such a fix? Mother and Dad trusted her and she'd let them down. Suppose Friendly had gotten to her and the news had gotten out? She pictured it: "Main Line socialite raped by star of 'Wake Up and Live.'" Or, "Main Line socialite impregnated by Broadway star."

Her sobs decreased as she thought that on the other hand, she'd handled the thing rather well. No one would ever know except Friendly Fred and he certainly wouldn't tell with jealous wifey around.

But she cried again when she thought how alone she was. What was she doing in this lousy hotel room away from those who loved her? She didn't belong with these people. Martin was right. She felt like having the security of his arms around her. She needed someone who cared, who knew who she was. And he was close by. He had his faults, but beside some of the creeps she'd been running into, he was a prince. Particularly beside the 'would-be rapist' star. He was better looking, too.

Her hand was on the phone to call Martin when it rang. It would be Martin, of course, checking up on her. Damn it, she resented that. She wasn't a child. She didn't need a chaperone. Anger dried her tears.

She let the phone ring. Wouldn't he be delighted to know what had happened? He'd have her where he wanted her. She could picture his "I told you so's." The hell with it. She'd weather it through alone.

Saved by the bell!

When at last the phone stopped ringing, she took it off the hook. Without undressing, she crawled between the covers and fell into a deep sleep, proud for being strong and grown up and handling things.

It was noon when Brenda woke with a terrible hangover. She had no sooner put the receiver on the hook than the phone rang.

She lifted it to Martin saying accusingly, "Why was your phone off the hook all night? Did you have a man in your room?"

Her head was pounding.

"Of course not."

"I was worried. I knocked on your door. There was no answer."

"I didn't hear you. I was asleep."

"You must have been drunk not to hear me."

"Oh, Martin, shut up."

There was a silence. He must have realized he was on the wrong track.

"I'm coming to your room."

"You are not. I'm not up yet."

"What difference does that make?"

"I don't feel well."

"No wonder, with all you drank."

She was too weak to make a comeback. A great yawn overcame her. It almost split her head.

"What you need is food," he said. "Come to the coffee shop. I'll buy you breakfast."

That sounded like a great idea.

"Give me twenty minutes."

In the mirror, she discovered she'd aged. Could that be? All features seemed to sag. Were those dark circles under her eyes just smudges of mascara? It turned out that was so. She got to work unsmudging herself. The cold shower helped somewhat. She suddenly discovered she was ravenously hungry. She dressed hurriedly and glanced in the mirror. Still not so good, but a slash of lipstick helped.

In the coffee shop, Martin rose from the table and kissed her hand. His eyes scoured her face.

"You look terrible."

"Thanks a lot. Get me some juice."

She collapsed on the chair, her head aching.

Sitting opposite her, he looked stern.

"You drank a lot, didn't you?"

She gulped ice water.

"Didn't you?"

"What's this? An inquisition?"

"Didn't you?"

"No."

Her best defense was silence, she thought. Besides, in her hung over state, talking was difficult.

She ordered oatmeal, bacon and eggs, waffles and coffee and gulped them down while Martin lectured her.

What would the family think if they knew she was out all night drinking and carousing? He'd promised Mother he'd come to the opening and take her out afterwards. It hurt that she wouldn't go after the trouble he'd gone to, taking off from his job and bringing her an orchid, which she hadn't even bothered to take, she was so anxious to go with those women.

"I'm sorry," she muttered.

Her family was worried about her, he said. Mother thought she wasn't looking well. Maybe she was working too hard. He'd promised to keep an eye on her and was planning to try and get to New York every weekend. But he saw now she didn't really want to see him.

While he was talking and she was stuffing, she was thinking Martin wasn't so bad compared to some of the schmos she'd been running into. That new suit looked sharp. In his foreign way, he was rather good-looking and he certainly had charm. She'd been lonely these past weeks. All the girls had men and she had no one. Maybe she should hang on to Martin, for a while anyhow.

Thoroughly stuffed and feeling better, she pushed back from the table. Yes, Martin didn't look so bad, even if his neck was too short.

"Thanks for breakfast."

She saw that soft look come into his eyes.

"Darling, why are you such a child? Why don't you understand that I love you and want to protect you?"

"I know, Martin."

He reached over and took her hand. At his touch, she felt that warm, whatever it was he could do to her, creep through her.

'Not that again,' she thought. 'I don't want that.'

But maybe she did. Why deny it? The attraction was there and he knew it.

"Darling, I've missed you so. Let's go to my room." His grasp tightened.

She knew what would happen in his room. Did she want that?

She stalled, "What time is it?"

He consulted his watch. "One-thirty."

"Oh, my God! I've got a rehearsal!"

"Skip it."

"I can't. It's important. The director wants us on stage to clear up loose ends." She got up.

"Damn you," he said.

But on the other hand, she didn't want to lose him completely.

"Pick me up tonight after the show."

At the theatre, everyone was in a state of wild excitement. There had been rave reviews: "WAKE UP AND LIVE wakes up Broadway. Gorgeous girls, terrific songs, a barrel of laughs."

But into the buzz of excitement came their Director, looking like a thundercloud. He sat the ladies and gentlemen of the chorus down in the auditorium and gave them hell.

"Don't let those reviews go to your heads. It wasn't that great. In fact,–"

He launched into everything they did wrong and a dozen changes that were to be made before tonight's performance: dance numbers and songs thrown out, others put in. The composer, lyricist and choreographer were on hand making copious notes.

"So," said their Director, "prepare to be here the rest of the day and all night if necessary. Nobody leaves. If you want food, send out for it."

Then, with his utterly charming and ingratiating smile, which he knew the exact moment to turn on to melt their craven little hearts, he said, "As a matter of fact, it wasn't all that bad. Some of you even looked pretty good. And Brenda from Philly finally learned her right from her left."

Laughter from all.

'Okay,' Brenda thought. So, she was the whipping boy again. Fine. Anything to please their Dear Director and to ease his sick woman-hate. Nevertheless, she turned red and ducked under the seat in front of her, pretending to pick up something.

By the time Martin got to her after the evening performance, she was wrung out with the endless day of waiting and being herded on and off stage to get better lighting effects. God, being cattle chorus in theatre was boring! No wonder the girls took up knitting.

Martin was at the stage door with an orchid, probably the one she didn't collect the night before.

"Look," she said. "I've had it. I've got to get some sleep."

She was staggering with fatigue and the hangover was still with her.

He was understanding, fed her dinner, and then took her to her room.

"Can I come in one minute?"

"I'm exhausted."

"Just for a minute. I've waited all day. I'll massage your neck. You like that."

In her weakened state she said, "Okay."

He sat beside her on the bed and massaged her neck. It felt good. Soon, he was uncinching her cinch. Then he was massaging other things. She was too exhausted to resist. It was the familiar routine. After, she fell asleep in his arms. Guilty but without the worry of Dad coming in on them.

Martin quit his job and moved to New York. She guessed he'd saved some money or else that woman was keeping him. She didn't ask. It was nice to have someone take her out after the show instead of going back to the lonely hotel room.

He was at the stage door every night to pick her up. The girls noticed, especially Sally Winsome.

"He's cute, Brenda. If you don't want him, I'll take him."

"He's a pain. You're welcome to him."

'Like hell,' she thought. 'Just try and get him, Bitchy.'

It felt good having a man of her own that someone else wanted, until she noticed him giving them the eye. It made her jealous.

"Don't be silly," he said. "They can't hold a candle to you. Why would I be interested in them?"

To reward him for this observation, she let him come to her room.

It all started again, the passionate kisses, the climaxes in which they clung together in frustrated and sometimes-messy intimacy. Often, he would come to her room in the afternoon. He had to be with her, touching her. But Brenda held out against the Real Thing.

They fought.

"This is no good," he said. "I'm a virile guy. You're ruining me. Soon I'll be impotent."

"I don't know why."

"You're such a child. You don't understand. You're driving me crazy. I want to marry you."

"I can't help it if you haven't any money."

'Or a lot of other things,' she thought, 'like honesty, class.' Who was he anyhow? Where did he come from? But still, he had a hold on her. She wasn't strong enough to kick the habit.

Then, one afternoon in her room between the matinee and evening show, she noticed he was not so eager; his kisses lacked their usual fire. She immediately suspected his needs were being taken care of elsewhere and accused him.

He looked sullen. The wide-apart eyes avoided her.

"So what if I am?"

She felt a flood of hate. "You're horrible. You say you love me. How can you do this?"

"You don't want me. Maybe someone else does."

"Get out of my room!"

He flung open the door and slammed it behind him.

Brenda threw herself on the bed, dry-eyed, furious. How dare he do this! This liar, cheat! But she had set herself up for it by getting involved again. She lay there feeling the narrow walls of the room closing in, listening to the alien noises of the city. Honking horns, screeching brakes, shrill protesting voices of myriad beings challenging one another, struggling for space. And suddenly she had a longing for Upsan Downs, the serenity of tall trees and open sky and most of all, Mother and Dad's arms around her and Ted's welcoming smile with the accompanied, "Hi, kid, big city too much for you?"

It was Saturday and after the evening show she could catch the late train for Philadelphia and take a taxi home.

She put in the call and drank in the sound of Mother's voice.

"Oh, Brenda dear, it'll be wonderful to see you. Dad'll be so pleased. He just got home from his trip today."

It was Sunday afternoon and they had just finished dinner when the doorbell rang. Ted went to answer and they heard him say, "Oh, hi Martin, this is a surprise. Come on in."

Brenda felt her heart lurch. Was there no getting rid of him?

Mother was all smiles as Martin bent to kiss her hand.

"How nice to see you. We thought we'd lost you for good, though Brenda did say she'd seen you in New York. I'll have Jancy get you a plate."

"Oh, no," Martin protested. "I can only stay a minute. But I couldn't leave without saying goodbye."

'What now?' Brenda thought. 'Some new trick?' But why was she upset? She wanted to get rid of him, didn't she?

"Goodbye?" Dad asked. "Where are you going?"

"To California."

"Well, draw up a chair and tell us about it," Mother said. "And will you have some coffee?"

Martin pulled a chair next to Brenda. She avoided looking at him, and when his knee grazed hers, she moved. As he drank the coffee, Martin informed them that a friend, a screenwriter (was he inventing him?), was driving to Hollywood and wanted him to go along. Even offered him a place to stay.

"He liked my play and felt it would make good screen property. It seems he has some pull out there and I thought it too good an opportunity to pass up."

"I should say so!" Mother exclaimed.

"That's wonderful, Martin," Dad said.

"So, all that sweat next door didn't go for naught," Ted put in.

Brenda said nothing and all eyes went to her.

"Yes," she said. "Good luck."

She was tossing a few thoughts around, like: How come she'd never heard of this screenwriter friend? And, was it the New York woman he'd conned into giving him money for the trip, and was she going with him?

Martin said he'd borrowed his friend's car so he could say goodbye, but he should get back to New York immediately. They were leaving at the crack of dawn.

"At least we got a glimpse of you," Mother said. "How long will you be gone?"

"Quite a while, I guess."

Martin got up. He seemed uneasy as he said to Brenda, "I wonder if I could talk to you a moment?"

"Yes," Mother said. "You and Brenda have been such good friends. I'm sure you have a lot to tell her since you won't be seeing each other for a while."

The family adjourned to the parlor to listen to the radio. Brenda followed him, reluctantly, to the library. She stood with her back to him and stared into the empty fireplace.

He gave a little laugh.

"Could we sit?"

He sat on the sofa. Brenda resisted that and perched stiffly on the straight-backed chair.

The far-apart eyes examined her.

"I'm sorry about what happened. That woman means nothing to me. I love you and always will, but I can't bear being near you with the way things are. That's why I am going away."

In Brenda, a void seemed to open. Why? She didn't want him. But the thought of never seeing him again bothered her.

"Tell me what you're thinking," he said.

She shrugged.

He knelt in front of her and raised her hands to his lips.

"You're young. I've been pushing you too hard. Maybe in a year you'll feel ready for a commitment. Do you think you'd marry me if I made good?"

She made a stab at honesty.

"I don't know how I'll feel a year from now."

His hands were on her thighs, caressing. She felt the pleasure his touch could always bring and thought she might never meet anyone who loved her as he did. It might be better to have a spare to count on.

"You haven't answered my question."

She got up. "Maybe in a year–"

He rose. "I know we'll be together again. I just hope you won't stay with that show too long. Those people–"

"What about those people?"

"They're just not–"

"Not what?"

"Someday, you'll know what I mean."

"I doubt it," she said snippily.

He shook his head. "Darling Brenda. You have so much, but you always go for the off-beat, the unusual."

"Sure. Why not?"

He just smiled.

She made up her mind that she and Martin would never make it. She was glad he was leaving.

# CHAPTER 11

▼

# HANGING OUT WITH BETSY

The show ran for a year. What had seemed so exciting a few months ago was no longer so. Brenda thought if she had to hear the star sing 'Things' once more, she'd gladly throw the pie herself. And sometimes cooped up with the Gorgeous Ones and listening to their babble about sex, men, bodies and how to improve them, she thought, 'What am I doing here? What kind of a maverick character am I? Do I really want to parade myself indefinitely in front of strangers as a dancer, singer, poet, comedian and as the grand climax, a singing show girl with falsies?'

The audience had been thinning and suddenly the show ground to a halt. A decision was made to take it to Philadelphia and Brenda, offered more money, decided to go. Some of the girls dropped out, didn't want to leave their hotshot boyfriends. Worse squeakers replaced them, and Brenda had to redouble her efforts to drown them out.

They opened at the Forrest Theatre and it was a kick to see Mother and Dad in the front row with Grandpa. He waved at Brenda and kept looking around the stage for Buster Keaton.

To pep things up, Brenda prevailed on Mother to give a cast party. Probably, it was the high spot of Mother's life. Members of a hit New York show coming to her house! For a week, she had Jancy and Aya polishing floors and silver. On the great night, she amazed Brenda by coming out of her shell and having a wonderful time. She flirted with the 'Things' star who, amazingly, came out of his shell, kissing her hand and calling her "Duchess." Handsome Dad made a hit with the girls with his courtly manners. Brenda's stock soared.

"Gee, Brenda. Your family's the greatest!"

Betsy Fulsome, a singer, had joined the cast. She was a pretty Southern blonde, except for a rather large nose. Education-wise, she seemed to be a notch above the other girls and at the party, charmed Mother with stories of her social background as a member of the Horsey set in Richmond, Virginia.

"A delightful girl," Mother remarked later. "Quite well born. Do invite her out again. Not that the other girls aren't nice, but Betsy seems more your type."

Mother always knew how to pick a lemon.

Brenda had no reason to believe Betsy wasn't all she said she was but soon discovered she had an odd behavior pattern. She couldn't say, "No," and that meant to anybody. On joining the show, she lost no time in launching into a hot and heavy affair with a good-looking chorus boy.

So what else was new? Only prudish Brenda didn't indulge.

When the show left for Detroit, Betsy talked Brenda into rooming with her. She managed to hold her libido in check for a while, but by the time the show closed, she was ready for action.

It seemed she had a boyfriend, Al, in Buffalo. And since their leading man and his girlfriend were driving to New York via Canada and Buffalo, Betsy begged a ride for them in his rumble. Ten hours in heat and dust, they arrived in Buffalo looking like members of a darker skinned tribe. Dumped at the hotel, and after a wash and change, Betsy was raring to go.

Brenda tried to beg off.

"You can't," Betsy said. "Al's bringing a date for you."

Betsy's date wasn't all that bad. Tall and well dressed, an insurance salesman she'd met in New York. Brenda's date turned out to be a massive muscle man named Harry who ran a health club and was a little lacking in the upper story. It seemed he was also gung-ho for fun and frolics.

After dinner, the four of them repaired to Betsy's suite, provided by Al. Betsy and Al immediately popped into the bedroom, closed and locked the door.

In the living room, Big Harry removed his jacket and tie and drew Brenda on his lap while trying to fondle her front.

"Stop it," Brenda said.

"Come on, Sweetie," Harry wheedled. "Al said you were in that show."

"So, what's that got to do with anything?" Brenda retorted, trying to claw her way out.

"I thought all you show girls liked to have a little fun."

Before Brenda knew it, she was being crushed in those massive arms while his big sexy lips were working on her small, pinched up mouth. His hands were everywhere.

Mother's militant training catapulted Brenda into action. She let out a scream you could have heard across Lake Erie, broke free and rushed to batter on the bedroom door with her fists.

"Open this door, Betsy. Open up, damn it!"

She kept battering until Betsy finally opened, wrapped in a sheet. Brenda saw Al under covers, looking annoyed.

"What the hell's the matter?" Betsy demanded.

"This sex fiend, Harry, attacked me! Get him out of here!"

"Are you nuts?"

"No, but you are. Get them both out of here!"

"I didn't know you were such a prude," she snapped.

Brenda had broken in on some hot agitating. Betsy was panting and lipstick was smeared all over her face.

"And I didn't know you were such a damned bloody sex maniac!"

"Aw, come on, Brenda," she whined. "Don't be like that."

She was dying to get back under those sheets with Al. But Brenda was planted in front of her, adamant.

"I tell you, get them out or I'll call the manager and have them thrown out!"

Harry, staring at Brenda open-mouthed, remained silent. Betsy retreated and closed the door behind her. She must have conferred with Al and they decided to humor Brenda.

The men left hurriedly. Betsy apologized, probably thinking of the nice meals at Upsan Downs and how it would be a good place to keep in reserve as a hideout when things got tough in New York. Even if Brenda was a prude, she could be a useful prude.

"Al spoke highly of Harry," Betsy said. "I didn't think you'd mind him coming on to you. After all, it's all in fun."

"I'm not about to jump in bed with every dope I run into, even if you are. I think your lifestyle stinks."

"Oh, Brenda, I'm sorry. Let's be friends. You know how fond I am of you."

Betsy looked pathetic standing there in the sheet, her touched up hair tousled, her long nose reddened as tears started to roll. She was undoubtedly a nymphomaniac and couldn't help herself.

"I need you, Brenda," she wept. "And you're right. Men are no damn good. They louse up my life. I'll try to change. Honest."

Poor Betsy. Brenda was fond of her in spite of her sluttish ways.

"Oh, forget it."

When the show closed, Brenda didn't feel like going home. What was she going to do there? So when Betsy suggested that they share her apartment and the rent, Brenda decided to stay in New York. Betsy had her good points. She was kind-hearted and fun and things were always happening around her.

They partied a lot with unemployed theatre types Betsy knew from other shows. She hauled Brenda out on double dates with ex-lovers and new prospects. Brenda managed to fend off advances and earned a reputation for being a cold fish.

So it was up all night and sleeping most of the day until the next drinking bout. Sometimes it occurred to Brenda she was wasting life. But look, wasn't she alone at last and living in tune with the exciting pulse of the Big City?

During this time, Mother shelled out a small stipend so Brenda could continue her singing lessons and look for a job. After a couple of unsuccessful visits to agents, Brenda gave up. Did she really want to be a singing showgirl again anyhow?

Betsy wasn't getting a job either and decided her nose was standing in the way.

"My nose is too damn big," she moaned.

"It's not that bad."

"Anyhow, I'm getting rid of it. I've decided to get a lift, too." She paused. "Don't tell anyone, but I'm almost twenty-eight."

"No!"

"Look at these lousy lines."

Brenda hadn't noticed before, but in the afternoon sun of the breakfast nook and without any makeup, they looked like little trenches.

"I can hardly wait to be done," Betsy said. "They can do everything. Breasts, flabby arms, the works. And they say a face lift can take off ten years." She examined Brenda's lineless face. "How old are you?"

"Twenty-two."

"You're a virgin, aren't you?"

"So what if I am?"

"Imagine! I lost mine at fifteen." Betsy had a warming smile. "Stay as sweet as you are, darlin'. Men aren't worth the trouble."

"So, why get yourself carved up for them?"

"I love 'em, darlin'. Love 'em."

It seemed Betsy had already consulted a Park Avenue nose bobber, a Doctor Samuel de Stine, supposedly the best in the business.

"He's real cute," she said.

'Uh-oh,' thought Brenda, 'here she goes again.'

"But those face jobs are expensive. Where are you getting that kind of money?"

"Oh, I've saved some and it's for a good cause." She paused. "Actually, Sammy goes for me. He's making me a special offer. Knocking it way down."

So, it's "Sammy" already. That's where she's been for the last few nights. Sammy'd probably be knocking her way up if she didn't watch out.

"Anyhow, I have another appointment to finalize things. How about going with me? I need some moral support."

'Immoral support, more like it,' thought Brenda.

But she went.

The waiting room of Dr. de Stine was spacious and luxurious, decorated in an Art Deco manner. Swedish modern, beige carpeting and abstract paintings in harsh and militant colors. Spider plants climbed the walls. Otherwise, the room was empty.

"Isn't it super!" Betsy exclaimed. "Sammy's spent a fortune on it. And he has his own operating room, anesthetist, nurses, the works!"

"If he's such a big shot, where are all the patients?"

"This is his day off. He squeezed me in before his golf game."

'And that's not all the squeezing he'll do,' thought Brenda.

From behind a mirrored door, a beautiful but rather stiff-faced blonde appeared. Her white uniform clung tightly to her curves. Had she been done?

"Doctor will see you now, Miss Fulsome."

Alone, Brenda perched on an uncomfortable piece of Art Deco. Why so many mirrors on the walls? she wondered. Were they to remind one of defects needing to be fixed? And how about that creepy-looking Picasso painting? It was bald and had two faces. Did it have some hidden meaning? Such as, we all have two faces? Or, that the doctor could change the one we have for some other? She wondered what the doctor would look like. Tall, thin, distinguished, kind of a god-like figure who could make people more beautiful than God intended.

Presently Miss Beautiful returned, seated herself and began typing. Brenda got up the nerve and asked if she'd been done.

"Oh, yes. Everything. Nose, eyes, arms, breasts, inner thighs. Would you believe, I'm over forty?"

"No! The man's a wizard."

Miss Recycled smiled, a little stiffly, as if her mouth couldn't quite stretch all the way. "Indeed he is."

Betsy was in the doctor's office quite awhile and Brenda wondered if she might be doing a little more than finalizing things.

At last a buzzer sounded. Miss Done-over said, "The doctor will see you now, Miss Marr."

'Why me?' thought Brenda.

In the examining room, a surprise awaited her.

Doctor de Stine was very ungodlike. A plump, cocky, youngish-looking little man (one suspected he was older than he looked. Could he have done himself?). He had a brown beard (dyed?) and alert, bird-like eyes. On his fingers were gold rings, on his wrist a gold bracelet. He wore a handsome sports shirt in the deep V of which a heavy gold chain dangled among lush black (dyed?) chest hairs. Checkered slacks and tan boots completed the ensemble. A 'with it' get-up if Brenda ever saw one. She supposed it was hard for him to find ways to spend all those big bucks that poured into his coffers every day.

He grasped Brenda's hand in warm, stubby, efficient-feeling fingers. Apparently Betsy had primed Doc Sammy that a new prospect eagerly awaited his wizardly works. And the Doc wouldn't be one to pass up the smell of new money.

Before Brenda could protest, he'd whisked her into the examining chair. He then proceeded to prance around her like a cockatoo getting ready to mate. He took soundings of her chin, nose and jowls. He took her measure with his thumb, like an artist preparing his masterpiece.

"Doctor Sammy really is an artist," Betsy remarked as she stood by. "I've seen his work."

'You haven't seen half of his work yet,' Brenda thought, noting the intimate way Doc Sammy's hand brushed her thigh as he passed. Maybe there'd be a little trip to Acapulco after she'd been done. After all, she'd be helping pay for it. He had a good thing in Betsy. She was even helping recruit a candidate.

Brenda sat docile and unspeaking while Doc Sammy summed her up. She'd need a couple of tucks here and there, nothing major really. But, of course, her eyes would have to be done.

"We just slit under the eye and pull up the skin. It eliminates those bags."

Brenda wasn't aware of having bags. Whatever her eyes needed had already been done, and those stubby little hands weren't about to slit up her eyes.

Doc Sammy then ushered them into his luxurious inner office, seated them and looked at Brenda expectantly. She surprised him by saying she'd have to think it over.

"I think she's just scared, Sammy," Betsy apologized.

Sammy was all smiles. "Nothing to be scared of, dear. A simple procedure, nothing organic involved, just stretching the skin. You'll be delighted with the results. Let us know soon. Understand, I'm terribly busy." He added, "A friend of Betsy, I'll make you a good price."

As they walked down Park Avenue, Betsy lit into her.

"What's with you? He's making a special price, opportunity of a lifetime. You got a screw loose?"

'No, but you have,' thought Brenda. 'And it's not only in the upper story.'

"I don't need it. And, I wouldn't do it if I did."

"He plans to do my face. He does wonders with faces. Then he'll do my nose. I've always wanted a little one."

'You better watch out he doesn't give you another kind of little one,' thought Brenda.

She said, "I suppose the Doc's married. I noticed a picture of wifey and kids on his desk."

"So, what else is new?" Betsy didn't sound discouraged. "Besides, he says they are about to get a divorce. He's crazy about me."

Suddenly Betsy's enthusiasm evaporated. "He's going to operate Monday. I'm real scared. You will stand by me and hold my hand, won't you?"

You couldn't help feeling sorry for Betsy.

Brenda patted her hand. "Have I got a choice?"

"Sammy's such a dear. He's promised to take me on a trip when the ordeal's over."

"Acapulco?"

"How'd you guess?"

Brenda was on hand at the recovery room when Betsy, groggy with sedatives and bandaged to the eyebrows, was propelled in a wheel chair by a nurse, down the elevator and into Doc Sammy's chauffer-driven limo.

At Betsy's apartment, the plump, motherly nurse thrust a card in Brenda's hand.

"Call this number if you need help."

"Help! Could something go wrong? Don't you think you'd better stick around?"

"Oh, no," she said cheerfully. "Just keep her sedated. She'll sleep most of the time. We've got two more to deliver today." She grinned. "We haven't lost one yet. Hang in there."

Brenda hung in through administering the pills, hand holdings, bedpans and Betsy's complaints. "I'm hot. I hurt. Get these damn bandages off me, I can't breathe."

When 'Plump and Motherly' returned several days later, the bandages off revealed Betsy's bruised eyes, scraped skin, scars behind the ears and on the neck. She looked a mess.

"Oh God, he's ruined me!" she groaned. "I'm going to sue! I'll never survive this!"

The nurse gave Brenda a sympathetic look. "I hope you survive," she muttered.

They survived, and everything finalized including the nose, Betsy came out without a wrinkle or sag, skin pink and smooth and nose diminished to a saucy button. She looked twenty or younger, and when they sauntered down Fifth Avenue, admiring male glances followed her.

Betsy was ecstatic. "Sammy says I'm gorgeous and I am."

She didn't seem too disappointed when Sammy "postponed" their little trip, pleading divorce problems.

"I'm through tangling with married men," she announced. "I deserve better."

On occasional trips to Upsan Downs, Mother was beginning to pressure Brenda to come home. "I can't keep supporting you over there, and you don't seem to be getting anyplace."

Brenda didn't want to go but at this point was wondering if she hadn't had enough of hanging out with Betsy. As well a face change, Betsy seemed to be having a personality one. Easy going, warm-hearted and friendly was being replaced by sullen, irritable and conceited.

"Listen Brenda, it's all right for you to just loaf around. You've got a rich family to support you. I've got to get ahead. Now that I've got the looks, I'm going to quit going around with losers and find somebody rich, famous and successful. And, I'm worth it."

One day she announced she'd just happened to run into what she was looking for.

"Who's he?"

"His name's Curtis Wicks, the rich and famous director of the big band, Vital Voyagers. He and I started a little thing once. Unfinished business. Anyhow, he's invited me to a bash at his apartment tonight."

"Can I come, too?"

Betsy looked doubtful. What was in it for her? But, remembering Brenda's handholding when she needed it, she guessed it would be okay.

# Chapter 12

## Kicks With Curtis Wicks

According to Betsy, the apartment house on Central Park West housed a lot of the rich, successful and famous: opera singers, actors and writers. Curt's place had a living room as big as a skating rink. Furniture was pushed back for dancing and a pianist was drawing good sounds out of a baby grand.

Brenda and Betsy were gussied up in new, second hand designer outfits scrounged from discount houses. Betsy's was a pink ruffly arrangement to match her pink cheeks. Brenda's was a slinky black job, which bared one shoulder. This went interestingly with her severe Madonna hairdo. It said "Come and get me, but I can't promise anything."

A lot of people had arrived. Not seeing a familiar face, they made for the bar. Brenda downed her martini, which gave its usual high-powered zing.

"There's Curt," Betsy breathed excitedly. "Isn't he cute?"

Their host came in with a group of men in evening dress, probably members of his band. Brenda wasn't too impressed. He was short and stocky with a blonde crew cut, which didn't do much for his blunt features. His suit was well cut, but in workman's clothes, he could have passed for a 'not bad looking' bricklayer.

He caught sight of Betsy and worked his way over. Betsy gave him a buss on the mouth.

"Looking sharp," he said to her and turned to Brenda.

"Say, what happened to the rest of your dress?"

"What?"

"You've only got one shoulder."

"I ran out of material."

"You should have run out of more."

He had great eyes, blue, clear.

They had a warming effect on Brenda. What was this? Chemistry?

"Let's dance," he said.

His assertive hand took her wrist. Betsy glared at her. "Damn you," she muttered and stamped off.

Brenda felt a momentary twinge. But why should she feel guilty? It wasn't her fault Curt had chosen her.

She was taller than Curt, so she stooped a little. His lips grazed her cheek.

"Where are you from?" he asked.

"Philly."

"Main Line?"

"How'd you know?"

"It's written all over you. What are you doing here with Betsy?"

"What's wrong with her?"

"Nothing. Except, she ought to be getting paid for it."

What a lousy thing to say. Still, Betsy earned it and Brenda was enjoying that stocky body pressing her. Unmistakable chemistry.

He said, "The big city is no place for unsure little girls from the Main Line."

"What do you mean unsure?"

"The way I read it, as well as being beautiful, you're oversensitive and afraid of life."

"Sez you."

"Sez me."

They were laughing. Brenda got bold. Martini bold.

"Truthfully, I'm in the Big City because of fate."

"What fate?"

"Don't you know?"

"You mean me?"

"What do you think?"

He kissed her cheek.

"I think you're right. Why don't we go find out?"

Brenda was floating. Maybe this Curt was what she'd been waiting for.

"Let's go," he said.

"Where?"

"I've got something in mind."

He was working too fast.

"What about Betsy?"

"What about her?"

"She likes you."

"I hardly know the girl."

Brenda looked for Betsy and saw she'd latched onto a man she recognized as a well-known entertainer. He had fuzzy black hair and swarthy skin. He was breathing in Betsy's ear and she seemed to be enjoying it and to have forgotten Curt.

"Come on," Curt said. "I want to see if you pass the test."

Damn! He was taking her for a pushover like Betsy.

"What test?" she stammered.

He smiled. "I see what you mean. But no, not yet that is. I want you to meet a couple of pals."

He steered her to the bar, to his pals Mike Dorn and Jim Manning. Mike was tall and skinny, with a hooked nose and glasses. Jim was good looking, a male model type. Both were big shots in advertising.

"Look what I found," Curt said.

"Wow," Jim said.

"Just my type, voluptuous brunette," Mike put in.

"Hands off," Curt said. "I saw her first. Please note the aristocratic Main Line nose."

"I'm noticing, I'm noticing," Mike said.

"She seems to have a few brains," Curt said. "Shall we adopt her?"

"And how."

Several nights a week, they picked up Brenda at the apartment. Betsy, involved with her dusky entertainer, couldn't have cared less. After dinner they would start their rounds of the nighteries, not ending until dawn. Once more, Brenda saw the nighttime city through a glorious alcoholic haze. Her three men said they adored her. More and more she adored Curt, her witty little Irishman.

Their favorite haunt was the Stork Club, the "in" nighterie of the times. Curt was a drinking pal of the owner and sometimes they were even invited to the Cub Room, that inner sanctum that even hosted such luminaries as Ava Gardner and Orson Welles.

'This is really living,' thought Brenda. 'It's got it all.'

Curt got her a singing gig on a local radio station. Here, she moaned 'Speak To Me Of Love' into the mike. Yes, this was making it. But what she really lived for were those nights on the town with her celebrity boyfriend. She became known as Curtis Wicks' girlfriend.

But there was a puzzle. Except for handholdings and kisses in cab, Curt hadn't made a real pass. He never took her to his apartment. She began to wonder if he were gay.

Mike clued her in. It seemed Curt was not only married and trying for a divorce but had been having an affair he was trying to get out of.

This was a shocker, but Brenda reasoned maybe Curt wanted to start them out with a clean slate. Could it mean he was serious about her?

She decided he should meet Mother and Dad and took him to Upsan Downs for Sunday dinner. It was not a success. Curt was stiff with them, even seemed bored. They could find no meeting ground. Dad tried politics. No go. Curt was a democrat. And where was Curt's wit she'd told them about? It occurred to her Curt was missing his martinis. He was out of luck. Liquor was only served on Christmas and New Years.

Things got worse when Mother said, "Isn't it wonderful that Brenda is doing so well with her singing job?"

Curt said abruptly he didn't think Brenda was too well suited to a stage career.

Mother got pink in the face and said, "I don't know what you mean. I've seen to it she's had the best training for a stage career."

Curt shrugged and continued to eat and after dinner said he had to get back to New York right away. This was news to Brenda, who'd planned an afternoon of wandering under the trees, hand in hand.

On the porch, waiting for Curt's cab, she asked what was the matter.

"I'll tell you when I see you next."

To his set profile she said, "I wish you hadn't said that to my mother."

"Why not? It's true, isn't it? You're not really interested in making it in the theatre. If you were, you'd be working at it harder. Am I right?"

His eyes could be cold and challenging.

"I wish I hadn't brought you here."

"I'm glad you did. Now I know what it is."

"What what is?"

"I'll tell you when I see you."

The cab drew up. Damn. She couldn't let him go like this. She wanted to be in his arms. What she got instead was Uncle Jake driving up behind the cab in his new Cadillac, no doubt coming to try and make a touch on Mother to help pay for it. The grandparents were hard up this month.

Brenda had to introduce Curt.

She saw Jake's critical eyes go over the sharp cut of Curt's suit and his other un-Main Line attributes.

As Curt drove off, Jake said, "Who's the New York Irishman?"

He was an expert at needling. Brenda resolved to not let him get her.

"He's the director of the big band Vital Voyagers."

"Whoever they are."

"I guess you wouldn't have heard of them. They're world famous."

He grinned. "Looks like a shanty Irishman to me."

Anger flared as she imagined Jake sharing this delightful news with Aunt Margot and the girls.

She started away. His words stopped her.

"Is he your sweetie?"

"He's my agent. He's promoting my singing career."

"Are you sure that's all he's promoting? Maybe a little hanky-panky on the side?"

"Uncle Jake, get your mind out of the gutter. You're no one to talk with your reputation."

He smiled slyly. "Maybe we have something in common, you and I."

She snapped. "We don't have a damn thing in common! Just because you mess around with every woman you can find doesn't mean that other people live that way."

"Oh, Miss Purity, huh?" he paused. "So, you're singing now. I guess you have plenty to sing about."

"What is that supposed to mean?"

"You were a show girl, weren't you? I understand they're pretty hot numbers."

"No hotter than your home-grown Main Line debutante types."

He laughed. "My, my, what a spit fire. Tell you what; we'll call a truce. I won't tell on you if you don't tell on me."

His eyes were dancing with malicious glee. She saw why women were attracted to him. He would challenge and excite them.

"You know you're a pain in the neck," she retorted and started away.

She knew he'd always been fond of her, probably found her tart come-backs titillating after the dullness of his household of bland, disapproving women.

He stopped her with, "It's too bad your mother let you go on the stage. It certainly hasn't done you any good."

"Really?"

"Your Aunt Margot and I always thought it was a mistake on her part to let you do that."

So, old Aunty Margot and the cousins had been kicking that around. Well, shitty-dit-dit on them!

He added, "But then, Lillian never did have any judgment."

Infuriated, she spun around.

"I'll thank you to keep your dirty mind out of my business! You're a God damned bigoted snob like the rest of your breed!"

She yanked open the screen door.

"Hold on there! I came to see your mother!"

"She's busy. She doesn't want to see you. Why don't you go get on a horse!"

She slammed the door on his surprised face. Insufferable jackass! Let him go home and tell that one to Margot and the girls.

She heard him cursing and stamping off and speeding away in his magnificent not-paid-for Caddy.

She hoped to escape to her room, but Mother and Dad were waiting in the parlor.

Mother said, "Come in here, Brenda."

She stood in the door stiffly.

Mother said, "That man, Curtis Wicks or whatever his name is, is very common. He certainly won't be of help in advancing your career."

"He is being a help. He got me my radio job."

"He strikes me as being a New York smart-alec type," Dad said.

"Oh, for God's sake," Brenda retorted. "He's the successful producer of one of the biggest radio shows in America."

Dad looked worried. "I hope you're not getting involved with him."

"Don't be absurd, Jason," Mother said. "Though I don't know why Brenda takes up with these half-cut people."

"I don't want her to get hurt," Dad said. "I think that young man could be tough and unscrupulous if it suited him."

"Damn it!" Brenda exploded. "You treat me like a child and I'm sick of it."

"Brenda, I forbid you to see that man!" Mother commanded.

"Forbid," Brenda said scathingly. "I'll see him if I want to."

"Don't let her, Jason."

Dad shook his head. "I'm afraid there's nothing I can do. Brenda's a woman and has to make her own decisions."

"And I intend to do it."

Brenda stalked from the room. At that moment, she hated them.

She could hardly wait to get back to New York.

Usually when Curt knew she was back, he'd be on the phone planning their evening. Brenda waited afternoon and evening. No call. Betsy must have been off someplace with her boyfriend. The next day, still no call. When Brenda called his office, his secretary said he was out. Did that mean to her? Brenda called Mike, who was evasive. He said Curt was awfully busy. Had Mike been programmed to say that?

Three days later, Curt called.

"Hi kid, how about a drink? I'm tied up tonight. How about tomorrow?"

Maybe she should play this busy bit, too. But her voice took over too quickly.

"Sure."

They picked her up and, as usual, they started on their drinking rounds. But things were changed; no handholding with Curt and the others seemed constrained. The evening ended earlier than usual, Mike and Jim begging off. "Big day tomorrow."

In the cab, Curt was quiet. Brenda was a bundle of nerves. Was this really the end? Her drinks gave her courage.

"Say, what is all this?"

"All what?"

"What's happened with us?"

He shrugged. "I just realized a few things."

"What—things?" Her voice trembled.

"I don't think you're going to like this."

Her heart gave a thud.

He said, "Look, Bren, you're beautiful and fun to be with. But I'm afraid it's no go."

"Why?"

"I didn't know what was wrong till I met your mother."

"What's she got to do with anything?"

"She's got you under her thumb."

"I don't know what you mean."

"Sure you do. Over twenty-two and you're still a virgin."

"How would you know?"

"It's written all over you. The thing is, you're a passionate girl. You're holding it all in. You've got these hang-ups."

He kept on. She was flawed; she didn't know how to give. Those were the girls he steered clear of. They were immature, messed up.

While Brenda listened, she was thinking he was right and this was silly. She was her own boss and she wanted him. Nothing else mattered.

"Shut up, Curt," she said. "Kiss me."

All her anger, frustration and misery exploded in that kiss.

"God," he muttered, "You are hot."

In his apartment, he unzipped her dress, yanked it off her shoulders and bent her back roughly.

"Wait," she protested.

"What for? What are you saving it for? Your old age?"

"This standing up is no good."

"You're right."

He pulled her to the bedroom and while she slipped out of her dress, he peeled down to his shorts. Then it happened.

In his clothes, Curt's shortcomings were minimized to conceal short chubby legs, slightly bowed, and a paunch. His shorts were flowered, the Hawaiian kind. Brenda's eyes settled on these objects. He looked ridiculous. The freeze began.

While he watched from the bed, she made herself undress but took a long time.

"Hurry up," he urged. "Let's go."

What, no loving words? At least Martin supplied those.

She got in beside him slowly. His thing pressed against her. No lack in that department. But those shorts!

She began to laugh. He pulled away.

"What's funny?"

She couldn't stop laughing. Why did chubby legs and flowered shorts turn her off? He was still Curt, successful and charismatic. Had she only been in love with a suit of clothes?

The laughter was beginning to sound hysterical. He sat up, his face white.

"What's the matter with you?" he snarled. "As if I didn't know. Snotty society brat wants to run home to Mama? Well, this time it won't work. You're out of your depth, kid. Time to take your medicine."

He shoved her on her back and went to work.

There was the panting, puffing, poking. He was strong, but her muscled dancer's legs remembered Friendly Fredly and gave a violent kick. It tossed him off. She broke loose and was up. He was right with her. He caught her, spun her around and hit her across the face until her teeth rattled.

"You bitch!" he yelled. "Main Line society bitch!"

He lunged for her, but she escaped to the bathroom and slammed and locked the door.

She wrapped a bath towel around her shaking body, then sat on the john and waited. It seemed like forever. Then, hearing no sound from the bedroom, she peered out. Curt had dressed and gone.

In a daze, she dressed and took a cab to the apartment. There, she took a long look at herself in the mirror, confronting what seemed like a changed person. Her eyes were wide and, it seemed to her, more knowing, as if they'd looked on something ugly and it had marked them. Was this what all the preparing had been for? To prepare her to avoid this?

Once again, her dream of perfect love had collapsed. She was naïve and romantic, ill equipped to play the games of Curts and Fredlys. Maybe the things Curt said about her were so. Maybe she had provoked him. Maybe he was sensitive about his shortcomings. But was that a reason for such brutality? Dad was right. The Irishman was tough and unscrupulous. He'd spoiled everything with his crudeness and those damn shorts. He looked like an ass in them.

She took a belt of Scotch and went to bed and slept.

The next day, back from a trip with her entertainer, Betsy was her old kindly self, now that she had her man.

"Poor Brenda from Philly, in trouble again. Dry your eyes, you're better off without him."

Her bobbed nose quivered sympathetically. To Brenda, it always looked kind of rabbity.

"Damn men," Brenda said. "They always mess me up."

"Ain't it the truth, honey."

Taking pity on her, Betsy began taking Brenda to listen to her dusky lover sing at one of the tonier nighteries. Bored and depressed, Brenda drank too much and had awful hangovers.

One morning, around ten, Dad called to say he was in town on business and how about having lunch?

"Fine," Brenda said weakly. She'd had about two hours sleep.

At twelve, she staggered into the Algonquin lobby. Handsome Dad rose to greet her.

"Brenda, you look awful. What's happened?"

"A touch of flu," she muttered.

At their table, Brenda ordered a martini.

"Martinis before lunch?" Dad raised an eyebrow.

People stared at Dad, so distinguished looking, black hair, graying at the temples. People stared at Brenda, too. She figured she looked like Camille in the last stages.

Her hangover was so bad she didn't trust herself to speak and when the martini came, her hand shook so she spilled it.

"Brenda, you're not well. What is it?"

"I'm okay, Dad." Her voice was shaky.

Dad gave her a long look.

"It's that Curt, isn't it?"

She bowed her head.

"So I was right about him, tough and unscrupulous. That bastard, he didn't–"

"No."

"Thank God for that."

Seated beside her, his arm came around her.

"My poor willful little girl, you had to find out for yourself, didn't you?"

She was crying. What a relief to let it out to Dad who always understood. He didn't say, "I told you so. How could you be so silly?" He was always there with the kindly advice.

"I think you've had enough of this town," Dad said. "You're coming home with me today."

"I have and I am."

Yes, enough of trashed-out city streets, the hot anxiety of metal, the thrusting, jostling humanity with their weary 'trying to make it' look.

Betsy was agreeable to her leaving. She'd decided to move in with her singer.

Bye, bye, Betsy. So long show biz. Brenda was glad to go home.

# CHAPTER 13

▼

# OLÉ

In a short time, the comfort of Upsan Downs seemed smothering. Aya babying Brenda, Jancy making sure she got her hot oatmeal for breakfast. Brenda realized she'd grown away from all this. The New York experience had changed her. She didn't fit here anymore: the same old boring Main Line, the Club, Wanamakers. She'd managed to bluff it as a dancer, singer, and actress. But who was she? Mother had created her from walleyed, pudgy and pigeon-toed. Maybe she should have left her that way. Maybe that's the way she really was. The Main Line Madonna was a phony and a failure. As for men, that seemed a dead end.

Why had she always met the wrong ones? She could blame it on Mother, throwing her to the wolves of Broadway or encouraging a foreign no-good-nic like Martin. Innocent Mother, what did she know?

And so, Brenda slumped around the place in old jeans, smoking, feeding Grandpa's ducks.

And Mother, puzzled and upset, watched her and worried.

What had happened to the talented beauty she had worked so hard to create?

One morning at breakfast, unable to restrain herself, she took off.

"Brenda, you've got to get busy!"

"Doing what?"

"I don't know. You didn't like life in the theatre. I don't know why. You had a wonderful chance. It was that awful Curt what's-his-name that messed you up."

"Mother, for God's sake!"

"Don't swear, Brenda." She paused. "So, what are you going to do now?"

"I don't know."

Dad peered over his newspaper. "Let the child alone, Lillian. She'll find her way."

"I think she should go back to her dancing."

'Damn,' thought Brenda. 'The same old cracked record.'

Mother went on, gathering a head of steam. Aldo could fix up the old barn for a dance studio. Brenda could teach there.

"Don't you think it's a good idea, Jason?"

"If Brenda wants it."

"What am I supposed to teach?"

"Spanish. You were always a lovely Spanish dancer. I'll even pay for some Flamenco lessons for you in New York."

"Olé," said Brenda.

But having nothing better to do and with Mother footing the bill, Brenda invested in a polka dot skirt and thick heeled Spanish shoes and entered into her new career. The Madonna hair-do could double for Flamenco, with a couple of spit curls thrown in.

Once more, she went to the shoddy old Roseland building where she'd once howled for Mrs. Tacconi. The dirty corridors still throbbed with the bleat of rehearsing bands and the jostle of striving young with their dance bags.

Everyone in the crowded class looked of teenage vintage. When they began with the whirls and heels, Brenda had to move fast to keep from getting stomped by sweaty senoritas. However, she was able to collect steps, which she wove into routines of her own.

"Now, who am I supposed to teach?" Brenda demanded.

"Oh, you'll find someone," Mother declared impatiently. "Don't tell me I invested in all those lessons for nothing. I'm going up and do my vibrations."

Brenda watched with affection and irritation as Mother bustled off. She was getting plump from too many of Jancy's good cakes and pies. When Dad remarked on her rounded figure ("Getting a little broad across the narrows, Mom."), she'd invested in a hip vibrator. Hips encased in a canvas belt she'd stand, shaking, for a half hour each day. Nothing happened to her hips, but Brenda guessed it strengthened her character. You had to hand it to Mother, she was always trying to improve herself. Much as Brenda loved her, she saw her little faults and how she manipulated to achieve what she might have wanted for herself.

Always resourceful, Mother suggested that Brenda might get some pupils by running an ad in the 'Main Line Tattler.'

"A good selling point might be to say it's a good way to reduce," practical Mother said.

Brenda didn't think much of this idea, however she ran an ad, which proclaimed in large letters: LOSE WEIGHT. LEARN THE FLAMENCO.

Brenda was amazed at the response. It seemed that along the Main Line, a bunch of women had just been waiting for a chance to stamp their heels to lose weight. Soon, she had eight enlistments.

In Aldo's fixed up studio in the barn, she labored over these female bodies. Charging them four dollars and to the music of the 'Pasa Doble' on her tape recorder, she attempted to teach them one of her creations, 'The Bull Fight Dance.' In this, with swirling capes, they were supposed to portray matadors in action. They looked more like hefty charging bulls.

Brenda suspected that what weight they might have sweated off, the hefty ones soon replaced by a dash to the nearest martini lunch haven.

One by one, these big ones dropped out, claiming ailments such as sore feet and spinal injuries.

However, unlike the martini group, it seemed that several of the women were dead serious about learning the Flamenco. These were middle-aged gals, bored with marriage and looking for some kind of fling.

Brenda gave it to them.

She clothed them in ruffles and polka dots. She cajoled them into clicking heels and castanets. They responded as she urged them to catch the furious rhythms of the dance. It was all fun until one discordant note appeared in the form of a take-over artist.

This was Ruby. Fortyish and blonde, with a big front, grown children and a terrible itch for fame. She wasn't much of a dancer, but she had a sexy hip wiggle that apparently intrigued the men. It was rumored among the girls that Ruby slept around.

After several months, the girls were looking fairly good. Brenda, with Dad's help, managed to scrounge up a country club date for her troupe, for which they would be paid a paltry sum. Brenda did her rhumba and found she could still "wow" 'em. The footwork wasn't Carmen Amaya, but the spirit was there. What the heck did the country club set know about Flamenco anyhow?

Unknown to Brenda, Ruby was bursting to do that rhumba. And when Brenda returned from her summer vacation, having allowed the girls to practice in the studio, she found that Ruby had taken costumes, music and several girls to perform with herself soloing that rhumba at some club she managed to snare.

"I didn't think you'd mind," Ruby said.

"I do mind. Get my costumes and music back on the double, and you and those girls can be replaced."

The loyal girls said Ruby tried to grab them, too and thought it was a dirty trick.

Hearing that Ruby was performing at a local high school, Brenda and her faithful ones went.

Four plump male guitarists were seated in the background. To announce the coming of Ruby, they launched into a rush and clamor of bass chords fit to proclaim the entrance of Queen Isabella.

Ruby slithered on in tight black velvet, a large gold chain glinting in her cleavage, which seemed to extend down to her nether regions. Ruby's dancing had not improved. She was still doing the same hip wiggle and passionate looks to the steps she'd learned from Brenda. Her only improvement was the support she got from the frenzied strummings of her guitarists.

"Anyone would look good with all those guitarists behind them," one of the faithful remarked. "She's probably slept with all of them."

Ruby was soon replaced by Mercedes Gantz, another lady not in the first flush of youth and given to wearing heavy eye makeup, boots and mini skirts. She'd had dance experience and Flamenco looked good on her. Another attribute was that she seemed to worship Brenda, praising her terrific talents, dance expertise, her hands and her feet. Brenda began to worry. Was Mercedes coming on to her? But no. Mercedes was just a gusher. Why knock it? Everyone needed a little ego boost every now and then.

When Brenda told Mercedes how Ruby ripped her off, Mercedes seemed shocked silly.

"How could she? How rotten!"

Mercedes brought to the troupe a young Italian named Johnny. There was conjecture among the girls about whether they were sleeping together. Of course they were. But one wondered how shy and somewhat backward Johnny ever got down to business. Probably aggressive Mercedes took care of that.

Johnny liked to be called José and he certainly was a dead ringer for Greco. There, the similarity ended. He had two left feet. He was also a little vacant in the upper story. No matter how strenuous Brenda's effort to pound a routine into that noggin, José would invariably have forgotten the whole thing by the next lesson. Still, he looked good. Good? He looked super. If his footwork wasn't so hot, he had great shoulders, slim waist and no hips. And how about those tight Flamenco pants that revealed a wonderful development, which automatically drew the eye.

Brenda once heard him tell someone before he danced, he never ate anything but two hard-boiled eggs. Quipped the wit: "I wondered what those things were."

Brenda decided José didn't have to dance much, just bang his heels, look like Greco and let the girls swirl around him.

One of the girls, Sharon, did more than just swirl. At every opportunity, she let her long, lithe, leotard-clad body with its outstanding front, brush close to José's beautiful body structure. Their eye contact was hot enough to start a brush fire.

'Why waste a good thing?' thought Brenda. She got them to work on a Flamenco in which their bodies writhed in unison and their legs entwined, giving a startling erotic effect.

So what if José had two left feet? Who was looking at the feet?

All this threw Mercedes into a twit. She began giving Sharon a lot of glaring Flamenco looks to the effect: "Of course I'm sleeping with the brute. How dare you try and grab him?" At this, Sharon grabbed harder. Brenda had a diabolical idea. How about a number in which the girls competed for José?

This worked out well. Stamping and circling like fighting cocks, the girls fought for their man.

One day it got out of hand. Mercedes flew at Sharon and ripped the front of her leotard to the waist, revealing Sharon's bra, padded to the hilt. Sharon grabbed a hunk of Mercedes' luxuriant black hair. The wig came off in her hand. Roars of laughter from the class as José blushed and bowed his handsome Greco head. Mercedes and Sharon stalked off, and soon after, Sharon quit the troupe. No doubt she'd found a replacement for too-hard-to-get José.

After some months, Brenda's Flamenco troupe found jobs on the Main Line in women's clubs, homes for the aged and anything for which they got paid, or not paid. Mother was happy with Brenda's dancing career. She herself had found her calling. With money inherited from her parents, she was turning a pretty profit investing in the stock market. Dad, who couldn't keep his bank balance straight, was heard to mutter, "Wonderful woman. I always wanted a financial genius in the family."

Sometimes, as Brenda soaked her aching feet, she wondered about her new career. True, they were the hottest Flamenco troupe in town. But then, they were the only Flamenco troupe in town.

That is, until the coming of Lolitata.

Lolitata had been at the Flamenco since the age of five and had lisped her way out of Andalusia to open a Spanish restaurant in Philadelphia.

When Brenda heard the news, something told her, "Uh-oh, there goes my troupe."

Mercedes jumped forward with the suggestion. "Let's go see Lolitata dance. Wouldn't it be great if she invited us to one of her Huergas?"

Brenda recognized her own shortcomings in Flamenco. No way was she about to display them in front of this luminous Lolitata.

"You go," Brenda said. "Tell me about it."

A couple of Brenda's faithful went to a Huerga, that gypsy mad fling in which inspired dancers suddenly leaped up from their seated circle to stamp and swirl. Her girls declared that Brenda looked as good as Lolitata. Apparently Mercedes and José didn't think so. They began showing up late for class and forgetting to chip in with their four dollars. This pissed Brenda off, particularly when she heard they were studying with Lolitata who was charging twenty dollars a half-hour.

She decided to drop Mercedes and José. Who needed these phony Flamencoers? The years were whizzing by, and what was she getting out of all this heel pounding but a few wrinkles and tired feet? She needed a change. Something was definitely lacking in her life.

When Dad suggested she get to her writing, she whipped out a short story called 'Loss Of Love.' It was about a woman who seemed to be in love, but as in Brenda's Curt experience, when she saw the male stripped and ready for action, love faded away.

'A bunch of crap,' she thought and put it in the bureau drawer. She certainly wasn't going to show this stuff to Dad. This junk certainly wasn't filling that lack she suffered.

Then, in the library one day, that lack was taken care of. It seemed that what she'd needed was a new friend, and Teeny Tyler filled the bill.

# CHAPTER 14

▼

# TEENY TAKES OVER

Teeny was a Main Liner with artistic leanings, a striving writer. She and Brenda clicked at once.

Teeny wasn't teeny. She was six feet tall and wide and had a great appetite for food, drink and probably sex–and gossip.

She spent hours a day passing on choice morsels to her friends, of which she had many. In spite of her unsparing tongue, everyone loved Teeny. She cozied and comforted, filled them with good food and drink. She was the earth mother and welcomed Brenda into her warm embrace. Brenda was more than willing to be there.

Teeny had a large husband and two large sons who trailed in her energetic wake. Her charming husband, Winston, also old Main Line, was unable to hold a job. Fortunately, he had rich relatives who conveniently died and left him a bundle just as the Tyler funds were getting low. The bundle went for a sports car and a trip to the islands and soon the Tylers were eating beans again. But what matter? They were enjoying life.

Teeny liked to organize. She had her religious group, her drinking group and her writing group. These assorted women didn't mingle too well. The hard drinking socialites wouldn't stand those "queer religious persons" and the writing group didn't warm up to the other two. Teeny drew Brenda into all of them, saying how nice it was to find a friend who fitted in everywhere.

Brenda couldn't seem to talk in tongues, so she dropped the religious group. A developing tendency to Grandma's 'Woodruff stomach' disqualified her for the martini bunch. But she did well in the writing group. This consisted of a young tongue-tied male poet, a gal who was trying to write mysteries and an elderly Jewish lady who successfully sold her romance novels.

All these came in for great encouragement and praise from Teeny.

Teeny's claim to fame she owed to a short story published in a woman's magazine. It was called 'My Husband the Failure.' Fortunately, Winston never read anything Teeny wrote.

Brenda let Teeny read 'Loss of Love,' which Teeny pronounced "neat."

"Let's send it to Women's Lib Magazine," she suggested.

Brenda sent it. Got rejected.

After her third rejection, she gave up.

"Give me the postage," Teeny said. "I'll sell it for you."

Teeny sent it once, got it rejected and gave up as well.

Brenda was depressed. Failure again. But Teeny was in no way ready to quit, even if it meant a change of pace for her friend.

As she sat with disconsolate Brenda over afternoon tea, she declared, "I think what you need is something to rattle up your hormones. You need a man in your life."

"But I don't get along with men that well. In fact, I'm practically a virgin."

"What!" Teeny exploded. "That's pitiful! I lost mine at thirteen. I suppose your mother, like mine, filled you up with that Main Line Victorian crap about sex being rotten. Forget it! I did a long time ago."

For sometime now, Brenda'd been wondering if maybe Winston wasn't the only recipient of Teeny's favors. Of course he wasn't.

"Sex is great," Teeny said. "It's time you dropped that virginal Madonna image of yours and got some fun out of life. And I've got just the guy for you, this neat Englishman, Bertie. He grew up in India and used to wrestle tigers. The secretaries love him, but you're more his type. I'll give a party.

### Bertie the Burly Brit

Teeny gave good parties. The Main Line social kind and her mixed bag variety. At the mixed baggers, you could meet almost anyone. Quite a few were secretaries Teeny was trying to fix up with odd bachelors. Bertie fitted right in to that bag.

Bertie had a big, pink English face and a blue eye. The other was covered with a black eye patch. He claimed he'd lost it to a tiger's claw. He was about six-six and broad as a wrestler. At the party, he performed slight of hand tricks, read palms and sang bawdy songs. He could give forth with a blood-curdling rhumble deep in his throat, which he claimed was a tiger's mating call. He could also trill like a canary. When the party lagged, he produced a sword and swallowed it.

The secretaries clustered around him adoringly. Brenda sat in a corner nursing a drink, content to be entertained. Several times she caught Bertie's eye roving in her direction and wondered of she was going to turn out to be his type. Kind of a scary thought.

About twelve o'clock, people began pairing off, disappearing upstairs or out onto the terrace. Winston was getting bombed and Teeny was off someplace with the tongue-tied poet. As Brenda rose to leave, Bertie left his circle of females and brought his three hundred odd pounds in her direction.

"Not leaving, are you?"

"Yes."

"Can I drive you anyplace?"

"I have a car."

"Why don't I follow you to see if you get there all right?"

"I think I can make it on my own."

"Why don't we make it together?"

Brenda liked the twinkle in the blue eye. Oh, what the hell.

At Upsan Downs, he got her out of the car. As he walked her to the door, he began to trill like a canary. Was this a mating song?

What did he have in mind, as if she didn't know?

Inside the house he seemed bigger than ever and she thought this could be hazardous.

"Would you have a bit of whisky about?" he said, the blue eye twinkling down.

In the pantry she'd hidden a bottle from Mother, in case of emergency.

Bertie poured the whiskeys, tucked her under his masterful arm and led her to the dining room.

"Lovely antiques," he said. "Which reminds me, did you ever hear this one?"

"Mary had a little lamb; its fleece was black as soot. And everywhere that Mary went, his sooty foot he put."

Brenda laughed. "What's that got to do with antiques?"

"Nothing. It's just one of my cleaner ones."

He roved about, his one eye peering at the family portraits.

"What's with the eye patch?" she asked. "Did you really lose an eye to a tiger?"

He grinned. "Like to see it?"

"Not really."

"Most girls do."

He pulled up the patch to reveal an empty socket. It made Brenda feel slightly ill.

He said, "As a matter of fact, it was clawed by a jealous woman in India."

Brenda began to think she'd better get rid of Bertie.

Bertie had other ideas.

Her mistake was taking him to the library. The couch heaved a deep sigh as he settled in. He removed his jacket and kicked off his loafers.

"Aren't you going to sit down?" he said. "Don't be a stranger."

"I am a stranger."

"That can be remedied."

The bright eye took her in. Then from his throat rumbled the tiger's mating call. It was creepy.

"Come sit on my lap. You look silly standing there."

"I'd look sillier on your lap."

"I like you," he said.

"That's nice."

"Could you give me a kiss?"

"No."

"Why not?"

"You might have something catching. I understand you're into one night stands."

Damn it. That ought to get rid of him.

No way.

"I'm careful who I kiss," he said.

"So am I."

He didn't grin.

"I'm healthy as a horse." He flexed his muscles to prove it.

"I'd like you to go. It's late."

"I thought you were nice."

"I'm not."

"You're missing a bet."

"I'll take that chance."

He took his whisky down in one gulp.

"Well, it's disappointing, but I guess I'd better leave if that's what you want."

Thank God he wasn't going to make a big deal out of it.

Wrong. As she started away, he was on his feet. He grabbed her and gave her a big open-mouthed sloppy kiss, which seemed to engulf her whole face. She gave him a push. No avail. He was a block of granite. She tried again. His grasp tightened.

Her face muffled against his huge chest she bleated, "No, Bertie. No! Can you understand no?"

He held her away. "Sure. And can you understand this?"

He cut loose with a rear end boomer that would have knocked the socks off Coco, Aya's parrot, and over his face came the delighted, mischievous look of a child.

She was furious.

"Bertie, you are a disgusting slob."

She should have her head examined. He could have pulverized her with one blow.

He only smiled mockingly.

"Well now, did I shock the lovely Main Line lady? What a shame."

"Let me go."

"Sure. All you have to do is give me a kiss."

"The hell you say."

She tried pummeling his chest. No good. He lifted her and pinned her down on the couch. God, he was heavy! Then he got down to his business. What did Teeny mean, "Sex was fun"? This mammoth was going to do her in.

She tried pleading. "Listen Bertie, I never give in. You wouldn't like me."

"I like you, I like you," he said, chewing her ear.

"I'm a tease."

"I love teases."

"I've got a bad back."

"I love bad backs."

He was getting very excited. He held her with one hand and unzipped with the other. Like old Friendly Fred, he was a whiz at this. But oh! What was on top of her was a frightening monster.

"You're too big," she panted.

"Most women like that."

"You're squashing me."

"Most women like that."

"Damn it, Bertie! Get off me!" she screeched.

He laughed. "I don't think you like me."

"I don't. Go wrestle a tiger."

He laughed more. He was getting down to real business. She saw no escape. The more she hove, the more he squashed. Then she remembered the Brenda maneuver she'd used on Friendly Fred. With this heavy weight it posed more of a challenge. But she was desperate. She managed to wriggle her leg into a strategic position between his legs.

She drew up her knee and let him have it.

From burly Bertie's mighty lungs burst forth a roar that would have brought a female tiger to heel. He reeled back, clutched himself, rose up and cursed in several languages. Clutching, zipping, grabbing loafers and jacket, Bertie bolted.

Brenda collapsed on the couch.

"What's all that noise down there?" Mother called from upstairs.

Dad usually snored so loud, he wouldn't have heard.

"Oh, nothing," Brenda said weakly.

"Well, don't forget to turn off the lights."

The next day Teeny called, annoyed. She said Bertie complained Brenda wouldn't put out.

"He didn't appeal to me," Brenda said.

"You should put out more. You don't want to be a virgin all your life, do you?"

Brenda thought maybe she did.

"That's the last time I'm going to try and fix you up, Brenda."

"Okay," Brenda said and hung up.

### The Clam Man

The rift with Teeny didn't last. She couldn't stand being on the outs with one of her best friends. Soon she was on the phone urging Brenda to come on over. And Brenda, bored on a Sunday afternoon in February, decided she needed a little friendly distraction.

She found it listening to Teeny's 'Mart' wives. Apparently, their visit to church had no leavening effect. As their second martini took over, gossip fleeted from their tongues.

"Did you know John was having an affair with Mimsy?"

"And his wife just had a baby, poor thing."

"The question is…whose baby?"

As Brenda sipped her light Scotch, she wondered if these people could all pass the stone-throwing test. And how would it feel to be on the receiving end of these pebbles of malice?

As the noise level increased, the front door suddenly opened letting in a draft of frigid air and a man in a straw hat, carrying an electric fan. Odd. But Teeny's friends were often odd.

The newcomer's arrival was greeted with howls of delighted laughter.

"Hey Robert," Ralph said. "Why the fan? Didn't anyone tell you it's winter out there?"

Robert removed the straw hat and said with dignity that he was delivering the fan to his cousin Cissy, from whom he'd borrowed it last summer.

They all seemed to know Robert and to appreciate his oddness. 'All old Main Liners together,' Brenda thought. She felt left out of it.

"How's Trish?" Teeny asked Robert.

"She's in Florida visiting her mother."

"Lucky her, out of this weather."

"I don't like Florida," Robert said, and looked at Brenda. "Do you?"

"No, I don't like Florida."

"I didn't think you did."

Under this nutty exchange, Brenda felt something happening. What?

Robert put down the fan and accepted a drink, to clear his sinuses, he said. Brenda thought he was rather attractive in a spare, aristocratic, high-nosed way. He had thin lips, curved down slightly, as though tasting something bitter.

Brenda sat quietly in her corner listening to the cocktail chatter and from time to time, Robert glanced at her curiously. Her sad Madonna profile seemed to intrigue him. Presently, the others left and Teeny said she and Winston wanted to listen to a radio program in their bedroom.

"Why don't you guys stay awhile? Finish your drinks."

"Thanks," Robert said. "We will."

When they left, Brenda said she had to go.

"Oh, don't," Robert said. "Stay while I finish my drink."

"Well, just for a minute."

They drank and he asked what she did with herself. She said she taught dancing. He said he'd thought she did something unusual and he would like to see her studio sometime.

"Fine. Come watch a class."

She rose to go.

"Don't go. Where's your husband?"

"I don't have one."

"Divorced? Widowed? You're too attractive to be husbandless."

She shrugged and held out her hand.

"Nice to have met you, Robert."

He looked at her with nice dark eyes, put down his drink, came over, put both hands on her shoulders and kissed her on the brow.

She drew back. "What was that for?"

"Because you're lovely looking, have a beautiful brow, and because you seem sad."

"Thanks for the compliments. And I'm not that sad."

"The trouble is, you're too pale. What you need is some clam juice."

She laughed. This was a new approach.

"Why?"

"It's good for the blood."

"My blood's good enough."

"I can recommend it. I take it all the time. I'll bring you some."

He helped her on with her coat.

"It's starting to snow," he said. "I think I should follow you home."

What was this? Another Bertie ploy? God forbid!

"Thanks, I can make it okay."

He picked up the fan, put on the straw hat and followed her. It was dark and snowing quite heavily. Dreary. He put her into her car.

"I'll follow you. If you're not too busy, I'd love to see your dance studio."

"Maybe some time."

She drove fast thinking she could lose him. She didn't need this married clam man wanting to build up her blood and she didn't feel like coping with another wrestling match. But this Robert kept his headlights on her and drew up behind her in the barn.

She'd get rid of him in a hurry.

She turned on the lights in the studio. It was cold. Robert admired the pictures of her troupe and the tall mirrors. He wanted to know if she taught ballroom dancing.

"I can."

"When?"

"How about now?"

Maybe he'd had a couple of drinks before Teeny's. Anyhow, this distinguished-looking Robert put his arms around her but not to dance.

His kiss was tender, gentle. She slid away with a laugh.

He looked upset. "I don't know what made me do that."

"I've got to go to the house. My family's waiting."

"I wonder. Could you give me a cup of coffee? I mean later? I'll deliver the fan and come back."

"Why?"

"I want to talk to you."

"Why?"

"I don't know."

He seemed breathless.

"I'm married, have been for eighteen years. I have children but you–"

"But me what? You mean, I love my wife, but oh, you kid?"

That shook him. He really was odd, and did she need odd?

"Let me come back," he said.

Oh, why not let him come? He seemed harmless. It might be an amusing way to kill a lonely Sunday evening.

"Okay but just one cup."

"I'll be right back."

He didn't come right back. After Mother and Dad had gone to bed, Brenda waited awhile in the kitchen with the coffee cups. She was a bit disappointed, but maybe it was just as well.

She was in bed reading when she heard a car enter the drive, swoop up the hill, past the barn and out the upper drive. It happened three times, Robert trying to find her. She smiled and went back to her book.

The phone rang later. Teeny.

"What's going on?" she said.

"What is?"

"Robert just phoned and wanted your number. I think he has the hots for you."

"Nonsense."

"His wife's a good friend of mine, you know. They go to my church. She does a lot of social work. She's a fine woman."

"What's that got to do with anything?"

"I just thought you should know."

"If your suggesting fun and games with me and Robert, forget it. His wife's got nothing to fear from me. I think he's some kind of a nut."

Brenda hung up. What a busybody Teeny was. She turned off the light. The phone rang again, insistently, for a long time. She pulled up the covers and went to sleep, smiling. He might be a nut, but it sure built up the female ego to be wanted.

Robert called the next morning.

"I couldn't find you. Where is that damned studio? I think I hit one of your stone gateposts. I think it made a dent in my car."

"Do you plan to sue?"

"I think I can find you now. Can I come over this afternoon? I have some clam juice for you."

"I'll be out."

"This evening?"

"I'll be out."

"Some other time, then?"

He sounded kind of pathetic. What gave? Trouble at home? Lonely?

"Maybe sometime."

The next afternoon, he appeared. He was wearing another funny hat, a peaked Sherlock Holmes contraption. He was bearing a large jar of clam juice.

"May I have my coffee now?"

"I was just going out."

"Where's the kitchen and my coffee?"

She was glad Mother and Dad were out for the afternoon. Mother wasn't keen on those odd men Brenda met at Teeny's.

She led Robert into the kitchen. As he drank, he talked–a lot. It seemed he had an unusual number of cousins, aunts and uncles. They seemed to be of great interest to him. He went into their lifestyles, histories, all of them Social Register types from Boston. While he talked, his eyes sought the wall, tables, and his cup.

Suddenly he stopped with the aunts.

"I'm infatuated with you. I can't look at you without trembling. It makes me nervous. I want to kiss you."

What was this? His wife not putting out?

"Ridiculous," she said. "You don't even know me."

"When I saw you sitting in the corner, something hit me. Nothing like this has ever happened to me. I've only been in love once, and that's with my wife."

"You're probably just in a mid-life crisis and think it might be fun to have a little on the side."

He looked shocked. "Mercy! I'd never do that. I'm not a philanderer. I don't want anything from you, just to see you once in a while. I feel you're lonely. Maybe I could help."

"I've got to go, Robert."

At the door, he kissed her brow; tender, comforting. She felt a burn of tears. Why couldn't she find someone like Robert, a gentle man?

"Goodbye, Robert," she said.

It wasn't goodbye. There were many phone calls and deliveries of clam juice. She began calling him Clammy. This offended his dignity, which was its purpose. She enjoyed taking him down because he really was a snob. He liked to brag about his thrift shop clothes, as if wearing them was a badge of distinction. 'See how humble I am in spite of my princely antecedents.' He looked new acquaintances up in the Social Register to see if they were in.

"Did you look me up?"

"Yes."

"So, I passed muster?"

"You would in any event."

When his wife was visiting her mother, he would come in the evening. They'd sit in the parlor, hold hands and listen to Sibelius recordings. On leaving, he'd bestow a chaste kiss on her brow. He said he loved her and couldn't help himself. Sometimes Brenda felt she was acting out a Victorian romance. She saw no harm in it as long as no one got hurt. It was comforting to have a man care if she lived or died.

This went on for several months. Then one night as the music played, Robert said, "I told my wife there was someone–"

"What did you say?"

"I had to."

Brenda had never met his wife and had always pushed the thought of her away. Suddenly she loomed up large and accusing.

She jumped up. "Damn it, Robert, you must be crazy!"

"I didn't tell her who it was." He got up and turned off the music. "I can't go on like this. I'll get a divorce."

"And put me in the middle of a scandal!"

How Margot and the girls would love that!

"Brenda darling, please—"

She pushed him away and started for the door. He caught her. The kiss felt good. Too good. Victorian romance? Hell! This kiss rang a bell, which gave a tingling aftermath.

She gave a thrust and a shout.

"I'm not a home wrecker! Get out of my house and don't come back!"

Robert fled and she went up to her top porch and gazed at the cold stars. Damn him and his tenderness. She realized she'd begun to care and she was hurting. Add this up to another zilch. But let's be sensible. Did she really care? It was just that she was lonely. This Robert with his foolish hats and snobbery would have worn thin. Why had the right one, someone like Dad, never come along? Now he never would.

Teeny was on the phone the next day.

"I heard about you and Robert."

"What about us?"

"Trish told me Robert confessed he'd been seeing you. I think it's awful. You turn down the men I find for you and go after the husband of one of my best friends."

"I didn't go after him."

"What do you call it then?"

Brenda banged up the phone.

This caused quite a rift. Mother was pleased. She didn't care for Teeny. (A tinge of jealousy?) "These queer men Teeny introduce you to are a waste of your valuable time."

Brenda was beginning to wonder how valuable her time really was. Mother didn't approve of what she called Teeny's "coarseness." "The way she sits with her legs apart. You can see way up." "Probably just cooling off her crotch?" Brenda suggested. "Brenda! You see, her coarseness is influencing you!" Mother took off to play Chopin.

# CHAPTER 15

▼

# PAPA PEPTO

This rift with Teeny didn't last either.

She called one day, full of enthusiasm, to say that on one of Winston's last failed jobs as a taxi driver, he'd met this really neat Frenchman called Pepto Levine.

"He sounds like some sort of a Jewish stomach soother. What do I want with him?"

"He's right up your alley," Teeny enthused. "Plays the guitar, sings, has been in show business and writes TV scripts. He's looking for a collaborator to write with. Maybe he can unstick your writing. I'll give a party."

Brenda'd been missing Teeny's parties. At least it might be good for a laugh.

The usual contingent of secretaries were there and foreign car buyers on the prowl. Brenda found a quiet corner to watch the happy hunting when Pepto Levine appeared.

He came in with a flourish, lugging a battered looking guitar case, stamping snow off his boots and announcing himself loudly.

"Here's Pepto Levine and his singing guitar, folks. I would have been here sooner, but my Hungarian Cadillac broke down and I had to hoof it up the hill."

He rushed to Teeny, put her in a deep back bend and kissed her lustily. Everyone applauded.

Pepto had luxuriant black hair, olive skin and was dressed in a navy sports jacket with a red scarf knotted at the white open-necked shirt. He was gorgeous and young. Very young.

"That's my date? How old is he? About eighteen?" Brenda asked.

"Oh, around twentyish. What difference? I've got to get my paella on the table. Go introduce yourself."

No way was she about to have a date with 'Twentyish,' or less, when she was creeping up on thirtyish. Why, he was almost young enough to be her son. No way was he going to unstick her writing or do anything else for her.

Teeny must have pointed her out because in no time, Pepto homed in beside her on the sofa.

"May I?"

"May you what?"

"You're supposed to be my date, n'est pas?"

"That's what Teeny said. But where's your kiddy car?"

Did he get the drift? Probably not.

He laughed, showing lovely white teeth. She noticed his brown eyes had gold flecks in them.

"I understand you write," he said.

"I like to think so."

"I guess Teeny told you I do radio and TV scripts."

As he went on about himself, Brenda decided that Pepto was a lot of bluster and push. She also noted his funny accent. Kind of Brooklynese with a French tinge. He kept throwing in "n'est pas". Another Schrull? Lord! He claimed to have graduated from a University Something-Or-Other in Canada.

He paused about himself to say he understood she'd been published and what was she writing now?

"Nothing."

"Pourquoi pas? Why not?"

"Because most of what I've written is reposing in a bureau drawer."

"That's bad. We must do something about that."

"We?"

"Sure, why not, pourquoi pas?"

Those soft brown eyes of Pepto had long lashes. She could imagine his melting women down with those eyes.

He said, "I've got some time right now. I'd like to see your stuff, maybe make some suggestions."

Brenda took a long, thoughtful drink of Scotch. She felt she was about to get into something she might regret. On the other hand, what good was the bureau drawer doing anything?

"Would you be interested in letting me read it?" he said.

She shrugged. "Maybe sometime."

"No time like now. What have you got in the bureau drawer?"

She told him about the short story, 'Loss of Love.'

"Great title. Tell me more."

The drink was warming, as was Pepto's enthusiasm. She told him more.

"Very commercial," he assured her, nodding his head wisely. "But I think it should be longer. Maybe there's a novel in it. I have a feeling great things are in store for you with this work."

Brenda noticed he sometimes forgot to be so French and became more Brooklyn. Did he really know anything about writing? Wasn't this Schrull again with his literary pretensions?

But Pepto's enthusiasm was hard to resist. She gave him her phone number.

People were pairing off early. This didn't suit Teeny. She liked her parties to keep roaring. Pairing off could come later.

She barged up to Pepto. "Hey, this party's dying. How about a song?"

He jumped up. "Anything to oblige the beautiful ladies, n'est pas?"

He uncased his ancient guitar, tuned up and announced, "Pepto and his singing guitar will now render an original."

He launched into a loud strumming. Flashy but not much technique.

'I hope he writes better than he plays the guitar,' Brenda thought.

Wild and passionate were Pepto's original songs. Did gypsy blood course under those handsome, swarthy looks? French, Spanish and sometimes a kind of guttural warbling issued. But it had pizzazz and grabbed Brenda off the sofa to stamp her Flamenco heels around the floor. Everyone yelled and clapped "olé."

When she collapsed on the sofa, Pepto rushed up and kissed her hands.

"Magnificent! What a dancer! What a team! Don't we make a great team?"

Everyone agreed they made a great team. Teeny embraced her and bragged about her Flamenco teacher. Brenda looked at her watch and was amazed. Where had the time gone? It was past one.

She drove home flushed and exhilarated. Life wasn't so bad. Even if nothing came of Pepto's brilliant schemes for their writing career. It had been a fun evening. And soon it would be spring.

When Brenda brought Pepto to Upsan Downs, Mother and Dad looked him over with a critical eye. What new oddity had she brought home this time? But Pepto soon won them over with his infectious smile and his enthusiasm. He entertained them one evening with his original songs and told of his promising writing career in radio and TV.

"I understand you would like to collaborate with my daughter on her novel," Dad said.

"I would like to, sir. It seems a shame she's not doing more with it. Her talent needs to be known."

"That's what I keep telling her," Mother said.

"I see no reason why you shouldn't give it a try," Dad said. "If that's what Brenda wants."

Conferring with Brenda later, they remarked on his youth.

"Are you sure he's had much experience?" Dad said.

"Teeny swears by him," Brenda said. "She's read some of his scripts."

"That Teeny," Mother sniffed. "I wouldn't put much stock in what she says. Still, if it gets you writing again."

Pepto came often to work on the novel. Mother began to feed him dinner. He pepped her up and made her laugh. He called her "The Chief." He had no money. He was Martin Schrull all over but with a difference. Pepto was no conniver. He was just himself. Honest and not too bright.

Brenda soon found he was no writer. She suspected he got his ideas from watching late night adult films. From 'Loss of Love,' he wanted to change the title to 'Lustful Love.' He said what it needed was more commercialism, more sex. Under his supervision, it grew novel length and steadily worse, larded with pages of steamy sex over which Dad would have blown his top. But why show it to dad? It would probably never get anyplace, anyhow.

And Brenda was having fun. They wrangled over every sentence. She picked on his lousy spelling. They laughed a lot and Dad, upstairs hearing this, was glad Brenda was getting out of her doldrums. Of course, the boy was very attractive. But Brenda was old enough to handle him.

Was she?

He called her Princess and insisted she call him Papa Pepto. Was this an attempt to establish a more equal footing between them age-wise?

She enjoyed teasing him about a young blonde she called Goldilocks. It seemed the girl wanted to marry Pepto and had a rich father who would supply them with a house.

"You better grab her," Brenda said. "That's an offer you shouldn't refuse."

"She kinda bores me," Pepto said. "But then, anyone would after you."

"Gee, thanks."

'My God,' Brenda thought. 'I'm beginning to sound like a teenager.'

After their evening wrangles, Pepto liked to entertain her with his passionate songs while gazing soulfully through the long lashes. Occasionally she felt a disturbing shortness of breath, probably indigestion. When this happened, she'd stop him.

"Pepto, you played a sour note."

"Did I, Princess? Papa Pepto wouldn't want anything sour to come between us, now would he?" He flashed the beautiful teeth and added meaningfully, "Or anything else."

She felt that annoying shortness of breath.

"Don't play it again, Sam," she said.

"You're mean to me, Princess," he muttered, packing up the creaky guitar.

Pepto took up a lot of Brenda's time. She decided she needed to see more of other people. She talked Mother into letting her give a party, to which she invited Jordan Kirsh and some of his friends, as well as Teeny and her crowd, and of course, Pepto. People might as well learn of the 'great collaboration.'

In the beginning, the party went well. Jordan and his friends seemed to mingle happily with the Teeny and Winston contingent over cocktails and buffet supper, and Pepto, told to behave, stayed discretely in the background. But after dinner, the rug was rolled up in the living room and Brenda's recordings of Latin music were turned on.

At the sensuous strains of a tango, Pepto, full of red wine, leaped to his feet, clasped Brenda and put her through some passionate inter-twining leg work, ending in a back bend and a kiss.

Brenda emerged dizzily to applause from Teeny's bunch but raised eyebrows from Jordan and his group. A glance at Jordan revealed to Brenda his perplexed look. Shortly after, he excused himself, saying he had to be in New York early the next day.

As he kissed her goodnight he remarked, "Who's your new young friend?" With emphasis on "young."

"He's a writer. We've been collaborating on a novel."

"Oh."

That "oh" said a lot. Jordan's disapproval really hit home. Baby wasn't living up to the Madonna ideal.

The staid group soon left and the party turned into a usual Teeny-Winston blast. Brenda was glad when they all left.

In the library, she lit into Pepto.

"You idiot!"

"What did I do now, Princess?"

"Why did you have to dance with me like that?"

"Like what? We were great. I loved dancing with you." He paused. "Besides, it's time people knew about us."

"What do you mean 'us'?"

"We're an item, aren't we?"

"Are you kidding? We're collaborating on the book. Period."

He looked sulky. "I don't know why you're making such a big deal out of it."

"It's no big deal," she retorted. "And, even if it was what you suggest, do you think people on the Main Line would accept us as a couple? You're crazy."

"What do you care what people think?"

"I do care." (God, wouldn't Margot and the girls like to kick this one around?) "The subject is closed. It's time you went home."

"You treat me like a child."

"You are a child."

Brenda didn't sleep well that night. Damn him and his kiss! Soon the book would be finished and that was just as well.

When the final chapters were submitted to Teeny, she pronounced them neat. "I think you've got a good chance with it," she said. "The sex is well written. It sounds authentic."

Her approving eye surveyed Brenda who seemed to be looking happier these days. Maybe Pepto had made the break through.

Brenda reddened. "Pepto's been handling the sex. I think he's been watching porno flicks."

Pepto grinned. "She's mean to me, Teeny. But I kinda like it."

"Masochist," Brenda said.

"Whatever that means."

"Now," Pepto declared. "What we need is a New York agent." He looked at Teeny hopefully. "A big city agent."

"Don't we all. Didn't you know agents are harder to come by than publishers?"

"Ah, but you're the miracle lady, n'est pas? Surely you know of someone."

Pepto went into his melt down with the eyelashes. Teeny was not immune.

"Maybe Yorky Bloame would give it a read," she said. "I'll give her a buzz."

It seemed Teeny had met Yorky Bloame at a conference of Publishers and Literary Agents of the Northern Hemisphere in New York. For a fee, Ms. Bloame would read unknown manuscripts.

Teeny gave her a buzz and Brenda, armed with pages of 'Lustful Love' and words of advice and heated encouragement from Pepto (who wanted to go but was discouraged by Brenda), she took off for the big city.

Yorky Bloame lived in a walk up in a decrepit building in Greenwich Village. Her small, book-cluttered apartment looked as though a good vacuuming wouldn't hurt. Yorky herself looked a bit dusty. A large woman, cased in voluminous black, she wore a turban, beads and hoop earrings. She smoked a lot and served herbal tea and cordiality. She boasted of clients in Science Fiction and the 'Kiss and Tell' fields. She thought the title 'Lustful Love' was very commercial and would read the pages immediately for a hundred dollars paid in advance.

Brenda gave her a check and left with the feeling this would never come to anything.

She was surprised when Yorky phoned to say she liked the pages of 'Lustful' and would Brenda come over Monday for a luncheon book auction. Teeny'd been to one of these and explained that books were often sold this way. The author read from his work. If a publisher liked it, he made a bid.

Pepto was ecstatic. "You see! I knew we'd get our break! When do we go?"

Brenda talked him out of it. With his big mouth, they'd be sure to blow it.

On Monday, escorted by Ms. Bloame to a restaurant on lower Fifth Avenue, Brenda found herself seated amid agents, authors and publishers. The publishers, seated together, all seemed to know each other well, drank martinis and looked very young. She noted one in particular, a handsome hunk in a Dutch boy hair-do and smartly turned out by his Italian tailor, looked younger than Pepto. 'Fresh out of Harvard or Yale,' she thought. Keen-eyed and sharp as a tack. What would the likes of him want with the concoction she and Pepto had spewed out?

She wished she hadn't come.

Avoiding her enemy 'the Mart,' she nibbled on melba toast and tried to find something to say to her neighbor, a girl who wrote children's books, like: "How long have you been writing?" She felt like saying, "And when did you graduate from high school?"

Suddenly she felt like getting sick, throwing a fit, anything to get out of here.

Too late.

Here was 'keen-eyed, sharp as a tack' calling her name.

"Ms. Marr, would you like to be the first to read."

He smiled in a kind of knowing way, it seemed to her. Probably so devilish clever, he could see right into the workings of her panicked brain. He'd probably figured her for some kind of middle-aged nanny goat with acid indigestion who didn't know her ass from the bottom of a Maalox glass, and had decided to get her over with first.

Fear triggered a surge of adrenalin and got her to her feet. She fumbled with the manuscript, almost dropped it, cleared her throat and took the plunge.

Drawing on her long ago experience as an actress she gave, squeezing every bit of drama and pathos out of the pages of 'Lustful Love.' But what was she squeezing? Drivel. As she read, shame, like an insidious burning, crept over her. Had she really written this tripe? Why hadn't she realized how terrible it was? Blinded by Pepto's enthusiasm, she'd blundered into this spot, presented herself as the author of these scribblings of unspeakable banality and bad taste. Thinking of what Dad would have thought of all this, she felt blood surge to her face.

Somehow she got through it and sat down.

There was a silence. The publishers conferred. In a quick glance, she thought she caught some raised eyebrows and faint smiles. Then little 'ole sharp as a tack cleared his throat and in a crisp tone, as much to say, "How dare you waste our time with such drivel," announced:

"Thank you very much, Ms. Marr, but I'm afraid this is not for us. My colleagues agree and wish you luck in placing it elsewhere."

Humiliated to the bone, she scooped up manuscript, pocket book and fled. The hell with steely-eyed word merchants! Thank God she didn't have to depend on them for a living. Sure the thing was tripe, but did he have to make her feel like two cents?

Ms. Bloame caught up with her on the sidewalk, hoop earrings tossing dramatically.

"I think it went pretty well. You didn't wait to hear other opinions."

"Were there more?"

"There are usually discussions. It just didn't happen to be for them. Of course with the war on, they're looking for something more timely. However, we'll try someplace else."

Brenda turned on her. After all, it was Bloame's fault for subjecting her to this fiasco.

"Let's not kid ourselves," she said. "The thing stinks. It doesn't have a prayer."

Ms. Bloame smiled. "Oh, I don't know. I've gotten worse things published."

"That's your problem," Brenda snapped.

"How about let's give it another try."

"No thanks."

"If you change your mind, you know where I am," she said cheerfully.

"I won't."

Brenda raced up Fifth Avenue and over to Penn Station. She could hardly wait to get out of this city that never brought her anything but trouble. And it was going to be tough to bring this news home.

Fortunately Mother and Dad were out, but Pepto was waiting in the hall in tennis togs, his face flushed with excitement and anticipation.

"Well, how'd it go?"

"Get me a drink," she said. "And you'd better get one for yourself."

In the library, she broke the news. He refused to accept it. What did she mean they didn't like it? What was wrong with it? Maybe she'd presented it wrong.

She took a gulp of scotch.

"Let's face it Pepto, it's lousy."

"What do you mean? You never said that."

"I was wrong not to tell you. I knew it was no good. But we were having so much fun."

"That's all you were doing, having fun? Amusing yourself?"

The brown eyes were reproachful. He was crushed.

She looked away. "I guess that's it—"

"But aren't we going to work on the book anymore?"

"What for?"

"Maybe if we make it dirtier," he said hopefully. "We could make it dirtier."

"I won't write that crap, Pepto. You go ahead if you want. Maybe you can do something with it."

"What could I ever do with it?" He shook his head. "Does this mean our collaboration is over, you don't want to see me anymore?"

"Sure, come up for dinner. Mother likes to feed you and—"

It was then Pepto threw himself on his knees in front of her.

"Don't you see? None of this matters as long as we're together. Don't you see I love you? I love you, Brenda."

Brenda looked into the limpid eyes with the long lashes, the open face, so young, so beautiful.

"Don't be ridiculous, Pepto. Get up."

He got up and pulled her up.

How long had she wanted to kiss that lovely mouth, feel that lithe body pressed to hers? The kiss seemed to last forever.

The reaction came on schedule.

She gave him a push.

"Stop it, Pepto!"

He was laughing.

"Why? You like it, don't you?"

"No."

"Care for another?"

He tried for another and missed her mouth.

"Damn it, Brenda, you tease me, drive me crazy! I want you–"

"What do you want me for?"

"I want to marry you."

Oh boy! Wouldn't Aunt Margot, Uncle Jake and the girls have a ball over that one!

"Marry me! My God!" Brenda snapped. "You must be nuts! Pick on some one your own size (age)! Pick on Goldy!"

"All right! I will!"

She started away. He slumped down on the sofa.

"You don't want me," he mumbled. "She does."

"Great! So get the hell out! Go to her! Good riddance!"

When she turned back, he looked up miserably. She knew she didn't want him. But she didn't want the teenager to have him.

'Come on, Princess,' she thought, 'grow up. You've had your fun. Maverick or not, you've lived long enough to be wiser than this.'

She saw he was crying.

"Pepto, you're wetting yourself."

"What?"

She sat next to him and he put his head on her shoulder.

She said softly. "Don't be sad, dear. You and I could never make it together. You need someone younger and more foolish than I."

'If the latter is possible,' she thought.

When he left, she went to her room and wept. She'd cared for Pepto. Oh, yes.

Bye, bye, Pepto.

Main Liners, even maverick ones, weren't supposed to fall in love with their almost young enough to be sons. It wasn't done.

There was no future in it.

# CHAPTER 16

▼

# YOU CAN'T GO BACK TO MARTIN SCHRULL

"Just put it down to experience," Dad said over breakfast as they discussed the fizzle of the novel and the fadeout of Pepto.

"He was an attractive boy," Mother said. "But I was right about him. I doubt if he'd ever make a success. He doesn't have the background."

"He had dirty fingernails," Jancy commented as she passed the scrambled eggs. "I don't think he took a bath that often."

Jancy didn't care much for Pepto. He'd tracked dirt on her kitchen floor a couple of times and he didn't slip her a tip once in a while as Martin Schrull had.

"Jason, I know you never cared much for Martin," Mother said. "But he did have beautiful manners and was always immaculate. Speaking of success, the last time I heard from him, it seems he's made it big. He's now head of a Fine Foods firm in New York City. Why don't you look him up sometime when you're over for your class, Brenda?"

"I think that would be a mistake," Dad said.

Brenda was at loose ends. She missed Pepto. Ted, in Washington, only came home occasionally. They stayed glued to the radio and the dreadful war news: Pearl Harbor; an American carrier sunk in the Pacific; the bombings in Britain. Except for blackouts, life at Upsan Downs went on its placid way amid green trees and lawns. How small its concerns compared to all that was going on elsewhere.

Their only happening was that Aya's parrot, Coco, was no longer with them.

He had succumbed to a heart attack while achieving a life long ambition. He caught up with Mother and bit her after chasing her down the hall. He died happily, laughing manically and yelling, "Go to Hell!" which no doubt is where he was heading. Brenda and Aya, in tears, buried him in the garden.

Dad bought Aya another parrot so she wouldn't grieve. Ted named him OcOc (Coco spelled backwards). OcOc didn't bite anyone, but he didn't talk much either. Ted finally succeeded in teaching him "go to Hell," which he yelled fitfully out the third story window. This was a comfort and consolation to Aya for her loss of Coco. Ted also, without success, tried to teach OcOc the words "screw you."

"I don't see why it would be a mistake," Mother said. "Martin might be a good contact for Brenda, now that he's a success."

"Contact for what?" Brenda asked.

"Oh, I don't know. He was always very fond of you. He might be able to help with the novel or something."

"Fat chance."

"I'm going to the greenhouse."

Brenda got to thinking, why didn't she look up Martin. It might help to get Pepto out of her system. Her self-image was at low ebb. A chronic virginity was finally getting to her, which no amount of passionate Flamenco dancing could ease. She remembered how Martin made her feel. Definite chemistry. Maybe her old love would be the one to awaken her. Of course he was married, but as Betsy used to say, "What else was new?"

She was also curious. What would he be like now? In any event, she might get a free lunch out of it.

On her next excursion to New York, she found him in the phone book: "M. Martin Schrull, Fine Foods Unlimited." Unlimited food, that figured. Martin had always liked to eat when he got the chance.

She called, gave her name and was put through at once.

"Well kiddy," Martin said. "What a surprise after all these years! How's Mother?"

She said Mother was fine and sent her best and that she, herself, was in town for a couple of hours.

"How about lunch?" he asked.

"Fine."

He hesitated a split second and then said, "I'm awfully busy, but I suppose I can shift things around."

The hesitation and that "awfully busy" should have told Brenda something. It didn't. She was gung-ho for that lunch with ole' Martin.

She met him at a place called The Peek Hole Club in the East Fifties. He wore a hat and a handsome camel-haired coat and saluted her cheek with a kiss. The young and pretty hat check girl was gotten up like a pussycat. She gave Martin a warm smile and took his hat, which revealed that Martin was completely bald.

The place was crowded with prosperous-looking men in business suits, probably searching out a bit of diversion with their three Martini lunches. The diversion was well provided by the pussy-type waitresses who scurried about waving their tails and displaying expanses of thigh to their armpits. The kittens wore mittens and boots. They all seemed to know Martin and gave him a twinkle and a nod. They were very young. They looked about fifteen.

The head pussy, a real show stopper whose front seemed about to escape its moorings, smiled at him brightly.

"I've got your usual table, Mr. Schrull."

As she led them to a secluded nook, Brenda wondered if other female lunch companions of Martin had preceded her to this cozy spot.

The hostess bent to offer Martin the lunch menu and Brenda saw his appreciative scrutiny of her upper exposure. This place was really better than a topless. Here, there was an element of chance. Would that front pop out or wouldn't it?

Seated beside Martin on plushy velvet, Brenda saw the years had not been kind to him. However, he was a good ad for Fine Foods Unlimited. He had got fat and, except for the grayish fringe around his ears, he was hairless. His always-short neck now seemed swallowed by his collar. But he still had the charm, she saw, as he raised her hand to his lips.

"Wonderful to see you, kiddy. You look the same."

She noted that he still had the funny accent.

He said, "I see you still wear that severe Madonna hair style."

She thought his glance was somewhat critical. He used to love her hairstyle.

"Why don't you fluff it up more?" he said.

"I don't think I'd like that."

Another good-looking, very young pussy stopped by to take their drink order. She hovered close to Martin's shoulder. Brenda noted her hair was fluffed to a monumental blonde bubble, which rather over-powered her small, pretty face.

"Bonjour Lisette," Martin said.

They had a little French exchange. Brenda noted that Lisette flicked an imaginary something off Martin's left shoulder in a possessive way, which got her thinking maybe Martin had a little something going here that didn't involve food and drink.

"Martini?" Martin asked.

Brenda hadn't had one in years and knew it was a mistake, but she nodded. Martinis were in? So, she could swing as well as the next one.

"Two Martinis," he said.

Lisette's china-blue eyes skimming Brenda suggested she found no competition here with that flat hairdo. Who was Brenda, anyhow? Probably some dull out-of-the-sticks cousin of his wife he'd been told to feed.

To Lisette's departing shapeliness, Brenda remarked, "She's pretty, that Lisette. And seems fond of you."

He looked pleased. "She's a little doll, isn't she?"

"Aren't you a bit old to be playing with dolls?" It just slipped out.

His smile was strained.

"Still a quick wit I see, Brenda."

Brenda wondered if his wife knew of his cavortings at the Peek Hole. Probably not.

"You seem well-known here," she said.

"Yes. I have a small interest in the place. It's a good tax shelter."

'I'll bet,' she thought.

Cocktails were delivered. He lit Brenda's cigarette and she wondered what she was doing here next to this fat stranger. But after a couple of warming sips, she began to relax. Martin's friendly smile helped.

"I'm glad Mother is all right. A lovely lady. I've sometimes thought I'd like to see her again."

"She'd like that."

"And your Father?"

"Having trouble with his eyes. He works too hard."

"A wonderful man."

Conversation lapsed. Brenda sipped. "I understand you're married?"

"Yes, have been for a number of years." He gave a small smile. "Do you mind if I brag a little?"

She said she didn't mind.

He said that he was head of his own company and had a lovely daughter and a wonderful wife.

He looked at her as if to say, 'What have you got to show for the years?'

"My wife is a fine woman and has made me a lovely home." He added, "She gives a lot of her time to church work." He mentioned the name of a fashionable East Side Episcopal church in Manhattan.

Brenda thought, 'Maybe his wife does know about his cavortings and that's why she's so busy with the religious works.'

"My wife's from the Hamptons, you know. We have a nice home there, right on the water. We keep our yacht there."

While he went on about his magnificent life, the yacht club, the horses, the daughter in fashionable schools, Brenda found herself wondering how many lies and intrigues Martin had to engage in to accumulate this wealth and prominence? And was this big brag a pay back for that turndown she had given him so long ago? An eye for an eye and "a toot for a toot?" She thought it was. But let her not lose her cool.

"I'm glad you've done so well, Martin," she said.

"And you?" he asked. "How have you done?"

She said she'd been very busy recently writing a novel, sort of a fun thing about her experiences in show business.

She smiled. "Also, I suppose I've dabbled in a few romances. Nothing really serious."

He regarded her. "Of course you would have men in love with you, beautiful as you are."

She then said she'd been rather successful teaching and performing Flamenco dancing.

He seemed surprised. "Flamenco? Why that?"

"I love it. It's exciting."

He shook his head. "Dear Brenda, still seeking the off-beat, the theatrical. You don't need that. You were born to the best."

He went on to say he'd spent a lot of time in Spain and it might interest her to know the high-class Spaniards looked on Flamenco as a dance of the lower classes.

"They must be stuffy. It's a wonderful dance form."

Conversation flagged. They drained their Martinis. He ordered more, which Miss Gorgeous filled quickly.

"This terrible war," Brenda said. "Ted was aching to go, but his near-sightedness prevented."

"A fine man, your brother. Of course I'm over age for joining up, but my business has been helpful in supply foods for our boys overseas."

Brenda couldn't resist saying, "I suppose you're an American citizen now?"

He looked annoyed, then said stiffly, "Indeed yes, for sometime. A friend, highly placed in government, was able to take care of that for me."

Brenda wondered who that highly placed friend might be. Yes, Martin had come a long way since his starving playwright days.

Silence again. Things seemed to have reached an impasse. But then the second Martini began to work its mellowing magic on Martin.

His wide and sentimental gaze encompassed Brenda.

"Brenda, Brenda how I loved you."

She didn't much like that "loved."

"Beautiful Main Line Madonna, how lovely you were."

She really hated that "were."

"And still are," he added.

This was better. She drank.

He said, "I've thought of you often through the years."

That was better. How sweet the invasion of the second Martini.

Then she felt the pressure of his knee against hers and strangely, felt a sudden surge of warmth. God! Could this unattractive-looking man still make her feel something?

"Oh kiddy, kiddy, why have you wasted yourself?"

"What do you mean?"

"On these men who I'm sure weren't up to you, and that show business and Flamenco dancing. When I think of your beautiful poetry, your great potential. You were so talented and creative. You could have made it big. You should have fulfilled yourself and would have if–" he stopped.

Did he mean if she'd married him?

He sighed deeply.

"Ah well, water under the bridge."

Damn him. He was making her feel rotten now, as was the sight of gorgeous Lisette hovering over his shoulder with the lunch menu and getting to flick another imaginary something off his shoulder.

He said, "Ah yes, Lisette. We will order now."

Martin still knew how to order up a meal with flair. Brenda had often thought he might have been a Maitre'D at some point in his career. Her appetite seemed to have fled. When she asked for a diet special, she thought Martin's smile slightly disapproving. With this menu the size of a table top, which offered delicacies that would delight the heart of an Arab potentate, what does the lovely Main Line Madonna choose but cottage cheese and a hard boiled egg.

He said, "Ah, watching your waist line I see, Brenda. Well, that's smart."

He wasn't that smart. After hungrily eyeing the menu, Martin ordered a dozen oysters on the half shell.

'For virility purposes, no doubt,' thought Brenda.

"Then the quiche," said Martin.

'There goes another two pounds on you,' thought Brenda.

"My usual filet, very rare of course."

'Enough protein in you to make a lion roar,' observed Brenda.

"And the Caesar's salad with some extra dressing."

'So you can take a bath in it,' thought Brenda.

Miss Puss lovingly chronicled Martin's words, as though her boots and mittens depended on it. Brenda took these moments to study Lisette. Young as she was, Brenda noted a certain wary look about mouth and eyes, which might harden into habitual set as time carried her into future encounters with future Martins.

"And, oh, my usual wine, Lisette," said Martin.

"I'm already chilling your wine," she responded.

'And heating his blood at the same time,' thought Brenda as she watched him surrender the menu to her and touch her fingers in a light caress. Yes, unmistakably an item.

When the food came, Martin pounced on it passionately as though each mouthful were to be his last. Perhaps this was to reassure his innards they would not have to go hungry again. As Brenda nibbled her melba toast, she pondered that when one has once gone hungry, perhaps eating might become a focal point in later life.

Sated to the brim at last, Martin excused himself, off to the relief station, no doubt. And Brenda, bemused by Martinis and cottage cheese, watched the little cats hustling their boots off to please the male majority. She pondered the fate of these Peek Hole dolls. Unless lucky enough to snag a rich one, they would probably end up scraping the bottom of the barrel.

Martin woke her from her reverie.

"Sorry kiddy, must run. Important engagement."

"I have to catch the Metroliner."

"I'll drop you at the station."

Martin signed his credit card with, no doubt, a goodly tip for the stimulator of his heart and other portions of his anatomy.

"Isn't she a honey?" he said as they made their exit.

"Yes, but has she got a driver's license yet?"

He didn't smile.

However, as they sauntered in search of a cab, she felt she was glad she'd seen him. After all, they were old friends who had once loved.

Then, as they passed the St. Regis, she noticed a group of well-dressed women, all minked up, full of lunch and flushed with wine and gossip were descending the stairs.

Martin saw them too.

"My God!" he muttered, grabbed Brenda's arm, pulled her across the street, narrowly dodging a speeding car.

"Hey! What's the idea, Martin?"

He looked all shook up.

"Those women, they're friends of my wife and I. They belong to our club."

She gazed at him, wide-eyed. "So what?"

"You know how people are. See me with an attractive woman. My wife's very jealous."

"Well you didn't have to break my arm." She pulled it away. "Can't you be seen walking with an old friend? You should have introduced me to them."

"People gossip."

"Oh, for God's sake."

He hailed a cab. It drew up and he helped her in, got in and told the driver, "Penn Station."

Silence as the cab sped away.

"Brenda, I'm sorry," he said. "I should have introduced you, but my wife–"

She was thinking, 'You can't go back. Particularly when there's nothing to go back to.'

He said softly, "Oh Brenda, please forgive me."

She allowed him to take her hand. So what? She was curious as to his next move.

"Such a lovely hand."

He turned it over and kissed the palm. Once this had thrilled her. No more.

His long, sensitive fingers Mother so admired began to twine with hers. Once this had raised erotic goosebumps. No more.

He murmured, "It's really been wonderful to see you. When are you coming over again?"

She said she didn't know.

"Why not make it soon? We could go dancing like in the good old days. Make a night of it. You could stay over. I'll get accommodations at the St. Regis." He paused. "I feel we have some unfinished business to take care of, you and I."

What business? As if she didn't know.

She pictured it. The plush hotel room, the kissings by those soft girlish lips. Then the bed, Martin gently stripping her to the tuff and then, always a vain man, unveiling himself for her admiration. She pictured the expert tailoring falling away to reveal protruding paunch, witness to all those lovely meals as the Peek Hole. And then, the flab of arms and thighs, the hairy white chest. And how about the shorts? Flowered? No thanks. At least Curt had taught her that tailoring does not make the man of your dreams. And without love, what have you got?

He was staring at her.

"Why the Mona Lisa smile?"

"Oh, nothing."

His hand tightened on her thigh. "You could always get to me as no one else ever has. Please come over."

The wide apart, pleading eyes meant to melt any obstruction. She kept the Mona Lisa smile in place.

"Perhaps. But not the St. Regis, do you think? We might run into some of your wife's friends."

The charming smile stiffened. "Oh, can't you forget that?"

The cab drew up. As he helped her out, Brenda saw his eyes go to her legs, which he had always admired.

"You still have the beautiful legs," he said. "They're the last things to go."

"What does that mean?"

"You're no kid, you know."

She gave him a cool stare. "It may surprise you to know I can still turn a male head now and then."

"You're still a good looking woman. How old are you now, anyhow?"

She measured the words with care. "I don't think that's any of your business."

Couldn't the man do anything but smile? And, were those front teeth capped?

"Still spirited, kiddy," he said. "I'm glad. Never lose that. It will help you to survive."

"I'm surviving pretty well, thank you."

"Oh, indeed you are." He gave a fleeting kiss to her cheek. "Please give my love to Mother and do give me a call."

He kissed her hand and gave her a final once over.

"By the way, dear, this hair-do really doesn't do a thing for you. Too severe. As I said, why not fluff it up more?"

She snapped. "Why don't you fluff yours up more, or get a rug?"

She took off. She'd call him again in a pig's eye. And speaking of pigs, 'Oink, oink, Mortimer Schrullsky!'

But Martin wasn't quite through with Brenda. One day he phoned, to her surprise, all cordiality.

"Hello, kiddy! Why haven't you come over? I've been waiting for your call."

"I've been pretty busy."

"I hope you'll make it soon." Pause. "By the way, I have a favor to ask."

Surprise. 'What's he up to?' she thought. 'Watch it.'

However, she could show cordiality as well as the next one.

"Certainly Martin. What can I do for you?"

"My daughter will be coming to Bryn Mawr College. She will be bringing her horse."

'How chi-chi,' thought Brenda, 'if a bit ostentatious. Why not hire a local nag? Or wouldn't her pretty little Hampton ass fit the Main Line breed?'

He said, "I thought you might know of someone on the Main Line with a stable that could accommodate her."

'Who, the daughter or the horse?' Brenda thought nastily.

But let's show old Mortimer we harbor no ill for those cracks about the flat hair-do and the tolls of approaching age. Let's be generous. She said she did know a horsey gal who might answer the need.

"I'll ask around," she said.

"Good. I'll call back in a few days."

When he called, Brenda told him it was set. She'd found a berth for the horse. She gave a phone number for his daughter to call.

Then, in a final flourish of generosity, she said, "By the way, if I can be of help to your daughter, have her contact me."

His words came out crisp, clear and icy. "Oh, that won't be necessary."

He thanked her for the trouble and hung up.

She flushed with rage as she banged up the phone.

Why that son-of-a-bitch mongrel out of Lower Slabovia or wherever, that they took in their home and fed when he didn't have two cents! How dare he condescend to her? Was his fancy daughter with the horse too fine to rub shoulders with such as Brenda Marr?

Mother, in the next room, now claimed a hearing loss except when something grabbed her attention. Brenda's banging had.

"Who was on the phone, dear?" she called.

"Just some son-of-a-bitch we used to know."

"Don't swear, Brenda," Mother said automatically.

Sometime later, Brenda's anger faded and she considered it all objectively. Certainly Martin had wanted to give her the finger. But he'd also been scared shitless that Brenda might spill the beans and the daughter would find out that Daddy had been a penniless wanderer, who'd scrounged on others for his livelihood and made it by marrying a rich woman. And Martin's house of cards, yacht and mansion might come tumbling down.

'Okay, Martin. Understood. Bye-bye.'

# CHAPTER 17

## IMITATION OF LOVE

Brenda's meeting with Martin had not helped her self-esteem. His unflattering remarks about her looks dug deep and in the mirror she began casing her face for sags and wrinkles. She wasn't happy with what she saw, particularly when she ran into Betsy Fulsome one afternoon in New York.

Betsy had on a new mink and looked younger than ever. She looked fabulous.

She threw her arms around Brenda.

"Darling! I've been thinking about you. How are you anyhow?" She gave Brenda the once over. "You look–pretty good."

Brenda bristled. "Damn it, Betsy, I'm pushing thirty. What do you expect, gorgeous forever? And you must be at least thirty-five by now."

"Twenty-five, love. Not a day older."

"Another lift?"

"Why sure."

"Speaking of that, how's Sammy?"

"Who?"

"Sammy the lifter."

"Oh, him. Haven't seen him. But listen, I've got a real rich one now. Old but loaded. We've got a pad on Park. You'll have to come see it."

"Sure."

"Well, got to run." The critical look. "Darling, you must think about a lift. It'll do wonders for you."

They parted with hugs. And Brenda, noting Betsy's stretched smile, decided whatever wonders a lift would do, forget it. Betsy's smile looked as if it had gotten stuck and was glued on her teeth. Whatever love, if any ventured into Brenda's life, would have to take her as she was.

Still, talk about having low ebb.

One evening as she sat on the porch with Dad, she felt suddenly overwhelmed by a realization of life passing by and nothing accomplished.

"What am I going to do with myself, Dad? I'm a washout."

He smiled. "Far from it, Brenda. I think the time has come for you to develop your talent for writing."

"What talent?"

"Whatever happened to that novel you wrote about New York Café Society? I think it showed a lot of promise. Why not have a go at that?"

Having nothing better to do, Brenda searched through old manuscripts and discovered the original 'Imitation of Love' before it had been sexed-up by Pepto. She decided it wasn't all that bad and after some rewrites, Dad thought it clever and sent it to a New York publisher friend.

To Brenda's amazement, the novel was accepted. No doubt, having a father with some clout a plus. Also, the fact that the author was in her twenties might have been a selling factor.

A few reviews were forthcoming. "Strong, original novel," declared the Birmington Times. The New York Times came up with: "Skillful Portrait of Café Society."

Brenda was on cloud nine. Dad was happy and Mother conceded that maybe Brenda should be a writer after all. And things began to really look up when Jordan Kirsh suddenly appeared.

Jordan now had a plushy government job in Washington, as well as his flourishing law practice. He was making it big and Philadelphia hostesses reading of his prominence began inviting him to their dinner parties. Even if he was Jewish, he was certainly presentable. Charming and witty, he enlivened their parties.

The fact that Brenda was now a published author intrigued him and, thinking to give his interest a boost, Brenda dedicated 'Imitation' to him. This raised a few Main Line eyebrows. It even provoked an item in the morning news: "Brenda Marr dedicates tome to well known lawyer, Jordan Kirsh, who she says is just a friend."

This "just a friend" was true as ever. Jordan never ventured more than a chaste kiss on the cheek. This was fine with Brenda. If people wanted to think they were having an affair, that was their problem.

As always wishing to help a struggling artist, Jordan began taking her to parties where she would meet people who might further her writing career.

At one of these, he introduced her to Willi Schmidt, a literary agent.

Jordan prepared her for the meeting in advance.

"Willi read your book and likes it," he said.

In the crowded cocktail room, Jordan steered Brenda in Willi Schmidt's direction.

"Here is the extraordinary girl I told you about, Willi," he said.

Willi's eyes swept over Brenda. She was glad she'd worn her black figure-hugging cocktail dress.

Willi raised her hand to his lips. "She is extraordinary," he said.

Jordan smiled knowingly. "I'll leave you two alone. I know you have plenty to talk about."

And he was off, gathering speed and spreading charm as he circulated around the room.

Willi was tall, rather corpulent and in his forties. His eyes, magnified behind thick glasses, were intelligent and kindly. He was balding and a little fringe of soft brownish hair curled about his ears. His lips were rather thick and he had a gap between his front teeth. Not great to look at, but someone you could like at once, was Brenda's opinion.

And he seemed to like her right away. Apparently the sags and wrinkles were not too bad. At least they didn't seem to discourage him.

"You are even more beautiful than your picture on the dust jacket of 'Imitation of Love,'" he said.

She noticed his slight accent and a nervous giggle.

He went on. "No. That picture definitely doesn't do you justice."

'Maybe he needs new glasses,' she thought, 'but what an ego builder.' And she sure could use one at this point.

She smiled. "Jordan said you'd read the book. You must be one of the fifteen hundred that did."

"Your writing really impressed me. Very original."

"Thanks. I wish more people thought so."

"They will. It's a good start for a first novel. Most of the reviews were good. You are very gifted."

The intelligent eyes dwelled with softness on her face.

She thought, 'My God, he is coming on to me.' And had an instant of revulsion at the thought of kissing those heavy lips.

"What are you writing now?" he asked.

She had to admit she wasn't writing anything.

"That's not good. You must strike while the stove is hot."

She smiled. "You mean while the iron is hot."

He giggled. "Sometimes I get my English sayings confused."

He lit their cigarettes. His eyes could really caress. It was almost embarrassing.

"I have several authors whose books I've sold recently to Doubleday, Harpers and Little Brown," he said.

"I'm impressed."

He went on to say his authors were mostly people he had known in Europe, refugees, recently escaped from Hitler's Germany. They were Germans, Austrians, an Italian and a lovely girl from Belgium who was now living with an American family.

"I'd like to meet them," she said.

"You shall. Meanwhile, would you be interested in having me represent you? I'm sure we could make some sales."

"I would be interested. But I don't have any writing going at the moment."

"I'm surprised to hear that with your fertile imagination." He giggled. "Could it be you're a little lazy?"

"Could be."

"How did you write the last one?"

"I don't know. It sort of just came to me. I dreamed it up."

"Why not dream up another? Maybe you need an incentive."

"Like what?"

"A contract and an advance. All you need is a couple of chapters and a two page outline."

She did a double take. So this was how it was done.

"You mean you can sell a book on that, just like a piece of meat?"

"It's a product like any other. Naturally, it has to show promise and you must have a great agent. Have I convinced you I am that?"

His eyes were positively pleading. So, she'd made a dent in him without effort. It was a good feeling. He was nice, warm and a pushover. No one could have been more un-Curt-like. And he was offering her a passport into a new world, which she sorely needed. She didn't have to kiss those lips if she didn't want to. Him she could handle.

"You've convinced me," she said.

"It's a deal then?"

She raised her glass. "A deal."

"Could you let me see an outline by next week?"

"I'll try."

She went home and tried. An outline about what? She started thinking about the refugee, the lovely Belgium girl he'd spoken of, bereft, homeless, coming to live with an American family. The family could have a spoiled, bitchy daughter. Conflict. A man in love with the daughter, the refugee in love with the man, etc.

She slapped it out and sent it off.

Willi called back immediately. The outline was great. The idea of the refugee and family had a fresh timely feel. Now if she would just get her inventive mind to work on a couple of chapters, he'd see what he could come up with.

Inspired by his words, she tore into two chapters. And to her amazement, in a short time, Willi came up with a contract with a publisher and an advance on a novel to be called 'The Beautiful Refugee.'

What was so hard about getting a book published? You just had to know the right people.

Mother was delighted. Dad beamed.

"I always hoped we'd have an author in the family."

She went to New York every weekend and stayed with a friend of Willi's, Nora Dobson. This blonde, robust Britsher had just come from a harrowing time driving an ambulance in Belgium for the Red Cross.

Dad protested Brenda's going to New York so often. He also protested Willi's numerous phone calls. He had her on the phone by the hour and seemed to think he had to caress her every comma. Maybe his stable of authors needed his constant supervision, but Brenda found it annoying. Who the hell was writing the damn thing anyhow?

Dad said, "Look here, Brenda, aren't you getting in a bit deep with this new friend? Does he have to call you so often? And, this going to New York. I hope you're not getting into that heavy drinking again."

"Not a chance."

Each week, Willi picked her up at Penn Station and they'd taxi to a little restaurant in the Village called Club International. Here, Willi's stable hung out and drank on Friday evenings. Brenda allowed herself a couple of Scotch's while attempting to store up some material.

There was a lot of it. There was Helmut, white-haired, distinguished looking, who had made a harrowing escape from Austria. Madame Becker from Germany, whose husband had been shot by the Nazis. And there was Anna, the refugee from Belgium on whom Brenda was to base her story. Anna was tall and statuesque, an Ingrid Bergman type. Brenda suspected Willi was helping her out financially and thought Anna had her eye on him. But at this point, Willi only had eyes for Brenda.

All of them were writing furiously, with Willi getting them jobs so they could survive. They were devoted to him and looked Brenda over carefully. Did she belong among them? Finally they seemed to accept her.

She'd been seeing Willi several months when one night, after drinks with the gang, Willi said he'd take her to Nora's later but first had something in his apartment he wanted to show her.

Brenda was curious about that something and figured she could handle any move he made bed-wise.

He lived in a second floor walk up in the West Sixties. The apartment was small with only a bed sofa, table, two chairs and a curtained alcove, which sheltered a stove and a sink. Willi might be making money but certainly wasn't spending it on living quarters.

What he was spending it on was books. They littered everything. He apologized for the mess, poured a drink, pushed books off the sofa, sat her down and turned a light on a painting of a Madonna he'd bought years ago. He said he'd fallen in love with it and guessed he'd been searching for her in the flesh for years. Now he'd found her.

"I knew it the moment I saw you," he said. "Don't you think her resemblance to you is uncanny?"

She didn't think it was all that uncanny but, to please him, said she thought it was. Then he turned her hand over and kissed the palm. Where had she run into this before? Oh yes, the Maestro with the halo on top.

The way Willi did it gave her a slight quiver she had not felt since the days of Martin. Tender, loving, sensuous. His lips found her mouth.

Probably if she hadn't drunk so much, it wouldn't have happened. But here she was, still practically a virgin. She needed affection. She was starved for it. And, as a lover of Toulouse Lautrec once said, "Ugly or handsome, in the dark they are all the same."

Willi turned off the light.

He drew off her clothes gently. Then undressed and lay beside her. He was a wonderful caresser and she found herself responding. She thought she would never be in love with him. But he was so kind, sensitive and was helping her so much. She needed him. He was showing her a more mature kind of love, which had nothing to do with looks or charisma. She wanted to make him happy.

Their kisses became more impassioned and suddenly she felt wildly excited. Then he was on her, finding her.

At the moment of readiness, nothing.

He whispered frantically, "Hold me, darling!"

She held him. The little thing melted away. She tried to revive it, but poor Willi's manhood drooped.

Oh Lord, after all these years she was ready to give because she was sincerely fond of him. And what happened? His thing wouldn't work. Was she to blame? Then she thought maybe this was why he hadn't made a move. He was unsure of himself.

He kissed her eyes, her throat.

"I'm sorry, darling," he whispered. "I usually can. I guess I just got too excited. I love you so."

"It's all right."

"I wanted to make you happy."

"You will, sometime."

Damn sex, anyhow. Nothing but trouble.

She rose and groped her way to the bathroom and put on her clothes. It wasn't all right. She felt thwarted and miserable. Would she never find the right love?

When she came out, he had turned on the light and had on his shirt and trousers. He stood in the middle of the room with head bowed. He couldn't meet her eyes. She felt very sorry for him. Impotence, it seemed, was the ultimate humiliation a man could feel.

He went down on his knees.

"I'm sorry," he said again.

She stroked his poor, bald head. "It's all right. There'll be another time."

"Sometimes I can," he murmured.

"Did I have anything to do with it?"

"Oh, no. The fault is mine. You see, I had an accident once–"

My God! Shades of Hemingway's Jake Barnes!

He embraced her thighs and held his face against them and began to cry. Oh God!

"I love you so much. I would do anything for you, give my life for you."

She thought it was the combination of Romanian and Jewish that brought out the drama in him. Probably, he really meant it at the moment.

"I guess you'd better take me to Nora's," she said.

"Stay with me tonight," he pleaded. "Just let me hold you even if–"

Her drinks had worn off. She felt exhausted. His love was wearing her out. She wanted only to get away.

"No. I'm sorry."

Pity can be a strong emotion. Not love but akin to it. She pitied Willi deeply. And thus began her affair with him. She sometimes thought of it as her imitation of love.

One Sunday, against her better judgment, she invited Willi to Sunday dinner at Upsan Downs. It was not a complete success. Mother's later comment was the usual.

"I don't know why you always take up with such queer men, Brenda. I know he's helping you with your book, but you're a beautiful girl and he's so odd looking. You certainly don't look as though you belong together."

Dad said, "He's just her agent. They don't have to belong together, Lillian."

"Well, I'm glad of that."

Dad pinned a searching look on Brenda. "I'm sure it's not a romance, or is it? Your association with him is strictly business, isn't it?"

"Of course." She felt a flush of guilt.

Mother persisted. "I don't know why all your men friends have to be Jewish."

"Curt wasn't and you didn't like him."

"He was impossible."

"You like Jordan, don't you?"

"He's different."

"I like Jewish people. They're sensitive and artistic. You shouldn't have pushed me into the arts if you objected to them. They're nearly all you meet in the art world." She was getting fed up.

"Now, Brenda," Dad protested.

"It's true. Besides, your sister married a Jew and you liked him."

Mother looked horrified. "I hope you're not thinking of marrying this man!"

"Of course she isn't," Dad soothed.

"She's such a worry to me." Mother fled to the greenhouse.

They were polite to Willi that Sunday and he and Dad seemed to get along. But Brenda felt the strain and was glad when Willi left.

So, Willi continued to caress her commas and her, and she continued to write and feel unfulfilled.

At this point, Nora had found a live-in boyfriend and needed her place. So, Brenda began staying at Willi's untidy walk-up and lying about it to the family. She felt twinges of guilt but figured she was her own boss and deserved to be loved. Although she sometimes wished Willi wouldn't love her quite so much. It was a jealous, possessive love and she often felt stifled by it.

To celebrate the publication of Nora's magazine article, she threw a party at her apartment.

Willi's stable was there and a lot of gregarious European friends of Nora's. Among these was a Dutch someone called Hans Van Spielberg.

Hans was dark-haired, sleek and charming with an accent. He had a handsome, impassive, olive-colored face, which put Brenda in mind of some George Raftish villain in a Thirties flick. The sight of him lit up something in her imagination and she made a mental note for the novel. Why not have the bitchy girl run into someone like this, a louse type who gets her pregnant? That would pep things up a bit.

Now Willi, in addition to caressing her commas, had an annoying habit of jealously hovering over her shoulder at parties, afraid some new man would get to her. As this Hans bent over her hand, Brenda saw the jealous glint flair in Willi's eyes.

"Come on, Brenda. I've got someone I want you to meet," he said brusquely and took her arm.

'Damn it, you are a bore,' she thought but smiled sweetly and asked if he would mind replenishing her drink.

He left reluctantly, at which Hans said with a smile of very white teeth (God he was good looking!), "Does your friend always do that?"

"What?"

"Try to scare other men away from you?"

"Not always. I guess he thinks you're prime competition."

He took out a gold case and offered her a cigarette. He lit hers and then his own, then remarked, "It is, of course, a characteristic of theirs when they latch on to a gentile woman."

Oh, a Nazi type was he? That figured. She made a mental note of it for the novel.

She sprang to Willi's defense. "Oh, I wouldn't say that. Willi's a great guy and a good friend."

His clever black eyes admired her. "But not nice enough for you."

Good dialogue. She made a note of it.

"You are very beautiful," he said. "Are you an actress?"

"I've been on the stage."

"You should be. Why hide that beauty?" Then he said, "Are you sleeping with him?"

He had a nerve. She snapped back. "That's for me to know and you to find out."

He switched tactics to tell her he was in Philadelphia several days a week working in a lab with a chemist friend. Then, as Willi was sighted scurrying towards them, Hans quickly said, "Since you're from Philadelphia, I would be pleased if I might call upon you sometime. I have a bachelor friend, a Naval test pilot, I think you might enjoy knowing. He is recently divorced and, I think, rather lonely."

"Sure," she said, puzzled. "Bring him around." Why the friend? How strange.

"I will get your number from Nora." He bowed from the waist and left.

"What was he saying to you?" Willi demanded.

Brenda sipped her Scotch thoughtfully. "Nothing much."

"Helmut thinks he's a Nazi sympathizer. Don't get too friendly with him."

"I don't expect to."

It turned out Hans was a Nazi sympathizer and, along with his German chemist friend, was incarcerated in Texas during the war. It also turned out, according to Nora, that he was a homosexual. He didn't want Brenda. He just didn't want Willi to have her.

Brenda realized more and more that Willi should not be having her. Poor Brenny from Philly was messing up again. Though she dutifully went to him every weekend, she was not happy. But she liked the stable and the parties, and again realized the narrow existence of Upsan Downs couldn't hold her anymore.

Although she was bored with the novel, she kept at it doggedly. If she could make a success of it, she figured she could break free of everyone.

One night, passing Mother and Dad's door, she was arrested by Dad's voice.

"Lillian, I think what Brenda needs is a husband."

"Husband!" Mother exclaimed. "Would you have her marry one of those odd men she brings home? She'll never find anyone to come up to her artistically or any other way. Besides, she and Ted are too busy right now pursuing their careers to get involved with marriage. That can come later."

'Yeah,' Brenda thought. 'When I'm about fifty.'

Dad said, "I don't think Brenda's happy."

"Of course she is. She has her dancing and her writing. She has us. She's perfectly happy."

As always when troubled, Brenda went up to Aya's room on the third floor with its little homemade altar, a table covered with a white cloth on which stood a statue of Jesus.

With OcOc in his cage beside her, Aya sat rocking and saying her rosary.

Brenda sat on the floor and put her head in Aya's lap.

"Oh Aya, I'm in such a mess."

"What is it, Snooky?"

"I'm going with a man. He's a good man, but I don't love him. But I don't want to hurt him."

Aya's eyes looked pale and milky behind the rimless spectacles.

"Sometimes it's more honest to hurt."

"But I need someone. I'm not getting younger."

She smiled. "You're not that old. Never mind, the right one will come."

"I wish he'd hurry."

"You must have patience," Aya said. "I'll pray that the right one will come. The Lord will help you to what is right. Just have faith. Miracles sometimes do happen."

"Go to hell," OcOc murmured.

'That might be a solution,' Brenda thought, unless Aya and God could get her out of the mess she was in and put her life on the right path.

# CHAPTER 18

▼

# SUPER FLY GUY FROM THE SKY WITH A DIAMOND

One day, Hans Von Spielberg called to ask if he might bring his Naval Officer friend to visit.

'Oh, Lord,' she thought. 'With my life in such a mess, what I don't need is to meet a new man. But at least it might be a distraction.'

She invited them to come.

They arrived in separate cars. Handsome Hans, his olive face smooth as glass, had another engagement it seemed. In the hallway, he said with a flash of his beautiful teeth, "You see, I did not forget. This is Brad Colton."

The Naval Officer's handclasp was large and cool. He, too, had a smile of white, even teeth, in a face of strong, rugged lines.

"I'm sorry I must run," Hans said. "I'm sure you two will find much to talk about."

His eyes seemed to her to say, "I'm doing you a favor replacing your Jew friend with this."

"Have a pleasant evening," he said and left.

Brenda didn't know what that "much to talk about" would be. She knew little of the Navy and had never met a Naval Officer. This one was certainly impressive. Having just come from work, he had on his smashing Navy blues. And after Willi's looks, this tall blonde creature with the golden tan and the build of a Greek god dazzled her.

If Aya and God had sent this one, he certainly passed in the looks department. But what about the rest?

She'd told Mother and Dad about the man her New York friend was bringing, and they just accidentally on purpose happened by to look him over.

She noted Mother's critical look as she shook Brad's hand: nice looking but military. Not Brenda's type at all.

However, she surprised Brenda by saying, "Do offer Mr. Colton a drink of wine, Brenda."

Dad loved the Navy. His father had been a Naval surgeon. Dad never missed the Army/Navy game. Brenda saw his pleased look as he shook Brad's hand.

"Who's going to win the game this year?"

"We are of course, Sir," Brad Colton said.

As they trooped up to their bedroom, Brenda was sorry she wouldn't be at their door. Their comments would be interesting, she was sure.

She led Mr. Beautiful into the parlor. This had a character of formality imposed by Victorian furniture from Great Grandfather's house on Rittenhouse Square. This stiffened atmosphere suited Brenda, no sinking into the library's relaxed couch for this person and herself.

Seated and wine poured, he offered her a cigarette. They puffed at one another.

How long had he known Hans, she asked.

"Not long."

Silence. They puffed. She asked how he liked Philadelphia.

"It's a good place."

"Where are you from?"

"Kansas."

This drew a blank.

"What's Kansas like?"

"Scorching in summer, frigid in winter, silos, farms, cows, chickens."

She felt like thanking him for the statistics.

What was with this guy? Surely not dumb or dull. It took brains to get through the Naval Academy. But talk about a man of few words.

She made another try.

"I understand you're a test pilot."

"Yeah?"

Is this an interview, or what?

"What's that like?"

"Fun. Exciting."

"How?"

"Well, like today for instance."

He was off, talking a blue streak about how they give you a problem and you go up and try to solve it. It seemed he went up as high as the plane would go, then plunged toward earth, pulling out at the last minute.

"They want to know how much stress a new plane can take." He grinned. "So far mine have held together pretty well, except for today."

"What happened?"

"Had a windshield break in my face. Fortunately, I ducked in time."

"And this is fun?"

"Sure. Why not? It's challenging."

Brave? Foolhardy? Well, he was different anyhow. Something new. And she was up for something new.

Sparked by her interest, he was off again, all about flying with the Navy stunt team. With his strong, well-shaped hands, he illustrated how planes fly in close formation, roll and dive. He'd just finished duty on the carrier as a landing signal officer. Apparently, that was a tricky business, balancing on the rolling deck as, with his lighted wands, he signaled the planes in.

Out of the far reaches of the sea, they'd home in on the tiny target, the man below, whose guidance meant their safety or destruction.

"Those guys have been out there tangling with the Japs. You want, sure as hell, to get 'em in safe. Sometimes you have to wave them off when the pitch of the deck is too steep. And you've got to be ready to jump into the net at the ship's side if the pilot misjudges and comes for you."

As he talked, she watched his eyes. They were dark brown and piercingly clear. She wondered if the clarity came from looking into heights and distances unknown to mere earth-born mortals like her. No, he wasn't dull.

"You like flying then?"

"Yes. Up among the clouds and wind with nothing in your way, you can think your own thoughts. You feel free."

"But there must be storms, danger to face."

"Yes, you're in alien territory up there and have to adapt. Sometimes, you get thunderheads a mile high, full of hail, turbulence, fire. You damned well better go around them if you can."

Maybe in dealing with these elements, some of their properties had rubbed off on him. Behind the disciplined mask, were there forces in Brad Colton as turbulent as those winds?

And why was he sharing all this with a stranger? Perhaps, back from the sea and his world of men, he needed a woman with whom to share. Maybe he had to find one in a hurry because soon he'd be off again.

He awed her. What courage! Beside this god-like creature, poor Willi looked like chopped liver. This man would never be indecisive or procrastinating. He had the earthy strength of Kansas in his bones and the discipline of his hard Naval training. This was super guy. Here was someone to look up to and respect. Someone straightforward, who would never lie or play games. She was sick of games. This man lived fast. In his world, there was no time for procrastinating.

While he moved his graceful hands, her mind was doing a little moving, too. She found herself wondering what it would be like to be caressed by those hands.

Yes, she liked him and this giving of himself so freely. His clear eyes turning to her often for admiration and approval told her he was liking her very much and that it mattered what she thought of him.

All this seemed to be happening so easily, she was afraid of it. Nothing ever came easily to her.

He had to leave to be up at dawn to fly to Langley Field, where a test flight was scheduled. At the door, he kissed her lightly on the cheek. This was nice. No grappling.

She said, "Be sure and duck that windshield tomorrow."

"Don't worry. I will."

He took her hand. "I'm glad Hans brought me here. I feel that—" he broke off.

She waited, feeling something coming toward her. Something exciting, a thrill almost of fear, as one feels at the sound of an express train coming from far off.

He said, "Somehow I feel that you and I might need each other at this point in life."

What a strange thing to say. Of course, Hans had told her about his unhappy marriage and his divorce. Had he told Brad about her affair with Willi? Did he sense she was troubled?

"Maybe we do," she said.

"Shall we find out?"

The intense eyes, searching, seemed to be offering a challenge.

She looked away.

"Shall we find out?"

She forced her eyes back to his. "Yes."

Behind the curtain at the parlor window, she watched him go up the driveway to his car. His stride, which had mastered a rolling carrier deck, was unhurried, balanced, free. Watching, she felt a lessening of the tension of these weeks of deception with Willi.

Could it be that this man Aya had promised was going to set her life in the right direction? He had as much said they belonged together.

She thought of Aya upstairs, praying, telling her to have faith and all would be right.

She knew she was going to have to make it right and that was not going to be easy. Willi would be expecting her for her New York weekend with him. What to do?

It seemed that Aya or fate intervened. Willi called to say he had to be on the West Coast for a week to work out some film deals.

"I'm taking your outline," he said. "Maybe I can make a sale for us."

"Wonderful."

But somehow the prospect didn't thrill her as much as it might have a short time ago.

"I hope you'll have some new chapters for me when I get back."

"Oh, I will."

As Brenda hung up, she thought, 'I'm not going to worry about that now. At least I'll be free for a week, free to be with Brad.'

It was a great week. He took her to dinner and dancing. He had two left feet. She said she'd straighten them out.

"You can't teach a klotz from Kansas how to do the Cha Cha," he said.

"Try me."

She showed him her dance studio and told him of her love for Spanish dancing, and how she planned to train girls to perform the dance for charity.

The studio floor was old and saggy in spots. He said dancing on it was a good way to break a leg.

"I can fix it for you," he announced. "Would you like that?"

"Be my guest."

He seemed to always be around.

Sometimes she'd hear his plane roaring over the house. He'd make a couple of passes, panicking the neighbors who thought the Nazis were coming. Brenda and Jancy would rush out on the lawn and wave. Dad enjoyed all this.

"Quite a boy," he admired.

"I wish he wouldn't do that," Mother said. "It gives me a gas attack."

He took her to the Officer's Club where she met his test pilot buddies and their wives. The men were types like Brad, all drinking to ease off the day's hectic work. She learned Brad was involved in a "hush-hush" project. These men worked for him and it was apparent they looked up to him.

"Brad's a leader," one of them confided to Brenda. "He never asks us to take a risk he wouldn't take himself."

Sometimes life around Brad was a little too exciting. At the club one evening, he asked Brenda if she'd like to watch him practice night landing signals on the field.

"Don't do it, Brenda," one of the wives warned.

"Why not?"

They all laughed. She gave Brad a look.

"It's perfectly safe," he assured.

"What do you mean 'safe'?"

"Come and see."

A couple of Scotch's gave her courage.

"Sure."

"Don't say we didn't warn you." The girls exchanged knowing looks.

Brad drove her to the airfield nearby.

"Now you'll see what it's like landing a plane on a carrier, only there it's a little tougher."

He parked, gathered up his wands and she followed him out on the field. Landing lights on both sides illuminated the runway. It felt strange standing there, two dots on the huge field with the immense, starless sky above.

"Now," Brad said, "stand close behind me and when the plane comes, be sure not to move. It could be dangerous."

"Okay." Her voice sounded small.

Hell, she was scared shitless, hearing that plane circling then seeing those glaring lights coming at them out of the dark.

Brad held his arms wide, with the lighted wands slowly waving to the plane. It took everything she had to keep from dashing into the night and probably getting mowed down.

With a dreadful roar, the thing passed over. It seemed only inches above their heads.

Her knees were water and her teeth, chattering.

"That wasn't so bad, was it?" Brad said. There was a smile in his voice.

It occurred to her he was testing her to see if she had the right stuff. Damn him! He had no right to do this. But damned if she'd let him know she was a coward. All the girls must have been through this initiation. That's why they'd laughed.

She managed to squeak out, "It's kind of fun, isn't it."

Fun, hell!

She braced for the next onslaught of the glaring, thunderous demon plunging at them from the dark. She thought, 'What a way to make a living. Anyhow, if it hits, it'll get him first. Serve him right.'

But how she admired those steady nerves, that boundless courage.

They developed an easy relaxed friendship. To her surprise, he found something in her she hadn't known about. She'd always thought she was a poet, dancer, and singer, sophisticated and glamorous. He told her she was decent, sweet, humble, shy, real and also funny. He called her Foxy.

"What's that supposed to mean?"

"You're like a little fox, always ready to duck into your hole."

"I am not."

"I happen to like foxes."

During the week, Brad had not ventured more than a few gentle kisses. Then, one night after the theater, he asked if she would like to come to his place for a drink.

She hesitated. Was she ready for this? Why couldn't things stay as they were? But she was curious.

Brad's apartment was furnished in what looked like Sears' best, everything brown and plain.

Brad removed his jacket, poured their Scotch and sat beside her on the sofa. They sipped a moment then he pulled her to him and kissed her lips and neck.

The performance seemed so mechanical, as though he were doing something that was expected of him. The kisses seemed dry, unimpassioned. There were no words to excite response. After the expert lovemakings of Martin and Willi, he seemed like a shy, awkward boy. How could a man so sure of himself be so awkward with a woman? He'd been married. Surely he knew how to make love.

She noted there was no impotence being manifested as he pressed his powerful body against her. Why was he leaving her cold? She couldn't respond.

He drew away. "What's wrong, Brenda?"

"I'm sorry. I just can't."

He searched her face then reached for a cigarette.

"Don't worry about it. It's not important right now."

"I'm in a mess."

"Would you like to tell me about it?"

She told him about her dream of success and how Willi was helping her.

"It's not really a love affair with him. It's just, well, I just got into it–"

"It happens. You don't have to explain."

Her admiration for him grew. Here was someone who was willing to accept that people made mistakes.

He added, "But you have to decide what you want out of life."

"The trouble is, I don't know."

He took her hands.

"I feel we have something for each other. But it must be allowed to grow without stress, don't you agree?"

"Yes. The trouble is, he loves me. How can I tell him?"

"You'll find a way if it's important to you. Is it?"

Once more, he was challenging her. Saying, "Grow up, take responsibility for your life." She almost resented his putting this burden on her.

He waited. She felt her heart quicken. The dark eyes with their piercing clarity held hers.

"Do you want me, Brenda?"

"Yes, I think I do."

He took her hands.

"You see, I'm leaving for the Pacific in a couple of weeks so—" he stopped. "Will you marry me?"

Just like that. He proposed the way he flew his planes, all signals set for go.

She drew away.

"I don't know, Brad."

He waited.

"We've been having a wonderful time together but marriage. You don't really know much about me."

"I know enough."

"Your life is so different. I don't know if I'd fit in."

"Of course we don't have much money. We don't in the Navy."

"It isn't that. I've never thought much about money but—"

"What?"

"I can't cook."

He laughed. "I'll teach you."

"I've never made a bed or run a vacuum cleaner."

"I'll teach you."

"And there are other things. Like, my Mother has always been a big influence in my life."

"I can handle that."

"Also," she stopped. "I'm practically a virgin."

He gave her a long look, then smiled. "I can handle that. I happen to be an old fashioned guy off a farm in Kansas. I like 'practically virgins.' Now, if that's all, I see no problem. Come on, Foxy. Be brave. Marry me."

The words spoke themselves. "Okay, I'll give it a shot."

Yes, it was going to be rough to break it with Willi. But she thought she would write him a nice letter explaining it all. If he didn't understand, well, just too bad. She should never have gotten mixed up with him.

After Brad left, she saw Mother and Dad's light was still on. Pausing at the door, she heard Mother say, "Jason, I think Brenda's seeing too much of this Brad Colton."

"Why? They're having a wonderful time together."

"But he's not her type. A military man, he'd never appreciate her. He's not an artist. Also, those people drink a lot. He's probably a drinker."

"You don't know that. I think he's good for Brenda. In fact, I'd like to see her marry him."

"Marry! Do you realize she'd be traveling all the time? We'd never see her. Besides, the type of people she'd meet and sensitive as she is—"

Brenda knocked on the door. "Can I come in?"

They were sitting in bed, side by side.

"Hi folks, I've got some news."

Mother looked worried. "Now, Brenda."

"Brad just proposed and I've accepted."

"Oh, Brenda." Mother seemed about to weep.

"That's wonderful," Dad said. He laughed. "Those Navy boys certainly don't let the grass grow under their feet."

"I think he's rushing things," Mother said. "I think you should think this over carefully. He's already had a divorce." She added, "Besides, I don't think Brad cares much for me."

"Why do you say that?"

"It's just a feeling that I have."

Brenda was to discover that Brad did not care much for Mother.

One evening as they drank at the club, she remarked, "What's with you and Mother? You don't seem to like her."

"Actually, I don't care for mothers in general. I had a lulu. She was domineering and possessive, as well as being a religious fanatic," he paused. "You're a writer. Want something to write about? I'll give you a story."

He told her his mother and grandmother were very poor. They scraped up a living as entertainers. Grandmother played the guitar and his mother danced. It seemed they came to this little town in Kansas where his grandfather was a religious leader.

He grinned. "Apparently Ma put on her sexy dance act in front of the townsfolk and Grandpa came after her with a whip and threw her out of town."

"Good Lord."

"But Ma got even. Years later, she came back disguised as a religious healer. She put on a good show, got around the townspeople, even fooled my Grandpa. Moved in with him, took over his house, the town and even his son, my father. She married him."

"Quite a story."

"She really loused up my childhood. I was glad to get away from her and go to the Naval Academy. I never went back." There was bitterness in his voice.

"Poor you," Brenda said. "But all mothers aren't like that."

"Glad you think so."

He glanced at her then grinned.

"Enough of this gloom, Foxy. Come on, drink up." He raised his glass. "Here's to mothers. Who needs 'em?"

For several days, Mother worried and fretted about Brad and the marriage. But Dad finally convinced her that Brad was a fine man, highly thought of in the Navy and would go far.

"I must call Margot," Mother said.

Brenda couldn't resist listening in on the conversation on the upstairs phone.

Aunt Margot said, "You must be pleased with the match, Lillian." Implying, of course, "rather than to one of those awful men she's been going with."

Mother said coolly, "We are pleased. He's a fine man."

"The girls and I were wondering–isn't the marriage a bit hurried?"

'Damn old witch,' Brenda thought. Was she suggesting a shotgun wedding?

Mother's tone was cold. "Brad's being sent to carrier duty immediately. There's a war on you know, Margot." She added, "By the way, will any of your sons-in-law be going to war?"

"One of them has signed up for the National Guard. The others will be at the Navy department."

"Oh, desk jobs, how nice. Of course, Brad's highly thought of in the Navy. He's in line for becoming an Admiral, you know."

Aunt Margot gave a light laugh. "Isn't he rather young for that?"

Brenda hung up. "Damned old witch!"

Jordan Kirsh, surfacing from his latest romance with one of his glamorous ladies of the theatre, didn't seem too pleased about Brenda's engagement either. After meeting Brad, he remarked, "Those Naval Academy men are all cut from the same cloth, the military mind and all. Nice fellow. But you're so different, Brenda. You're an artist."

Brenda was disappointed. She'd wanted her old friend's approval. Could it be he was a little jealous? Baby slipping away from him? Maybe he was irked she hadn't consulted him. He liked to be in control in these family matters.

"Wouldn't want my Madonna to make a mistake," he said.

Brenda just smiled.

Brad thought a simple ceremony with a Justice of the Peace would do it. Mother would have none of this.

"We'll have the wedding at Upsan Downs," she announced on the verge of a gas attack. She was more than ready to do battle with Brad.

His grin disarmed her.

"Whatever you say, future mother-in-law."

Great preparations were under way: scurrying to get invitations sent, caterers consulted, the parlor gussied up with ferns, a makeshift altar and folding chairs. Aya and Jancy wore themselves out polishing everything. Ted came up from Washington to help and Mother survived with the aid of Pepto Bismol.

Notices appeared in Philadelphia papers. "Brenda Marr, daughter of well known architect, Jason Marr, to marry Naval flier. He wooed her from the sky, the writer, dancer, actress declared." There was even a notice in the society column of the New York Times and Betsy Fulsome, who carefully scanned the Times for social events, saw it and rang Brenda up.

"Darling, I read the great news. Can I come?"

"Wouldn't get married without you."

There was an odd assortment of guests. Dad rounded up some Main Line golfing buddies and their wives. Ted produced a couple of artistic types. Teeny came with a few of the Mart group. Brenda sensed Teeny's nose was a bit out of joint since she hadn't been in on arranging the deal. The largest contingent consisted of Brad's officers and their wives. The fly-boys were magnificent in dress uniforms and clanking swords. Margot and her girls, without their husbands, put in an appearance, no doubt to look over this Navy man Brenda'd been able to snare.

Brenda wore Mother's wedding dress, a beautiful ivory satin, so ancient that every time she drew a deep breath, she felt it split a little under the arms.

"You look lovely, dear," beautiful Dad, in his cut-away, whispered as he guided her between the folding chairs and expectant faces.

Brad and the Navy Chaplain waited at the improvised altar and as Brenda said, "I do," she felt another split under her arms.

'I must remember to keep my arms down,' she thought.

Over Champagne and buffet, Dad's cronies and the Navy men eyed one another. And Aunt Margot and the girls eyed everyone, particularly Betsy Fulsome, who was blonder and more lifted than ever and twinkling with gold chains and bracelets (loot from former conquests.)

After Brad and Brenda cut the cake with his sword, the party began to heat up. Betsy tried her charms on Jordan and when this didn't take,

offered to do a strip tease, egged on by the flyboys and Teeny, who offered
to unveil, too. At this, Margot dragged the girls away and Dad's pals made
a quick exit. In the library, rugs were rolled back and dancing began to the
new tape recorder. Brad, Ted and Dad waltzed with Brenda. Mother drank
Champagne, giggled and made a hit as she always did when she came out
of her shell. Brad invited her to dance and told her she looked pretty as a
rose in her pink dress. Mother blushed. It seemed Brad was going to know
how to handle Mother. Outside, a soused Lieutenant fell in Mother's
goldfish pond. Everyone thought this hilarious.

Then it was time to go. Brenda didn't want to. The party was just
getting good. But Aya and Jancy rushed her upstairs and into her going
away clothes for the honeymoon in Williamsburg, Virginia.

"You looks real sharp, Miss Brenda," Jancy said, giving a final zip-up to
Brenda's new suit.

"You see, Snooky," Aya said. "I knew the Lord would send you a good
man."

As she hugged them, Brenda felt a pang. This time she was really leaving
Upsan Downs, her childhood and this place she loved. Where had those
years gone? What lay ahead was unknown. Anyhow, it was a new adven-
ture. Hadn't she always been up for new adventures?

Kisses for Mother and Dad, then she and Brad ran under the Navy's
upraised swords and pelting rice and into Brad's new second hand
Oldsmobile with the Navy's tin cans attached behind.

As they drove off, amid voices calling goodbye, Brenda heard another
voice, OcOc's, ringing out from the third floor window. It seemed he'd
finally conquered Ted's magic words.

"Screw you!" OcOc yelled. "Screw you!"

Brenda hoped this might be a happy omen.

They had dinner at Wilmington's best hotel and after, went up to the
bridal suite. The flowers were there and the Champagne in a bucket. Brad
uncorked the Champagne and they toasted each other. Then Brad
bestowed a light kiss and withdrew to the dressing room to change.

Looking around the room with its pink and white décor to delight a new bride's heart, Brenda thought, 'What the hell am I doing here?' She called home.

Ted answered, sounding a little drunk.

"Hi, big shot bride. Been laid yet?"

"Shut up." Her voice sounded small.

"You sound more like a funeral than a wedding. What gives?"

"Nothing."

"Listen Bren, if you don't like him, you can always come home."

"I do like him, you idiot."

"You just had to get married, didn't you? You were so afraid you wouldn't catch a fish, weren't you?"

"Shut up."

"Well, anyhow, he's better than Mortimer, isn't he? Or ole' Pepto, or how about Clammy?" Ted had taken a dim view of these.

"Yep."

"Well then, hop to it, sexy. Give the ole' Lieutenant a break. The poor guy probably hasn't had any for a long time. Do your wifely duty."

"Thanks for the brotherly advice."

"No charge."

She hung up and was still sitting and staring at the bridal bed when Brad appeared. He looked gorgeous, if somewhat military, in his stiff new blue pajamas.

"Hey, Foxy, what's with you?"

"Oh, nothing."

"Care to undress?"

In the dressing room, she took her time unpacking her bag and putting on the new white satin, lace-trimmed nightgown. In the mirror, she thought she looked more virginal and Madonna-like than ever.

Hopeless.

She wandered back into the bedroom and stood looking at Brad, already in bed.

He grinned at her.

"What's funny?"

"You are, my beautiful love."

He held out his arms to her satin-clad, shivering body.

"Come here, Foxy. You look cold."

She found a warm nest beside him. He smelled good and it seemed pretty natural to be there.

At his kiss, she thought she heard a bell begin to ring in the distance. She drew away.

"Tell me something. Do you think I look like a virginal Madonna?"

"Hell no."

He took the pins out of her hair and it cascaded over her shoulders.

"You look like you. Unique. One of a kind. Now, do you think you'd like to make love with me?"

"I think I can handle that," she said.

Mother wasn't always right, was she?

Or was she?

For that night, OcOc's encouraging words didn't pay off. This was no doubt due to Brenda's practically being a virgin and Brad such a quick performer.

Mounting, Brad came on without much warm up and with deft military precision. Brenda's rhythms were slower and she didn't quite catch up for the grand finale.

"Sorry, darling," Brad murmured. "Guess I beat you to it."

He kissed her, turned over and went to sleep.

Brenda felt cheated. She realized she'd hoped for the 'Great Fulfillment' at last.

'Maybe with time and practice,' she thought.

She lay awake a long time, uncomfortable next to Brad's scratchy new pajamas. Finally, about to drift into troubled sleep, OcOc's words sounded in her ears.

"Oh, go screw yourself, bird!" she told him.

# CHAPTER 19

▼

# TAMING OF THE MAVERICK

Other nights were better. She learned to endure Brad's rough caressing and it even seemed that at times, he tried to please. But she was glad when the honeymoon was over.

Though Brad's apartment was small and cramped, he decided they should stay there for now. The war was heating up and he might have to leave at any time to join his squadron.

He had invested in a double bed, which took up most of the tiny bedroom. And on their first night back, Brad's restless body and snoring kept Brenda awake most of the night, strengthening her resolve to agitate for twin beds.

Having finally fallen asleep, she was rudely awakened by Brad showering and buzzing his electric razor in the bathroom. The bedside clock told her it was six-thirty. My God, the middle of the night! She was used to sleeping until ten. Morning was not her best time.

She lay limp and sulky, listening to Brad gargle. Sure, he had to go to work but she didn't.

He began to whistle. Damn it! Why didn't he shut up?

His cheerful face popped around the door. "Come on, Sleepy Puss, up and at 'em."

"What for?" God, she hated heartiness in the morning.

"To cook my breakfast, of course."

Brad had never mentioned that she would be expected to get his breakfast. It came as a shock.

He was pulling on his trousers. "Eggs, bacon, toast and coffee."

"I don't know how to do that," she said.

"You'll learn how," he said cheerfully.

Shitty-dit-dit.

He leaned over and pulled the covers off her. She curled up in a ball. The room was cold.

"Come on. Most of the world is stirring by now."

"Let 'em stir. I'm sleepy."

"You can sleep later."

"That ruins my day."

He stared down at her a moment, then said crisply, "Brighten up, girl. The world is about to blow up. People are already out there getting killed. And all you're thinking about is indulging your laziness."

"I am not lazy."

He gave her a light swat on the behind. "Well, come on then."

He departed for the kitchen.

Grimly she rose. Clever of Brad to shame her this way. She took her time, brushing teeth, washing face and putting on lipstick. When she made it to the kitchen, still in her robe, he had already made his breakfast and was sitting at the kitchen table, eating and reading the paper.

So, he had cooked. Good. Just be slow about getting to it and he would soon catch on she wasn't about to cook his breakfast.

She said sweetly, "I see you did the cooking and a lot better than I could."

He glanced up from the paper. He looked fresh and alert. No doubt morning was his good time.

He said, "It's not so much that I want you to cook. I just want your pretty face beside me to start my day off right."

"I'm afraid I'm not much good in the morning," she said.

"No one is," he said pleasantly. "It's a question of discipline. You'll get used to it."

'In a pig's eye,' she thought. She poured herself some coffee and slumped down at the table.

"I didn't sleep well," she said. "You snore and move around all the time."

He looked amused. "You'll get used to it."

How unfeeling could you get? Would Martin or Willi have treated her like this? He was making her feel like a spoiled brat and she resented it. And he was doing it on purpose. He knew what he was about. Breaking her in right, was he? Well, we'd see about that.

"Come on, smile," he said. "You have pretty teeth and I have a long day. Have to fly to Langley and break a couple of windshields, so cheer me up."

Now she really did feel rotten. Him risking his life and she grousing about no sleep.

"I'll try to do better tomorrow."

"I know you will. And how about getting to work on your book?"

"I will," she said unenthusiastically.

"I've got a heavy day and probably won't be back until after dinner. Can you manage?"

"Sure."

He gulped down his coffee, kissed her on the cheek, grabbed his cap and briefcase and took off.

She rinsed the dishes and went back to bed.

She felt deserted. Why did he have to be away so late with his work? Was the Navy more important to him than she? It took her quite a while to realize that it was. The honeymoon was over and it was just a question of settling in, writing and waiting for Brad to come home. The prospect did not thrill her. She knew why. Who was she kidding? She didn't really look forward to his coming home.

But she'd made the choice and would learn to live with it. For a while anyhow.

Brad had bought her a new typewriter and set it up in what he called "her writing room." There waited the half finished manuscript of 'Refugee.' She read it over and decided it stank. A piece of junk! Without Willi caressing her commas, how could she finish it? She had to. She owed it.

She sat at the typewriter and tried to pick up thread of the story. Nothing. She was completely blocked. No wonder, cramped in this lousy little room. It dried her up.

She thought longingly of her big room at home, the piece and quiet of Upsan Downs. Why didn't she take 'Refugee' out there and work on it? Brad might not like this, but he wouldn't have to know. She could get back to the apartment before he did.

She found Mother and Dad in the library listening to the war news on the radio. It was bad, Hitler gobbling up everything.

It seemed strange to see Dad home on a weekday doing nothing, with Mother beside him knitting instead of at her usual stand in the greenhouse.

Dad turned off the radio.

"Welcome home, bride."

Brenda felt a pang. What had happened to him? She had only been gone ten days, but he seemed to have aged overnight. Or was it that she'd been so preoccupied with her affairs, she hadn't noticed his graying hair and how his shoulders sagged?

She sat beside them.

"Dad, are you all right?"

"I'm fine."

"He isn't," Mother said. "It's his eyes. He has glaucoma."

"What's that?"

"It can lead to blindness."

As Mother knitted, her long fingers sparkled with Grandma's diamonds.

"She's exaggerating," Dad said. "It can be controlled with drops. The only thing is, it puts a crimp in my work. I can't use my eyes much." He smiled. "Looks like your Pop's getting to be an old geezer."

"You are not!"

"He works too hard," Mother said. "There's no need for the money now that I have mine." Her knitting needles clicked impatiently. "He continues to drink coffee and eat rich desserts when he knows that's bad for his liver."

For years, Brenda had listened to Dad say, "I feel far from well." It was sort of a family joke. Not really a joke. He suffered from migraine headaches.

"Sometimes I get tired of telling him," Mother said.

Dad smiled. "Wonderful woman. Doctor Marr, my physician wife."

His eyes rested with love and annoyance on his beautiful nagging wife.

Brenda felt a thrust of sorrow. She'd never thought of Dad as old. He'd always been so active, going to his studio every day. Dad, always her rock to lean on. It seemed her rock was crumbling.

She said, "Brad's going to be away a lot, so I thought I'd bring my manuscript out here and work on it."

"Good, dear," Mother said. "And since Dad can't drive anymore, you can have the Buick to come out in."

For a while, Brenda's plan worked. In familiar surroundings, 'Refugee' went better. She hadn't told Brad what she was doing and was always back at the apartment before he got home. And what difference did it make where she wrote?

It seemed to him, it did.

One night he came home late. He hadn't phoned and she'd had his chili simmering on the stove for hours. She began to worry. She knew he was getting in his flight time, a trip to Jacksonville. Had he run into trouble? But the Navy immediately contacted wives in such cases.

When he finally came in, she saw that he'd had more than a couple of beers with the boys. He was loaded.

Without speaking, he brushed by her and tossed his cap on the living room table. At their makeshift bar, he poured himself a Scotch, downed it, and then turned.

"Well, I hope you had a good time wherever you were."

"What do you mean? I've been waiting here for hours. You might have phoned."

"I did phone, four times. You didn't answer."

"I had to go out."

"Sure." He bit out the word.

"I don't know why you're angry at me. I'm the one who's been waiting. Where were you anyhow?"

"I was celebrating," he said. "Not that you give a damn."

"Celebrating what?"

"Just a very important day in my life. A day when I might have wanted my wife at my side. But I guess she's not really interested."

"What are you talking about?"

"Just that I learned this afternoon that I've made Lieutenant Commander and also will head a squadron. Not that that means much to you."

"That's wonderful, Brad." He had wanted this so much.

She approached to give him a kiss of congratulations. He fended her off. He removed his jacket, threw it on the sofa bed, loosened his tie and went to the bar again.

"Don't you think you've had enough?" she said.

These were the wrong words. He turned. His mouth was drawn in a thin line.

"Don't you tell me what to do! You sound just like my Mother."

She watched him pour and down another drink.

He faced her. The look in his eyes was not pleasant.

"So, where do you go when you go 'out,' as you put it? As if I didn't know."

"Really Brad, you can't expect me to stay cooped up here all day."

"You go where you go everyday. To your parents, don't you?"

"Well, I do go out there quite often. What's wrong with that? I'm always here when you come home."

His eyes bored into her. "And what do you do when you go out there?"

"What is this? An inquisition? I mess around the place, help Mother in the greenhouse."

"Like hell you do." His eyes kept boring in. "Who do you think you're kidding?"

He stalked into the writing room and scooped up a handful of empty pages, which he brandished at her accusingly.

"You haven't written a word since you've been here. Deduction: you're writing at your former home and lying about it."

"I didn't lie. I just didn't tell you. I tried writing here and couldn't. I dried up. It's too cramped."

"Too cramped is it? You need luxury and comfort to write, do you?"

"You don't understand—"

He crumpled up the pages and threw them on the floor.

"I understand all right. This place isn't good enough for you. Well, you married a poor man, remember? Or, aren't we really married?"

"Brad, for God's sake—"

"It hasn't even been a month and already you can't stand it here."

"That's not so."

"Maybe you can't hack it that some men are pushed to the limit in their jobs and need stability at home, someone who cares and is not always escaping to comfort and luxury."

"I'm not."

"No? Well, get this straight. You married me and you're stuck with it. But if you want out, just say the word. Just say, 'Brad, I'm afraid to face life and marriage. I want to go home where I'm petted and pampered and where I can turn into a non-entity under my parents' wing.' Is that what you want?"

His voice was rising. He was advancing on her.

She backed away.

Maybe she was in the wrong. But did she deserve this tongue-lashing?

His eyes narrowed, his lips were pale, twisting with harshness. There was a wildness in his face. She wondered if she could make it to the bathroom and lock the door if he started throwing things.

"Let's have it," he said furiously. "What do you want? Are you married to me or are you still married to that mother of yours?"

Her words came out in a spurt.

"Oh, shut up!"

"What did you say?"

"I said, shut up!"

"Don't you ever say that to me again."

"Shut up! Shut up!"

His hand came back. He slammed her across the cheek with such force her teeth rattled.

Her strange reaction was a kind of hysterical laughter. Could this be happening to her? Gutter people slammed each other around like this–or, crazies.

His fury lit hers. She flew at him, aiming for ripping his buttons. (Shades of Cousin Billy?)

He grabbed her wrists. A paralyzing grip.

"A wild cat, are you? I'm glad to see some spirit there."

"Let me go!"

"I'll let you go all right. I'll let you go for good if that's what you want."

He flung her wrists from him.

The Buick keys were on the silver dish on the table. Her impulse was to grab them and dash for home. He thought of that, too. He went for the keys, to take them, she thought. He was full of surprises. He tossed them at her. They grazed her and fell to the floor.

"There, take the keys and run home to Mommy like a good girl. I'm going to bed."

She stood, suffocated by anger, tears of humiliation starting.

To hell with him! To hell with him!

At the bedroom door, he turned.

"The moral of the story is, if you can't pee, get off the pot."

To her surprise, he spoke without rancor. His anger seemed to have evaporated. He didn't even seem drunk. It was as though the scene had never taken place, that he had already put it behind him.

He closed the door between them. Good thinking, because she was damned if she was going to share his bed this night or any other.

Her anger subsided. She picked up the keys.

His words "run home to Mommy" rang in her ears.

Damn him. Why should she make the long drive home in the middle of the night to wake and worry her family? It was rotten of him to challenge her like this. Common sense told her to go home and stay there. Who needs this treatment? Of course, he'd been hurt she hadn't been with him to share his success, and her deception about the writing had been wrong. But it was idiotic of him to fly into a tirade over such a trivial matter. Had the whole thing been a ploy to get his way? By putting the burden of things on her, was he making a bid for her to knuckle under him? And he really was a bastard to have hit her.

She concluded he was probably under strains she knew nothing of and decided this once, she would let it pass. Probably their whole trouble was they were not communicating enough.

She took a quilt from the closet, wrapped herself in it and fell asleep on the day bed thinking, 'Never let him raise his hand to me again or I will walk out.'

Brad left the next morning without waking her. He left a note saying he'd be gone a week on the West Coast and if she wanted to write at home, it was up to her. There was no word of "sorry I hit you."

If Brenda expected Brad to apologize, she'd better have another think. He never apologized. That would have been an admission that he was wrong. In his eyes, he was never wrong. Had he been too drunk to remember? She was to discover his mind functioned like a machine, even when he was paralyzed with drink.

At home, Brenda found no escape from troubling thoughts. Upsan Downs had become a sad place with Dad's illness. He took painkillers to deaden his headaches. This angered Mother who had no faith in medicines and hid his pills. This angered him.

"And where did you get your medical degree, Dr. Marr?"

Indomitable Mother! As others failed, she seemed to become stronger, bossing her estate, practicing the piano, working with her flowers. The world might be ready to blow up, but nothing disturbed her daily routine.

The week seemed long. Brenda tried to write but found it bored her. She missed Brad's coming back at night with exciting stories of his adventures and his cheery "What's Foxy been up to today?"

But what about that teeth-rattling smack? Could she just overlook that? It seemed she was married to a Jekyll and Hyde character. What to do? Dump him or hang on and hope he'd change?

She was still scurrying for an answer when he called.

"Hi Foxy! Coming in tonight?" Cheery. The 'good' Brad.

"I don't know if I can," she muttered.

"What do you mean, you don't know?"

"It's the family. Dad. He's not well."

"I'm sorry to hear it, but you can go back tomorrow if you want. But listen, I've got to see you. Your man misses you. The apartment's awfully empty." He added, "I think you'll like the dress I brought you from San Diego."

A peace offering?

"It's awfully late. The family will—"

He broke in, his voice urgent, pleading, his lover's voice.

"Darling, please come. I need you so much. I love you—" his voice trailed off.

She thought in a strange way, he did love her. And perhaps she should give it another try. And she did want to see the dress from San Diego.

"I'll come."

She was tense when she arrived. But there he was in the kitchen in his shirtsleeves, an apron wrapped around him. The table was set with candles and her wedding silver. Wine was in the cooler and he was cooking a steak.

Handsome, vital, his arms came about her. His kiss surprised her with its ardor. Something seemed changed. Had their quarrel somehow cleared the air?

He seated her, poured the wine and raised his glass to hers.

"Let's celebrate, Foxy. We might not have been able to. You might not have seen your little ole' Brad in one piece again."

"What do you mean?"

He told her he'd had a near miss when his prop failed during a test flight over the rocky coast near La Jolla.

"No place to make a landing," he said. "Too low to parachute out. But I managed to get the motor started just in time." He kind of laughed. "It was a lot of fun."

'My God,' she thought. While she was caressing commas and feeling sorry for herself, superman was up there wrestling with the grim reaper. 'Shame on you, Brenda, making such a big deal over a slap on the cheek.' What did she know of the terrible stresses of testing a plane? He was strung tight and it was up to her to understand. She married superman and if he got out of control once in a while, it was up to her to cope.

That night, she seemed to find a new tenderness in his arms. Maybe he'd been doing some thinking about their sex life.

She thought, 'Maybe this will work out after all.'

# CHAPTER 20

▼

# YOU COULD ALWAYS COME HOME

They were at Upsan Downs for Sunday lunch when news came over the radio that Pearl Harbor had been bombed and that a German U boat had been sighted off the Jersey coast.

"Oh Lord," Mother moaned. "Germans at our shores. I've got to lie down. I feel all dizzy."

"It's probably a false alarm," Dad said.

"I doubt that." Brad spoke briskly.

Brenda saw his annoyance at these mere civilians who could never understand his world. His training had been leading up to this moment. When he received orders to report to the West Coast to put his towing tests in action for the Pacific war area, he was eager to go.

He would have ten days to drive to the coast. There was a wild scurry to get packed and out of their apartment.

Mother and Dad were upset and the phone call from Ted didn't help. He'd enlisted in the Army and was stationed at Fort Dix.

"How could he do this?" Mother moaned.

"He had to," Dad said. "All his life he wanted to go to war."

It was hard to say goodbye to Ted. She told him on the phone.

"We're leaving for the Coast."

"Guess I won't see you then."

She felt a pang. "Guess not."

"Well, as the British say, keep your pecker up."

"I would if I had one."

He gave a grunt of appreciation.

"Love ya."

"Me, too."

While Brad tended to last minute details, Brenda spent her last night at home.

Mother came to her room and sat on the edge of her bed to give one of her "talks."

"Now, Brenda. We're entering into a bad time and I don't want you to get pregnant."

Brenda didn't particularly want to but for sake of controversy said, "Why not?"

She looked upset. "You aren't, are you?"

"Not that I know of."

"Brad will be going to war and if anything happens to him, you'll be stuck with a baby."

Brenda didn't really want a baby but said, "What's wrong with that?"

Mother shook her head.

"With all your show of sophistication, you're very innocent. You haven't really grown up or felt life's sting."

This sounded like a line Mother had read in one of her romantic novels.

'Haven't I, Ma?' she thought. 'What about those stingers, Martin and Willi? And don't forget that bastard, Curt.'

Mother continued. "Bearing children isn't easy and especially if you're married to someone like Brad."

"What's that supposed to mean?"

"You have a delicate nerve force like I have. Bearing children takes its toll. I almost died having mine."

Oh please, not that again!

"Are you telling me you don't want me to have a child?"

"I'm only trying to spare you." She paused. "Children complicate life. Brad's high strung. I shouldn't wonder if, when he's drinking, he could become violent. I'd hate to think of you and a child of yours being subjected to that."

As usual, Mother had figured it all out and was doing Brenda's thinking for her. It was annoying.

Brenda said, "I know you're not keen on Brad. But he is my husband and I think I'm capable of managing things."

"I hope so."

Mother's gray eyes looked deeply into Brenda's. She said softly, "You're very precious to your father and I. We want you to be happy."

"I am happy." She realized she was lying.

Mother, who seldom showed affection, leaned over and kissed her.

"Go to sleep, dear. You have a long day ahead. Dad and I will see you off. Remember to please wear your diaphragm."

"When, tomorrow morning?" The feeble joke could not hide Brenda's sadness.

When she couldn't sleep, she sat at her window. There was a full December moon. It glinted cold and hard on the panes of the greenhouse and poured over the empty space where the old house had been. She thought how short life was. That house, which had contained so much life, laughter, jealousy, hatred, sorrow. All gone now, living only in memory. The great Paulownia tree extended black skeletal arms over the glassy pond. Unsoothed by snow as yet, the dark earth of their place lay exposed to biting cold. All was closed by winter.

Her heart seemed closed, too.

Damn it. She couldn't stand leaving her aging parents who needed her. She couldn't stand leaving Ted. But how could she leave Brad when he would be in the war soon and said he needed her so much?

She decided to go. If things got too rough with him, she could always come home.

Early the next morning, they stood on the porch to see her off: Aldo, Jancy, Aya, Mother and Dad. Stoical Mother usually refused to cry. But she was weeping and as Brenda put her arms around Dad, she felt a shock. His body, always so strong and firm, felt flaccid as a sack of flour.

"Dad, I'll write often and Ted will be coming–"

"But I won't have my Brenda."

He shook his head and it hit her that maybe this was a last goodbye.

"Come on, Brenda," Brad called impatiently.

She stumbled into the car and as she looked back, knew that leaving them was wrong. She felt that somehow she was going to be punished for this.

Brad noticed her sadness and as he started up the motor, said, "Cheer up, Foxy. We've got things to do in the world, you and I."

The first few days were pleasant, the weather brisk and clear. The farmhouses of Ohio looked cozy, tucked up for winter, smoke coming from their chimneys.

Brad hummed and smoked his pipe, in good spirits, no doubt glad to see Brenda away from Mother, glad for a change of duty. And she soon got to know what a driven soul he was, how he pushed himself to the limit and drove everyone around him.

On the third day, she noticed he was driving faster.

"What's the hurry?" she asked. "We have ten days."

"I've decided to do it in seven. I may be needed at the base."

She saw he was bored. He needed the excitement of speed, the challenge to make it in seven days. In the towns, he'd go full tilt and slam on the brakes when anything obstructed him. Her foot was on an imaginary brake pedal most of the time.

When she protested, it aggravated him.

"I'm doing the driving," he snapped. "Your job is to read the map." He added sarcastically, "That is, if you think you can."

She quivered with anger but kept her mouth shut. She figured if she didn't, he'd get them into an accident.

One evening, as they pulled into the motel, she said, "I want my own room tonight."

"Why?"

"Your snoring keeps me awake. I don't feel well."

"What's the matter with you?"

"I don't know. I feel sick."

He considered her.

"I think it's all in your head."

She said angrily, "I know how I feel."

He gave her a funny look. "My mother would get you over that sickness in a hurry."

"What's she got to do with it?"

"We didn't believe in sickness in our family. She wouldn't put up with neurotic behavior. That was one good thing about her."

"You think I'm being neurotic?"

"You don't hurt anyplace, do you? You didn't break any bones?"

"Oh shit," she said.

He smiled. "That's better. That brought a little color to your cheeks."

She snapped, "Neurotic or not, I want a room to myself."

Surprisingly, he smiled.

"All right, Foxy, if that's what you want."

'You devil,' she thought. He seemed to enjoy it when she asserted herself. He seemed to thrive on strife.

In Kansas it began to snow, heavy flakes, which piled up in drifts. The roads were slippery and the car skidded from side to side, but Brad kept up the fast pace. He seemed to enjoy the danger.

One evening, they passed a car that had slid into a ditch and was tilted on its side. A man and a woman were sitting in it.

Brad pulled up and rolled down his window.

"Any broken bones?" he shouted, his favorite phrase.

The people stared back looking dazed. The woman had a bloody gash on her forehead.

"Hold on, I'll send help," Brad shouted and drove on.

"Couldn't you have done something for them?" Brenda said. "They could freeze to death sitting there."

"Any suggestions? The back seats are full of luggage. I suppose I could have put them on the roof." His tone was sarcastic.

She kept quiet. She felt he could have helped them somehow. He did stop at a gas station miles further on to report people in distress.

As the nightmare trip continued, her nerves were stretched tight. With his bad temper, her grievances grew. She knew now she could never stay with him. He would never change. Sometimes she thought she couldn't last out this trip. But she had only a few dollars with her. Hitchhiking? Forget it. Out here in this weather, people froze to death. Phone the family to telegraph money? He was with her every minute. That would really make him roar.

'Hang in there,' she told herself. 'Your time to cut out will come.'

It came sooner than she thought.

When they reached the Grand Canyon, the snow was left behind and with this, Brad's bad temper seemed to evaporate. They had made it this far in six days and that pleased him. It was dark when they arrived at the hotel on the edge of the canyon. She could not see it but felt keyed up, sensing the awesome presence of the great primeval pit. For some reason, Brenda felt a sense of foreboding. She could not seem to shake it off. She sometimes had such feelings, but they usually came to nothing. It was just that ghastly trip had her on edge.

At dinner, Brad noticed.

"What's the matter, Foxy?"

"I don't know. I have a feeling something's wrong–"

He laughed. He was on his second drink and feeling no pain.

Foxy with her wonderful imagination. What could be wrong? "What you need is a drink." His solution for everything.

Then, after dinner, the phone rang in their room. She answered to hear Ted's voice.

"Brenda–"

She held her breath. She knew but didn't want to know what he was going to say.

"How did you know we were here?"

"The itinerary you left. I took a chance." He paused. "It's Dad," his voice broke. "He's gone–at breakfast. He just slumped over, a cerebral hemorrhage–"

She felt faint. She'd known she would never see him again.

Brad hovered anxiously. "What is it, Brenda?"

Ted said, "Mother wants you to come home for the funeral. We'll wait. Can you come?"

"I'll come."

"Wire what train. I'll meet you."

"Yes."

She hung up. Brad was staring at her, a beer in his hand.

"Dad died," she said. "I'm going back."

Brad put down his drink, crossed the room and put his arms around her. She smelled the beer and pulled away.

"Brad, I'm going back."

He patted her. That released the tears.

"I'm sorry," he said. "I know what he meant to you. I know how you feel."

'Do you?' she thought bitterly, 'hard as you are?'

But he'd liked Dad. Maybe he was sorry.

"Of course you must go," he said. "Lie down and rest. I'll take care of everything."

He couldn't have been more kindly and consoling. Yes, she was married to two people. It seemed he needed some crisis to bring out his best.

During the trip back, she was hardly aware of anything, dwelling in a kind of numb suspension, putting off the time when she would have to face up to her grief.

There must be some mistake. Dad couldn't be gone. She'd find him there, waiting for her.

But he wasn't there.

It had only been a few days since she left; yet all was changed. Grief had moved in. It filled the space where Dad should have been. In the hallway, she seemed to hear his voice. "Welcome home, bride."

They were waiting for her in the parlor: Mother, Aya, Jancy. Their faces seemed to yearn to her as if she had the answer they wanted.

A hurt cry burst from her as she ran to Mother's arms.

Mother looked strange in black. Its darkness seemed to extinguish her. Perhaps she had wept too much. Now she was calm.

"Dear, I'm glad you've come," she said.

Brenda thought, 'I will never leave you again.'

Mother and Ted led her to Dad's room. He lay in Great Grandfather's beautiful old bed. He looked like a statue of himself. Peaceful. She wondered at the reserve and dignity of death, passion emptied, the heart of silence. Had they put a tinge of rouge on his cheekbones? She wanted to rub it off. She touched his brow with her lips. Its' cold seemed to sink into her marrow. She touched his silky beard with her fingertips and bent to it. The clean scent of Dad lingered there. She turned away from this copy of him and shook with grief, as she felt something drain out of her.

She knew it would never be the same.

Letters of condolence had been answered and Dad's will settled. Now Mother was ready to get on with her greenhouse and piano.

But she was changed, more withdrawn. She kept her sorrow to herself, but grief had left its imprint, little lines around her eyes and mouth. She still continued to apply her creams and lotions, and Brenda wondered for whom she took such pains to stay beautiful. There would certainly never be another man in her life. Perhaps it was just a habit, a matter of pride.

Since Dad's death, Aya and Mother would sit in Dad's study in the evening and listen to the war news as they sewed. Brenda supposed this comforted them. They had both loved him. His two widows.

Several weeks passed and Brenda made no move to go. She wasn't about to tell Mother of her projected break with Brad. At this point, she couldn't have borne her, "I told you so. I told you he was a mean man."

Once Mother asked. "Do you plan to go West, Brenda?"

She replied vaguely, "Brad's looking for an apartment. Things are crowded out there with the war on."

Mother said no more, but Brenda got the message. Shrewd Mother. She'd probably guessed the truth and believed her child had come back to her to stay.

But how hard it would be to come back to that closed little world of women again.

Brad wrote brief notes saying he was terribly busy. He hoped to find a place for them to live soon. He always ended, "I miss you. I love you, Brenda."

She tried writing to say that their marriage was no good and she wanted out. But it seemed too cold-blooded with the war waiting to gobble him up. So, she only wrote that she was still needed here. She seemed to be existing in a hiatus of numbness and inaction.

Then action came from an unexpected source. She had a letter from the publisher. How was she getting along with 'Refugee'? The subject was timely and they would like to publish it.

This was great! For the moment, it seemed 'Refugee' was to solve her problems. She had a good excuse to stay put and write.

Elated at the sudden widening of her horizons, her confidence returned. She seemed to see the direction her life would take now.

She decided to write Brad the "Dear John" letter when she received one from him.

"Dear Brenda, I'm going to be leaving for the war zone in a week. Could you possibly come out for a couple of days because God knows when I will ever see you again. I think you will like it here. The weather's great and it's an exciting place to be. Parties, friends meeting and separating, trying to forget they may not meet again. Please come. I need you so much. With you beside me, I cannot fail in my duty to serve my country."

Her first reaction was, 'I'll be damned if I'm going out there to get beat over the head. Here he comes with his challenge. Calling on me to be his strong woman. Well, have another think. He should know by now that pampered Brenda can't fill that bill.'

Then, she felt ashamed. How selfish could she get? He was going out to get shot at. And what about that "Who knows when I'll ever see you again."

To her surprise, Mother said, "Of course you must go, Brenda. You must stand by him and do the right thing."

In Mother's novels, the heroine always did the right thing.

Mother added, "You need to only go for a few days. But it seems to mean so much to him."

Brenda got to thinking, what would it cost her to go? Clever Brad had to put in the part about the parties and excitement. He knew how she loved all that. And how good it would be to be warm for a few days and to get away from this world of women.

It occurred to her that he would expect her to sleep with him. Sometimes it wasn't all that bad. And if you wanted to be down right cynical about it, let's say it would be her contribution to the war effort.

That really did sound hard boiled, but if she was getting that way, he was doing it to her.

# CHAPTER 21

▼

# IF ANYTHING HAPPENS TO ME

Brad, handsome in his Navy blues, strode down the platform to meet her. She thought of the unhappiness he gave her. So, why was she glad to see him? Had these few weeks so dulled the memory of that miserable trip?

"I was afraid you wouldn't come," he said. "You sounded so uncertain. But you're here. I've needed you so much."

His eyes searched her lovingly.

She thought, yes, he needed her. Who else did he have but naïve and forgiving Foxy? Who else would put up with what he dished out? If only he could control the drinking and that wild temper.

He was full of enthusiasm about his plans.

"I only have two days, so let's make 'em good ones. We're booked into the famous Del Coronada Hotel. Nothing but the best for my girl."

As they drove to the hotel, brilliant flowers smote her eyes used to the muted wintry shades of the East.

"So what have you been up to, Foxy?" he asked.

"The usual. Dancing, of course."

"Good. I know how you love it." He stopped. "If anything ever happens to me, you'll always have that—"

She was startled. "What could happen?"

"Don't look so worried. Nothing will. Your old man's tough. Now I've got some news. A bit of luck."

He told her Bobby Ashton, a classmate, was being transferred and had offered to rent them his house on the bay. She could stay there while he was away.

"We're meeting the Ashtons for dinner to talk about it. You'll like Lillian. She used to be in show business."

He wanted a drink to celebrate her arrival and lead her to the bar in the hotel. This was buzzing with activity. The Navy husbands and wives were here for a few days before being separated for who knew how long. Brad introduced her around. He was in his element of being near the action. And after her recent shut in life, she found she was enjoying the excitement, the war talk, the jokes. There was talk of a Japanese invasion of the West Coast. Everyone was here with a wild effort to enjoy. Who knew who was next on the list to go down with a ship or get shot out of the sky?

Brad ordered them Martinis. Brenda should have known better. 'Oh, what the hell,' she thought. 'Let's try to relax, have fun.'

"Here's to the love of my life," Brad said.

As the Martinis slid down, Brenda pondered what about her did he love: her so-called talents, her air of sophistication, her Main Line credentials? No, it was Foxy he loved, that immature, insecure kid. That's what appealed to him. Being insecure himself about women, under all that manliness and bravery, he could handle the raw material of Foxy. Just as he made fighting material out of unformed men, he would take that little Main Line Maverick and, yes, make her over the way he wanted her. It was a new challenge, something to overcome. She might struggle, but he would win.

Brad had taken a suite and after lunch, led her upstairs. The rooms were charming, all chintz and white wicker. There was a small bar on which she noted Brad had placed a bottle of whiskey. There was a double bed.

'So what?' she thought, recklessly.

"I'm sleepy," Brad said. "How about a nap?"

She hadn't slept on the train and was feeling bushed.

"I could stand one."

Passive with Martinis, she allowed him to lead her to the bed. While he was undressing, then removing her blouse and skirt, a Martinis-ridden dialogue was taking place in her head.

"Why are you doing this?"

"He's my husband. He's going to get shot at. It's the least I can do."

"You damned idiot. You don't owe him."

"He loves me."

"But you don't love him."

"You can't have everything."

Brad had a beautiful body, slender and strong with muscles in the right places. He was clean, good smelling and his skin was soft as a woman's. As he stroked her, she began to come unstrung.

As a lover, he was a great aviator, but she thought his lovemaking had improved. She wondered if he'd been getting some practice. Not if she knew him, straight arrow Brad.

His laboring breath and muttered exclamations were distracting as he went to work. But the liquor helped and she found she was able to respond a brief, not unpleasant spasm, while he went all out in a roaring finale.

She thought about how wonderful this might be if one were really in love.

As she was about to fall asleep with the soothing rustle of the sea in her ears, she thought, 'This isn't half bad.' Then another thought struck her.

'Oh God, I forgot my diaphragm!'

She rolled away from him.

"Something wrong?" he murmured.

"I hope not."

The Ashtons arrived on schedule. Lillian was blonde, too blonde. She wore too much makeup, even the false eyelashes. She had a fantastic front and talked with a kind of pseudo-Southern accent. Yes, she'd been in show business, a dancer in Las Vegas.

"Just for kicks, ya know, darlin'," she proclaimed. "Course ma family's from Virginia. Huntin' country, ya know."

Shades of Betsy Fulsome! Was this type to dog her through life? Brenda wondered. She could bet Lillian's family was from the hill country of Paduca, Kentucky.

In the crowded hotel bar, the Ashtons ordered Martinis. Brenda's luncheon Martinis had left her with a raging headache. Just the thought of them made her ill. To be sociable, she had a Scotch and soda and prayed the evening would end early.

Lillian wriggled out of her mink jacket, saying, "Isn't it a dream, darlins? Little ole' Bobby gave it to me for ma birthday, the sweet thang."

She gave little ole' Bobby's hand a squeeze.

"But then, he is a darlin'."

Her false eyelashes fluttered in Brad's direction.

"Lil' ole' Braddy's a darlin', too. I've known him since Naval Academy days. In fact, he and I had a little thing goin' at one time, that is, till my great, big, sexy Bobby came along."

Brenda wondered if she expected her to be elated at this news.

Big, sexy Bobby was good-looking in a chiseled profile way. He had an aggressive chin and thin lips, and he was silent. But none of them stood a chance with Lil rattling on. When Bobby and Braddy started war talk between them, Brenda was left at Lil's mercy.

"Darlin', I've just been dyin' to meet ya. I hear you're from the Main Line. I have friends there, haven't seen 'em in ages, but I visited their lovely estate once."

"Where was that?"

She looked vague. "Somewhere out near Bryn Mawr. I sort'a forget. Anyhow, you're gonna just love livin' in our little cottage by the sea. It's small but charmin'. I just hate to leave it, but ah know you'll take wonderful care of it." She sipped her drink delicately. Brenda took a gulp of Scotch.

"I'm sure you're just gonna love it here. We got a wonderful bunch of girls in our wives' club, good bridge team goin' and we play lots of tennis and we got a big bake sale comin' next week. You're just gonna love it, honey."

'Will you shut up?' Brenda thought. 'You're silly and pretentious and I hope I don't have to see you again.'

But she managed to keep a smile glued on through the evening. While they tanked up on wine, liqueurs and started the Scotch again, Brenda sipped soda water and conjectured on the state of their livers. Lil gave out with some raunchy jokes, of which she seemed to have an endless supply. The more the men drank, the more they talked about the war and the people they knew who had just taken off and returned, and those who hadn't returned. Lil entered into the conversation. She knew all the people. Brenda knew none of them. As she listened, it occurred to her that Brad would be much happier with someone like Lillian, who would drink with him and give him the kind of sex he wanted, frequent, vigorous and unburdened by the panty-waist notions of romantic Foxy, like being kissed and gentled into love.

At last the ordeal of the evening was over.

"Got to turn in early," Brad said. "Got an early flight in the morning."

They shook hands. Lillian gave Braddy a big buss on the mouth and they said they would get together soon. 'Not me, coach,' Brenda thought. 'I'll be long gone from here.' No way was she going to move into Lil's little cottage by the sea and get mixed up with the bake sale crowd.

By now her headache was raging. All she wanted to do was flop in bed. But Brad, who hadn't stopped drinking all evening, seemed prepared to keep on. In the living room of the suite, he took a can of beer out of the refrigerator and gulped it, then took off his jacket and lounged back on the sofa.

"How did you like the Ashtons?"

"Okay."

"You don't sound too enthusiastic."

"I'm just tired."

"Bobby is one of my oldest friends. We roomed together at the Naval Academy."

"Oh."

He glanced at her and took another gulp of beer.

"How about a night cap?"

"No thanks. I've had enough for one day."

She felt like saying, 'And you have, too,' but knew what that would bring forth.

She opened her suitcase, took a few things out and prepared to take them into the bedroom. Brad kept working on the beer. She thought, 'Oh God, do I have to smell that stink all night?'

She felt him watching her.

He said, "I thought you'd like Lillian."

"Oh, she's all right. Kind of—oh, I don't know—a bit much."

"How do you mean that?"

"I don't know. I guess she's not exactly my type."

"And what exactly is your type?"

His note of sarcasm irritated her. She couldn't resist saying, "You seem to be her type. She was all over you like a tent."

He grinned. "Lil does like the boys and they like her."

"Goody, goody."

She started for the bedroom to change into nightclothes.

His words stopped her.

"Not jealous of her, are you?"

This really did it. She snapped. "Me jealous of that bleached blonde feather brain? She's a typical service wife."

It just slipped out.

His eyes narrowed.

"Maybe the typical service wife has something you lack."

"What's that supposed to mean?"

"The guts to stand by her man when everything goes wrong."

"You think I lack that?"

He finished the beer, chucked the can in the waste bucket and went to the refrigerator for another. She noted his unsteady walk and thought, 'Watch it, this could get out of hand.'

He opened the can, took a swig and flopped down on the sofa again.

"Let me give you an example."

Brenda's feet were killing her. She was groggy. She hoped this example would be short and sweet.

He said, "A few years ago, Bob cracked up a plane. There was talk of negligence on his part. There was a trial, long, drawn out and nasty. Lillian stuck by him and finally, he was proved innocent."

"I'm glad."

She started for the bathroom. 'Please let him finish his drink and go quietly to bed,' she prayed.

"Foxy–"

She turned. He'd gotten to his feet and was standing in the middle of the room, swaying slightly. His expression was kind of sad, pathetic, lonely-looking.

"Come on, have a drink with me."

She said, "Really Brad, I'm bushed. Couldn't we call it a day? You say you have an early flight. You shouldn't drink anymore either."

The switch from pathetic little boy to snarling drunk was instantaneous.

"Oh, don't be such an old maid," he barked. "Why don't you relax and drink with me like a real woman?"

"I don't want to get drunk with you," she muttered.

"Old Carrie Nation," he sneered. "Boy, you're really a sour one."

He crossed the room and held out his beer can to her.

"Come on, drink."

She felt her temper leap.

"I'll be damned if I will. In fact, at this point, I'm beginning to–"

His eyes had a hard glint.

"To what?"

"To be sorry I came."

It slipped out, and why not? Why shouldn't she say what she thought? Why should she always have to hold back?

"Sure," he snapped. "Sure you're sorry you came. I knew you didn't want to come."

"No, I didn't. Who could blame me after the way you treated me on that trip?"

"That's just an excuse. The real reason is you don't give a damn about me. The whole truth is, you look down on me. I'm not good enough for you."

"What rot."

"The truth is you're a spoiled Main Line snob, while I'm just a Kansas hick. That's what's behind it all. The truth is, you just can't stand me. Well, you shouldn't have married me then!"

He was shouting now. She was backing away as he advanced, towering over her, his face twisting with drunken hatred. And a burst of newfound hatred rose up in her.

She flung the words at him. "I wish to hell I hadn't!"

"What did you say?"

"I wish I–"

The hand came back and slammed a good one across her cheek.

She spoke through clenched teeth.

"I told myself that if you ever did that to me again, I'd–"

He hurled the beer can to the floor and grabbed her wrists.

"You'd what?"

"I'd leave you."

The brutal strength of his big hands wrenched a gasp out of her.

"You won't leave me," he said. "You're afraid to. But maybe you want to look for someone else. Is that it? Well, forget it. You belong to me and don't think you can ever get away."

She tried to pull away, but the punishing grip tightened more. Was this the beloved of Dad and Mother, Ted and Aya, being subjected to this hideous treatment? Sure, she had faults, but she deserved better than this.

"You're a coward," he sneered. "You're afraid of everything."

She was petrified by the wild drunken glitter in his eyes. But she mustn't show fear. That's what he wanted. But suppose those punishing hands went around her throat?

"You're a coward," he repeated.

"I'll show you if I'm a coward," she blustered.

"You will, will you? All right, show me. Go running back to the dear old Main Line and Mama. She'll be happy to have you at her beck and call. Go on!"

"I don't have to."

"No? What will you do then?"

"Never mind what I'll do."

"You don't know what to do, you poor little sniveling rat!"

He threw her away from him and grabbed his jacket.

"To tell you the truth, I don't care what you do. Just stay out of my way."

"Don't worry, I will. This is the last you'll see of me."

"Good riddance! If any one wants me, I'll be at the B.O.Q.–drinking!"

He wrenched open the door and slammed it after him.

Exhausted, she'd fallen asleep and it was about noon when she awoke and dragged herself out of bed. She stared out the window at the beautiful impassive sea sparkling in the sunlight. It looked unreal and alien, as did this luxurious room. How she longed for the richness of trees and brown earth, and even the bleak snow of the East.

She felt a surge of panic. She must get away from here–Now!

It was an effort to dress and pack, but she finally made it and went to the dining room, feeling weak and without appetite. But heeding Mother's advice to "always eat well and keep up your strength," she ordered bacon and eggs. And in the attractive setting, amid the cheerful rattle of dishes and conversation, tried to collect her muddled thoughts.

Face it. This was it. There was no turning back. She'd married some kind of mad man and the sooner she got herself on a train for home, the better. Luckily, she had some money and a return ticket. But making the arrangements seemed like such an effort. She was used to having everything done for her. Now she was on her own and better get used to it.

With the comfort of coffee, her spirits rose. She thought of her slight success with 'Refugee.' Maybe she could still make it as a writer. Then she would be independent of Mother and Brad, and could make it on her own.

She was waiting for her bill when the waiter came and said she was wanted on the phone.

Her heart lurched. Brad, of course.

"Did the person say who it was?"

"A Navy Commander." He added, "He said it's an emergency."

Yes, Brad sobered up and was coming on with more of his brandishments. He figured she was in no mood to talk to him, so had dreamed up this "emergency" to get her to the phone.

But how could she not answer? Suppose it really was an emergency, something wrong at home.

She picked up the phone in the lobby.

"Mrs. Colton?" It was an unfamiliar voice.

"Yes."

The impersonal voice said, "This is Lieutenant Commander Ellis. I'm calling from Camp Callen. Your husband has been involved in an accident here."

She felt a twinge of fear.

"An accident…"

"The aircraft he was testing had to make a forced landing. He's had a nasty blow on the head." He paused. "We thought you would want to come out here."

She said nothing.

"Mrs. Colton?"

"Yes, I'm here."

"We will send an official car to pick you up in about twenty minutes. Mrs. Ashton will go with you."

Mrs. Ashton? How in the world did the Navy know she was the only person she knew here? It was sounding more and more like some kind of hoax. In her confused state, Lillian Ashton was the last person she wanted to see.

She said nothing. The clipped voice came in again.

"Mrs. Colton, I know you've had a shock. Did you understand me?"

"Yes, I'll be ready."

As she waited on the wide, old-fashioned porch of the hotel, sitting in the white wicker rocker among the other chair rockers on this bright, vivid, sea-sparkling California day, wild thoughts surged.

If Brad really had cracked up a plane and it wasn't some kind of a Navy joke, could he have done it on purpose to make her feel rotten? To bring Foxy to heel, to make her relent?

She ruled this out. No, Brad would never let down his beloved Navy to such an extent as to smash up an expensive plane just to spite her. More likely, his wild night of drinking and fighting with her had messed him up, so during the flight, he'd made some fatal error and come to grief. Damn his drinking and damn that silly Lillian who had kicked off the fight between them!

'Cool it,' she thought. 'Maybe it's nothing.'

But when the official station wagon and driver in uniform drew up and Lillian got out saying, "Brenda, I'm so sorry," she knew it was no hoax.

"How did you know?"

"Bobby called me. He's going to meet us out there."

The night of drinking hadn't helped Lillian either. Under her heavy makeup her face looked drawn and tired and her Southern belle effusions seemed to have deserted her.

"Is it–bad?" Brenda asked.

"They don't know yet. He's lost a lot of blood. But Brad's a fighter. He'll come through it okay."

She helped Brenda into the car and sat by her as they started off.

She searched Brenda's face. "Are you all right?"

Brenda knew she looked a mess. She hadn't even bothered to put on lipstick. Her stomach was churning and she felt cold.

Lillian put her hand over Brenda's.

"I've been through this. I know what you're feeling."

Brenda thought she couldn't possibly know. Guilt is what she was feeling. Couldn't she have handled the evening better? When she knew he had the important test, couldn't she have avoided fighting with him, prevented his drinking so much, even shared that beer with him? She'd only been thinking of herself, how tired she was. Now he was lying out there, smashed up, losing blood, maybe–.

Lillian's comforting hand remained on hers. Her words were kind. She'd thought her silly. She was the silly one. These Navy people were strong and loyal. They took care of their own. Right now she was one of their own.

Callen, near La Jolla, was an army camp that had sprung up during the war. It stood on a bluff above the ocean, a bleak-looking military installation with several brown barracks-like buildings and a small parade ground. From a distance, Brenda saw the plane. It seemed to be wrapped around a telegraph pole. One wing was completely torn off, and there wasn't much left of the rest of it. She felt sick. How could anyone have survived that wreck? She remembered this was where Brad said he'd had the near crash before. Not so lucky this time.

Lillian led her into the small hospital and went to confer with the nurse at the desk.

While she sat in the waiting room, a young J.G. who had apparently witnessed the crash sat near her. He was all excited, talking to another officer about it.

"Never saw anything like it," he said. "I was about to go into the barracks when I saw this plane circling the parade ground and rapidly losing altitude. I thought the prop must have failed and that the pilot had probably tried to land at the Del Mar racetrack. It's been done before. But the track's torn up for repairs. So he headed for Callen and the parade ground, hoping to land there. But he was too low to avoid hitting the barracks and the hospital. He knew the men would be inside the barracks having noon chow. I guess he made the decision then to crash land the best he could, to come across the road and hit the telegraph pole with his right wing. The impact would swing the plane around and avoid killing a lot of people and he might survive." He paused. "He played it right, came in on target, hitting the pole and swinging the plane around. Amazingly, the cockpit remained intact. But in the crash his head must have taken a hard blow and his metal goggles had snapped and dug him in the face. Really messed him up. But he was cool. Blood gushing from his head, he pushed back the hood, climbed out and lay on the ground. Of course everyone rushed out of the barracks to help, myself among them."

"'Stand back,' he ordered. 'Don't touch me. I'm going into shock.' He then looked up at me through bloodied eyes and said, 'Lieutenant, get a stretcher and get me on the operating table on the double.' Then he passed out."

He paused. "So cool. I never saw anything like it. I guess he planned the hospital bit too. Talk about nerve. Man, he's got that."

"Sure," the other officer said. "He's Brad Colton. Never heard of him? He's the Navy's ace test pilot."

The Lieutenant said, "It's a damn shame. Looks like he's had it."

"You mean—"

He shrugged.

The men suddenly noticed Brenda.

"You okay, Ma'am?" the J.G. asked. "You look real bad. I'm sorry, did I—I mean, are you a relative or something?"

She shook her head.

Lillian came with the nurse and they led her into the small room. A white-coated doctor stood by the cot on which Brad lay. There was a suspended plasma jar and a tube with the needle inserted in Brad's arm. His head was bandaged and there was a bandage around his throat. His face was white as the sheet, which covered him, and his mouth looked oddly twisted.

Her knees started to give. Yes, she was to blame. She could have prevented this.

Lillian's arm came around her. "Steady."

Brenda looked at the young doctor's tired, kindly face.

"How–is he?"

The doctor spoke measuredly. "He's had a nasty blow on the head and lost a lot of blood. We don't know how severe the injury. Are you his wife?"

She nodded.

"He's been asking for you."

Brad moved his head. His eyes opened and searched her face.

"Hello, Foxy." It was very faint.

His hand reached out. She took it. It was cold. Cold. He seemed to struggle for breath. She bent down. His twisted mouth formed the words, "I love you, Foxy." His eyes closed.

She gasped. "Brad, Brad–" She felt a rush of tears.

Lillian led her from the room. The doctor followed.

"I'm sorry, Mrs. Colton," he said. "It's a tough break."

She faltered. "You don't think–he's going to make it?"

"He's a strong man. But we'll just have to wait and see."

# CHAPTER 22

▼

# NOT THIS TIME

Brad made it and Brenda stayed with him. Sometimes she wondered why. Was it because he needed her and loved her so much? She knew he did, and there were times of compatibility, even happiness. But times of terrible stress.

She soon learned more of his fierce temper and that it only took some little thing to light his rage. The outbursts usually happened when he was drinking. And when he went out of control, he couldn't stop. He needed help, but the one time she suggested it, he flew into such a rage, she ran and locked herself in the bathroom.

She reasoned that his brutal childhood plus the harsh disciplines of military life had worked deep repressions in him, which had to burst out. And liquor was the catalyst that released the violent flood.

And, of course, drinking was expected of any officer and gentleman in the Navy.

They'd been stationed in San Diego near the Naval Hospital where Brad was receiving treatments for his injured eye. They needed the money so he continued to get in his flight time. He seemed in good health except for an occasional attack of what he called asthma. When this happened, he would grow pale, breathe heavily and have to lie down. Brenda was sure he never reported the attacks to the Navy and he seemed to come through the physical exams without incident. He now wore a black eye patch over his wounded eye, which gave him the look of a dashing pirate.

Mother wrote often. When was Brenda coming home? She was lonely, getting old and her arthritis was worse. And Brenda longed for the peace and beauty of Upsan Downs.

She was delighted when Brad announced one day, "Get packed, Foxy. We're going East. I'm due for surgery at the Bethesda Naval Hospital next week. You can stay home with your Mother."

It was wonderful to be home, to sleep in her own bed, to listen to the trees murmuring outside her window. Brad came to Upsan Downs on weekends and he and Mother seemed to be getting along. But Brenda was always apprehensive. She prayed there wouldn't be trouble between them.

But one day it came.

It was Mother's birthday and Brad had brought her a lovely gift, a silver bowl. Jancy outdid herself with roast duck and baked Alaska. And Brad, in the mellow part of his drinking, made an effort to be charming to Mother, drinking her toasts in sherry wine, the only drink she allowed. Mother was pleasant, and Brenda hoped she was softening to him.

After dinner they went to the terrace for coffee. It was cool, and Brenda went up to Mother's room for a shawl. Hearing voices from the terrace, she went to the window and looked down. Mother and Brad were sitting together, Brad drinking out of a large tumbler.

Brenda heard him say, "By the way, Mom, last time I was here I put up some curtains in the basement. I thought that little room down there would make a good darkroom."

Brad had showed some talent for photography and to please Brenda, was working at it to show he could be an artist, too.

There was a silence, then Mother said, "You mean you've already fixed it up to suit yourself?"

"I didn't think you'd mind."

"Well, I do. It's hard enough to keep up this place. But I guess it's all right as long as you don't make a mess."

"What kind of mess?"

There was an edge to Brad's voice.

"Oh, dragging in a lot of trash."

"I don't plan to drag in a lot of trash," he said sharply. "All I've done is to put up some curtains."

"The girls have all they can do to–"

"Oh, for God's sake!" he exploded. "Forget the whole thing! I won't do it then!"

"I think it's best."

Brenda saw him drain his glass then put it down on the table. He got up slow and unsteadily and stood over her Mother. Brenda had seen that look so often when the mellow phase had passed and the going out of control was taking over. She felt a twinge of fear and knew she should run down and intervene. But she stood, fascinated, seeming unable to move. It was like a scene in a play.

She heard him say, "You know what I think? I think you're a selfish pampered woman. You've always had everything your way and you've done a lot to ruin your daughter's life."

Mother looked up at him. Brenda saw her profile, hard as iron.

"What do you mean?"

"Just that."

She got to her feet with difficulty because of her arthritic knees. But there was no weakness in her voice.

"If anyone's ruined my daughter's life, it's you, with your drinking and bad temper and the rest."

"My drinking is my business," he barked.

"And my daughter's happiness is my business and it's obvious she's not happy with you. I knew you were wrong for her the moment I saw you. You've brutalized her until she can't hold up her head. You're a miserable man."

He said furiously, "I don't have to listen to this!"

"Well, go on then!" Mother shrilled. "Get out! Get out of my house!"

"I'll go when I get damn good and ready!" he bellowed and raised his fist.

Brenda plunged down the stairs and ran out to the terrace.

They were still in the same position as if posed for a tableau. His fist upraised, their bodies close, rigid with anger. Mother's face was very red; Brad's very white.

"What is this?" Brenda yelled. "What are you doing? Brad, stop it! Stop it!"

Brad lowered his fist. He spoke through clenched teeth.

"Brenda, I want you to go out and get in the car. We're getting out of here."

Mother swerved around. "Brenda, you're not to go with this man. Are you his slave?"

"More like your slave!" Brad clamored.

His eyes, with their wild glint, fastened on Brenda. "Get out to the car, do you hear me?"

Brenda's heart was pounding. The words jerked out of her. "Yes, I hear you. I hear both of you."

"Well, get the hell to the car!"

"Don't you do it!" Mother was screaming. "I'll never speak to you again!"

His voice cut in. "She's my wife, old woman. She belongs to me. You're trying to break us up. You've been trying to for years and–"

What fire there was in that seventy-seven year old body! She flew at him. He grabbed her wrists.

"Please! Please!" Brenda pleaded.

They didn't hear her, so intent they were on hating each other. What did they care about her, and that they were grinding her to pieces between them? It occurred to her that they were actually enjoying their dramatic scene. No, they were not for one minute considering her. Why should she consider them? Where was the maverick spirit she'd once had? Was it gone? Was she just a passive wimp, letting people push her around?

Hell no! Not this time!

As if something had come unlocked inside and was propelling her, she moved away from them. She went into the house and up to her old room. She threw a few things in a small bag then went downstairs, opened the back door and closed it silently behind her, and walked down the back hill to the train station. Fortunately, a train for town was just pulling in. She got on it.

The next morning she called Mother from the hotel.

Mother sounded frantic.

"Brenda! Where have you been? Brad and I have been so worried."

Oh, we were so worried, were we? United, for once, in worry were they?

"Are you all right?"

"Yes, fine."

"Where are you?"

"At the Bellevue."

"The Bellevue! You mean you've been staying there?"

"That's right."

"How could you do this to us?"

"How couldn't I?"

"What do you mean?"

"You'll never know, I guess."

"I was going to call the police, but Brad said to wait. He was sure you were all right."

Oh he was, was he?

"Now, Brenda, I want you to come right home, do you hear? You've had me worried sick. Poor Brad had to go back to Bethesda Hospital for a few days. He said to call him the minute I heard from you, which I will do. I couldn't understand him. He said, 'So, Foxy is finally declaring her independence. Bravo!' What did he mean?"

'You'll never know,' Brenda thought grimly.

"I'll be home later," she said.

"I hope you're not running up a big hotel bill."

"Don't worry, I'll pay it."

"With what? You don't have any money."

"Don't worry," she said. "And now I'm going to the movies."

"Movies!"

"Yes, the Marx Brothers. I need a good laugh."

"Really, Brenda. I don't understand you. And here I've been so–"

"Goodbye, Mother. I'll be home for dinner. Please tell Brad even a sniveling rat can eventually bite back."

She hung up and called Jordan Kirsh.

Jordan took her to lunch at the Bellevue.

She told him she wanted a divorce.

The sleepy blue eyes regarded her seriously.

"I thought this would happen sooner. You two were always completely mismatched."

"I can't stand it anymore. He's a good man in many ways but–"

"He drinks?"

"A lot."

"Has he struck you?"

"Yes."

He shook his head, his face distressed. "Beautiful, talented Brenda. What a waste. Your father would turn over in his grave."

"I think he has flipped over a couple of times by now."

"But why didn't you leave him?"

"I suppose I was afraid of him. He's frightening when he drinks. He vowed he would never let me go and with his violence–"

"The bastard," he muttered.

"I was sorry for him. Poor Brad, he's his own worst enemy. He suffers a lot since his accident and won't slow down. He's not well, been having these attacks. I think it's his heart. I've tried to persuade him to tell his doctor, but he just gets angry at me for even suggesting it."

Jordan put his hand over hers. "Dear Brenda, too caring, too sensitive, too loving."

Brenda felt a rush of tears and held them in. Sympathy she could not stand at this point. She also sensed that Jordan, esthete that he was, shied away from emotional outbursts. To him, the romantic Russian Jew, a woman should always be beautiful, dignified and unattainable. 'Touch me not' was Jordan Kirsh, bachelor, worldly, sophisticated and most decent. Always helping others but never wanting to be helped to live fully himself. He skirted the edge of life. At that moment, Brenda was glad she had never fallen in love with him. Many women had. It must have been like trying to grasp sea spume.

The blue eyes studied her.

"Do you still care for Brad?"

"No. I don't know. It's all mixed up."

"Women are funny creatures, their loyalties, the amount they can stand. I've gotten a lot of them divorces and I guess I'll never understand them." He paused. "Are you sure about this? I've had women change their minds at the last minute. It's not easy to break up a marriage."

"I think I know better than most. Yes, I'm sure about it."

Again the eyes studied her.

"How old are you now, Brenda?"

"Almost forty, I blush to admit."

"Different from the little girl in the Russian boots I once had lunch with here."

"Yes, so long ago."

"You haven't changed. You're still beautiful."

"That's debatable."

"More so. Your beauty has deepened. Suffering sometimes does that to a woman. It's not too late for you to make another life."

A little smile constricted her mouth.

"I'm glad to hear that."

"Very well," he said. "I'll handle it for you. Where is Brad now?"

"In Bethesda. But you could write him at the Navy Department."

"I'll take care of it."

"Thank you."

He raised her hand to his lips.

As soon as Brad received Jordan's letter, he was on the phone.

"I'm coming up."

"Please don't. I don't want to see you. I've made up my mind. It's over."

"Why?"

"You know why. Too many reasons to count."

"I'm coming up."

"No. It won't do any good."

"I'm coming," he repeated.

She hung up.

# CHAPTER 23

# THE LONG WALK TO GOODBYE

Brad arrived at eleven o'clock that night. Mother and Aya had gone to bed. When Brenda heard the car drive up, she had a dreadful foreboding. He was probably drunk. God knows what he'll do.

She let the doorbell ring a long time as she lay in bed in the dark. Then he began pounding on the door. She thought of calling the police but shrank from rousing the household and the neighbors. No, she would have to face it alone.

She put on her robe, went downstairs, turned on the hall light and peered through the curtained window.

"Brenda, please let me in."

She took a deep breath. "Remember you're brave," she told herself, "though that might be questionable. But Dad and Ted would want you to be." She opened the door.

She saw at once that Brad had not been drinking. He looked terribly tired, white-faced, thin and forlorn, standing there. He looked ill.

"Could we sit down?" he said.

He followed her into the parlor. She remembered their first evening there, the handsome, dashing man she decided to marry, without even loving him. So foolish.

He collapsed on the sofa. She saw he was having one of his attacks.

"Can I get you some water?"

"No. I'm all right."

She sat in the armchair across the room from him. His eyes went over her in a tender way that made her catch her breath.

He said, "You were right, Dr. Colton. On your advice, I had a complete physical. They found I have a bad ticker. In fact, it seems I've already had several heart attacks." He kind of laughed. "The Doc said if I don't slow down, quit work and take a long rest, the next one might do it."

"Do it?" Brenda said dully.

"Yep. Out. Fini. Done for, for good old Brad."

He took out a cigarette and lit it.

"Oh Brad, you shouldn't smoke."

"What's the difference now? Anyhow, I'm taking a few weeks leave, an early retirement I guess. Who knows? I'm still young, maybe I can get some kind of job."

"I'm sure you can," she murmured.

He smiled. "Don't look so sad, Foxy. It's not the end of the world." He stopped. "You sure gave Mom and me a start, disappearing like you did the other night. You really had us worried."

She started to say she was sorry. But damn it all, she wasn't.

"So, what do we do now?" he asked. "You want a divorce?"

"Yes."

He didn't raise a fuss, just sat there smoking. Surprising.

"What do you plan to do with yourself?" he said finally.

"I don't know. Teach dancing, I guess."

"That would be good."

He drew deeply on the cigarette, then said, "Brenda, I want you to be independent."

"What do you mean?"

"Independent of your Mother. I can leave you a little."

"Leave me?"

"Money. We can't all live forever, you know."

Was this a play for sympathy? He was good at that.

"Nonsense," she said. "You will live forever."

"I've looked into it. You can get a Veteran's comp, and after a while my social security–"

"This is a lot of nonsense."

"Could be. I'm pretty hard to kill. But anyhow, I'd thought I'd let you know. You're pretty hopeless when it comes to practical things."

He removed the eye patch and rubbed his eye. It looked red and shrunken, and the skin around it very scarred.

The sight made her flinch.

"Is it so ugly?" he asked.

"Of course not."

He held out his hand. "Come, sit by me, Foxy."

She sat on the edge of the couch.

He said, "Poor Foxy, can't say I blame you for wanting to be free of me. I haven't been much of a husband, but I hope we can be friends–" he stopped. "Though I've never let anyone know it, you've made me happy. As happy as an ornery ole' rootin', tootin' puddle jumper from the state of Kansas could be made happy." He stopped again and a faint smile twisted the scar on his lip. "This may sound corny and don't quote me, but–you see, Brenda, I love you. Always have."

"I wonder why. I'm really not your type at all."

"But you are. You try so hard to be fancy, the way your Mother wanted, and you're really just sweet, kind, loyal, decent and real."

Tears sprang. She quenched them.

Again the smile. "That'll be our little secret, won't it, love? That, and the fact I always knew you never really loved me. You didn't, did you?"

"I–"

"Don't say it."

He was very pale. She saw he was laboring for breath.

He said, "I've got this little pill I'm supposed to take–"

She found the green pillbox on the table. He took a pill and placed it under his tongue.

She went for water and when she came back his eyes were closed. There was something rigid in the way he lay there. Frightening.

"Brad–"

But his eyes opened. He grinned.

"Poor Foxy, I give you a hard way to go, don't I? But it'll all come out in the wash. Could you help me off with this damn jacket? It's hot in here."

She helped him and he lay back again.

"Foxy, I wonder, could you just lie down beside me for a minute?"

She said nothing.

"Please–just for a minute?" His eyes pleaded.

He made room and she lay beside him. He began to stroke her hair.

"Darling Foxy, so kind, patient." He kissed her face.

"Don't, Brad." She tried to pull away, but he grasped her, kissing her eyes, her throat. He was getting excited. He began to gasp.

She tried to pull away. "Stop it, Brad. You mustn't."

"But I want you to love me. I want you."

"Stop it! You mustn't! Your heart–"

"The hell with it!"

He held her with surprising strength, pulled her on top of him and tore away her clothes. Somehow he managed to bare himself, and his passionate mouth found hers.

She thought, 'Here is the love I once knew. And perhaps to him it is his last love.'

She gave herself to him as if in farewell.

But it was not farewell.

Mother, realizing that Brad was very ill, made an effort to be pleasant. She prepared the blue room for him to rest and had Jancy prepare dishes to tempt him.

Brad took to teasing her.

"I think your Mother's got a crush on me," he joked. "Is that true, sweetheart Mom?"

Mother flushed. "Brad, you really are impossible."

After a week, Brad seemed better and one day announced that since Brenda wanted to teach dancing, he'd decided to fix up the studio floor.

"It's in bad shape, lots of rotted wood. I can fix it, that is if her royal highness, Madame Mom, approves, of course."

"You're not strong enough to fix anything," Brenda protested.

"Oh, yes I am."

Madame Mom approved and Brad, as always with any project, entered into this one with enthusiasm. In spite of Brenda's protests that this hard labor was not doing his heart any good, he insisted on working long hours, tearing up the heavy rotted wood and hammering in new oak planks. Often he'd grow pale and have to stop and take a pill. It was as though he were racing against time to finish it before he was no longer able.

He seemed happier than she'd ever known him. And when the new floor was quickly and efficiently finished, his pride in it was touching.

"Now you can have your new career," he said.

They never discussed divorce and he sometimes spoke of finding a job when his retirement came through. She didn't think he ever expected this job to happen. But he seemed to be looking forward to a new life and he seemed quite well. Well enough to go to a party.

The party was given by one of Jordan's political friends, a Jewish gentleman of some wealth, new wealth, Brenda surmised. He and his wife had recently renovated an old Main Line mansion, a huge affair, abandoned by the owner when old wealth ran out, no doubt. A swimming pool and tennis courts had been installed, and manicured lawns and gardens were in evidence. The house overflowed with antiques, "imported from France," their host informed them. Portraits of ancestors, someone's ancestors, decorated the walls. Their host, portly and urbane, and their hostess, sporting a diamond as big as the Bellevue and wearing a little black creation so well cut and simple (it must have cost a fortune), were charmingly enthusiastic as they showed off their treasures to their guests. There were about ten of them, mostly Jewish, cultivated music and theatre lovers.

Brenda thought that what impressed her most about the house was the long, mirrored hallway, which seemed to have been borrowed from something in Versailles.

They were ushered into the large dining room where a beautiful dinner was served beneath a crystal chandelier. A butler in formal dress and two maids with white aprons and headpieces served them. It was like something out of Hollywood. Not since Grandma's dinners had Brenda been present at such a display of luxury. They drank toasts to Jordan's birthday. Brad, drinking sparingly of wine, charmed their hostess with tales of himself as a fledgling pilot, a few hair-raising events that made a hit with the non-flyers.

After dinner, they were led down the long, mirrored hallway to a charming smaller room for coffee and liqueurs and to watch a political rally in which Jordan and the other guests were interested.

Their hostess asked Brad if he would like a drink.

"Maybe a beer," he said.

His beloved beer.

This was served on a silver platter. For some reason, Brenda watched him as he raised the pale, sparkling liquid to his lips. The others were engrossed in television, but she saw Brad suddenly put down the glass on the table beside him.

"Excuse me," he said.

No one noticed as he got to his feet and left the room.

Brenda saw him walk down the long, mirrored hallway. His head was erect, his shoulders back, his steps unfaltering. It was a long walk and she saw him turn left and go into the living room. A strange thought struck her. 'He's going toward something.'

The others watched the rally. She sat and waited. It seemed a long time. Brad didn't come back. Jordan saw her strained look, as if she were listening for a sound beyond the room.

"Where's Brad?" he asked.

"He had to leave a minute. He–"

Suddenly she was on her feet, running down the hallway. It was like a dream, her reflection in the mirrors fleeting along with her as she ran down the endless hall, and hearing that sound, that sound from the living room as of someone gasping.

She rounded the corner and saw Brad. He sat erect in a big antique armchair, his head back, resting on green velvet. The gasping was his.

She was in front of him, putting her hands on his as they rested on the chair arms.

"Brad! Brad–"

For a second, his eyes flickered up to her and his lips moved.

"I love you, Foxy–"

A sob choked her. The words spoke themselves.

"I love you, too, Brad."

He smiled and his eyes closed.

She ran to the hall.

Her voice screamed down the mirrored corridor.

"Please! Someone come! Help! It's Brad!"

Then Jordan was there and the others. Two men lifted Brad to the sofa. He seemed to be breathing. Without thinking, Brenda threw herself on him and breathed into his relaxing mouth, breathed with all her strength.

Nothing. His breath faded away.

Still she tried until Jordan lifted her to her feet.

"It's no use, Brenda."

Their host felt for a pulse, which was no longer there.

An ambulance was called and everyone couldn't have been nicer, considering that someone had just messed up their living room by dying. They all said that Brad had died like a soldier and a gentleman, without making a sound.

Brenda thought that was a funny thing to say. But probably they couldn't think of anything else.

Since Brad's last duty was at the Philadelphia Navy Yard, it seemed logical that he be buried in their family burial ground under Great Grandfather's obelisk. A classmate of Brad's, Captain Brent, attached to the Navy Yard, took care of the arrangements and a military funeral was held in the Navy Chapel.

Mother and Jordan were with Brenda and several of Brad's classmates and their wives showed up, some flying up from Washington and as far away as Pensacola, Florida. Though Brenda knew them slightly, they treated her as an old friend and she was glad of their warmth. How lonely and pathetic the ceremony would have been without the Navy contingent. The Tylers, Brenda's only close Philadelphia friends, came too.

Mother, looking regal and matriarchal in black, entered the chapel with Brenda. As an officer tried to help her up the steps, she pushed him aside, though Brenda knew her arthritic knees could have used the help. Brenda saw that she was not accepting help from anyone belonging to Brad this day.

After the service, the funeral cavalcade drove to the old Laurel Hill Cemetery, overlooking the river. Brenda thought of Grandpa and Grandma and Dad sleeping there, under the obelisk, where Aunt Margot and Uncle Jake had now joined them. She thought of the plots there, which waited for Mother and herself.

Ringed around by the blue uniforms and the wives in their summer dresses, Brenda was proud so many had come to honor Brad. Many flowers and wreaths decorated the open grave. The casket was flowered and shots were fired across it by Marines. Then the bugle sounded Taps, and as the sad notes floated down the hill to the river, Brenda allowed herself to weep for Brad. She felt Jordan watching her. He understood much of the sufferings and inner conflicts of human beings. She was glad of the comfort of his arm under hers.

She had not lied when she told Brad she loved him. In spite of the ugly moments when she could have killed him, there were many things in him she did love and admire. He had been an extraordinary man, courageous, strong, clever and loyal to what he believed in. She'd loved his physical beauty and the kind things he often did, like using his last strength to build the floor, something for her future. She loved his awkward gentleness sometimes when they made love. And she admired his graceful entrance into the presence of death. She had always sensed that under his harshness lived a sensitive soul. He had overcome much in himself, but his brutal childhood had twisted him, left a mark he could never erase. He had spent his life trying to escape from it into the oblivion of drink, into the exhilaration and danger of tremendous speed and in the endless pursuit of trying to prove himself through heroic endeavor. He did not forgive weakness in others and seemed compelled to punish it. Nor did he forgive it in himself and meted out his own punishment.

People that knew him said he was marked for success. People that knew Brenda said she was marked for success. She saw now how they had killed that promise. Mismatched, their fierce clash of wills had done it. Their struggle together had been forged in pride, despair and misunderstanding. Perhaps if she could have bent a little more his way. If she had been willing to take that last drink with him in the Del Coronada Hotel, she might have prevented that catastrophe that had wiped out his chance of becoming an Admiral and of going on to glory.

She had been a strong-willed and spoiled child. He had chastened her and willed her to change. Peasant strong, with a different set of values, he had almost broken her. Never quite, because it seemed there were always currents seething within, willing her to be cleansed of the debris of fear, hate, and, oh yes, her own weaknesses. In spite of herself and because of him, she believed she had strengthened and grown.

Now he was broken. And now that he was irrevocably gone from her, she was able to appreciate who he really had been, and all that was ugly seemed to fade away. He had wanted her to cut free of Mother and grow up. She saw how right he had been.

The final notes of the bugle dissolved in the summer haze and she was handed the folded American flag, which had covered the casket. She thanked the Navy friends for coming and knew she would never see them again. She was glad that they would never know that she had been about to leave Brad. He had left her instead.

But one day she discovered that Brad had not left her completely. In his farewell lovemaking, he had left her with something to remember him by.

She was pregnant.

After the first shock, she began to think this might not be a bad thing. She had never particularly wanted a child, or even considered it. But her life seemed empty now, without direction. What would it be like to have a child?

Of course there was Mother to consider. Living at Upsan Downs, this would certainly cause a problem. But she could always get herself an apartment. Brad had taken care to make her independent of Mother. And he'd been right.

But she had a surprise in store. Mother received the news of the pregnancy very calmly. In fact, she seemed pleased. Of course, she fussed over everything.

"Now, Brenda, you must take care of yourself. We must be prepared. We don't want anything to go wrong."

"What can go wrong?"

"You never know." She paused. "I've been thinking. It would be lovely if you bore a girl."

Brenda smiled. "I'd love to bear a girl for you, Ma. But I'm afraid I don't have much influence over that."

"Yes," Mother went on. "It would be lovely. And I have a feeling it's going to be a girl." She stopped. "I've been thinking about this a lot. What shall we call her?"

"I don't know, Ma. But since you already know what it'll be, and you're always right, guess I'll have to settle for a girl. I think I'll call her Braddy Colt."

# Chapter 24

## Home

As per usual, Mother was right. The baby girl, Braddy, came along at the appointed time. She was a pretty little pink and white thing. Brenda just couldn't get over how tiny she was. Nor could she even begin to imagine all of the surprises raising a maverick daughter held in store for her in the many years ahead.

So, life went on at Upsan Downs. 'Well named by Dad,' Brenda often thought.

Brenda happily continued to turn Main Line matrons into bull fighting Flamenco dancers and when inspired, tried her hand at a new novel.

Still, Brenda's favorite daily activity was to walk the grounds of the family estate. She would reflect back on her life: the dancer, the showgirl, the loves, the marriage. Yes, she'd made mistakes. Who didn't when trying to discover themselves? She would look at the empty plot of land where the Grandparents' house had been and she'd think of the many people who had lived there: Grandma and Grandpa, the cousins, the maids, Aunt

Margot and Uncle Jake. She'd smile as she recalled the follies, bickerings and jealousies of her kin. She thought of how much life had been lived in that old house, now only living in her memory.

Wandering around under the ancient trees of Upsan Downs, Brenda thought that life wasn't all bad for this maverick, now that she'd come home where she belonged.

# About the Author

▼

*Other works by Sally Gibbs*

*Novels*

**You Don't Belong Here** (Doubleday)
**Not All Your Laughter** (Appleton)

*Short Stories*

**Intimate Strangers** (Aegina Press)

*Poetry*

**Beauty for Ashes** (Dorrance of Philadelphia)
**Soundings** (Aegina Press)
**Who Are You?** (Mellon Poetry Press)

*Plays/Musicals*

**The Plastic Surgeon**
**America, We Love You But...**
**Yucky U, University of the Dance**
**Comfort Her With Fury**